A DAWN LEFT BEHIND

MARK AESCHLIMANN

For Matthew, miss you every day little bro.

Chapter One
Formidable Opponents

'Got him! Right on the nose! HA!' Matthew exclaimed as he pumped his fist in the air, the man on TV having no idea of his apparent ridicule.

'Well done, Matthew. Another formidable opponent slain.' Justification from the man who's opinion Matthew valued above all else. Or was it? George hadn't lifted his eyes at any point away from the notebook he regularly wrote in.

'Grandad, I can never tell whether you're serious or just taking the piss. Did you even see it? The insane accuracy? Card flicking should be an Olympic sport. Guaranteed gold medal here... Grandad... Grandad... Pay attention to your talented Grandson.' Matthew dragged his lanky frame over the couch and waved in George's face, stealing attention from the notebook.

A long sigh ensued. George looked up slightly and peered over his glasses at Matthew like a teacher interrupted from their marking. 'Matthew, I would never begrudge you having any skill. You never know how it could help you in the future. But you need to have more about you, my boy.' The glasses had now been removed and the notebook closed. Time for the serious talk. 'You're all I've got, Matthew, and I won't be around forever. I want to be sure you can take care of yourself after I've gone.'

'What are you talking about? You've got at least twenty years left in you, old man. Nobody gets around like you. You've got more hair than I do,' Matthew reached over and shook George's neatly parted, white hair. George waving him away in agitation. Of course George had nothing on Matthew's thick, shaggy, dark brown hair.

'I'm serious, Matthew. There's a lot more to life than going to work, making coffee and hanging around with your mates. You need some direction. Some life skills. You need to challenge yourself. Sometimes I feel like you're just coasting through life. Don't hide away from the world. You've got so much to offer.'

'I'm just looking for my calling,' Matthew said defensively.

'Looking or waiting for it to hit *you* on the nose? If you don't explore what's out there you won't find what it is you're looking for.' After offering similar advice time and time again he wore the weight of a losing battle on his face.

'Maybe you're right, Grandad. I'll start by looking at the bottom of this bag of chips,' Matthew reached over to the coffee table and grabbed the bag of chips he'd started earlier. 'It's gonna be a bit of a journey to get there. I'll keep you updated. Anyway, I'm only eighteen. There's plenty of time.'

George shook his head in resignation and took a sip of his tea. He then stood and stretched his legs as he fixed up his beige cardigan, trying to ignore the constant, irritating crunch emanating from Matthew's mouth. 'I know it hasn't been easy for you, spending so long watching everyone else grow up with their parents. Not a day goes by that I don't think of them. I just want you to have the life they would have wanted for you. You're eighteen now and need to think about the future.'

'I know, Grandad. I know it's been hard for you as well but I think we've done OK,' Matthew replied.

'Yeah. We've done OK. Now go put a shirt on and stop rubbing yourself all over my couch.'

Matthew was once again sporting his usual shirtless, sweat pants combination at home that irritated George. His natural ability to stay slim and toned, along with his darkish, olive skin, which he inherited from his islander father, gave him no reason to be self conscious about being shirtless at home. George, on the other hand, felt it a little inappropriate and was confused at the contrariness of Matthew's outlook when in public.

'How about a story when you get back?' asked George.

'Nice!' came the reply as Matthew ran off to his room.

Even as Matthew got older he could never resist listening to one of George's stories. Somehow there was a new one every time. Matthew suspected that they were all linked but since George never used names for the characters, only descriptions, it was never confirmed and Matthew was never bothered enough by it to enquire. For Matthew, these were the only times he really felt like there wasn't anything missing. He loved the stories, he loved that his Grandad was telling them and he knew that his Grandad loved to tell them.

It was strange to him that George had never been a writer, instead being a carpenter after his stint in the navy until his eventual retirement. It wasn't that he was bad at his job. In fact, he was known around town as being rather good. The stories, however, seemed to be his passion and was what he, at least in Matthew's eyes, was best at. At the same time that made Matthew feel even more special. That he would be the only one to get to enjoy them made him feel privileged.

Matthew returned and launched himself onto the couch. The phone was switched to silent and the TV turned off. He rested his square jaw on one arm which was lounging on the back of the couch and fixed up the black rimmed glasses sitting on his long, broad nose.

'OK. Ready,' said Matthew. His thin lips stretched into a long, wide smile across his face, unable to contain his excitement as he awaited the next adventure.

George sat himself back down on his old, well worn armchair with a fresh cup of tea and began his story. 'Our hero washed ashore a strange land with nothing but the clothes on his back and the necklace he had found a few days previous. It was night time and the sky danced a peculiar dance. As he lay in the sand, attempting to catch his breath, the ocean water caressed his body. The reflection of the sky, along with something in the water provided a glow which faded as the water receded. The blood of the trees pulsed from a couple of clear patches in the rocky alcove in which he lay. As he fought to keep conscious he spotted the blurred outline of a woman quickly moving toward him. She knelt beside him as he faded to darkness.

'The man woke some time later amid the candlelight which shrouded the room in warmth. He was on a bed within a room of stone. He knew not where he was, but could see the furnishings came from considerable wealth. On a table beside him lay a bowl of water, cloths and objects covered in strange symbols. There was a single window in this room, however no light escaped around the curtains. The door opened and startled the wounded man. In walked a woman. Tall and elegant in the way she walked, very beautiful. Her red dress hugged her body closely. She wore a silver, metal headband atop her head which was shaped as leaves from a tree.

'Over time the man was nursed back to health and love blossomed between he and the woman that found him on the beach. However, the woman was already wedded to another and was raising little boys. For a short time the man stayed under her employ as a guard, however being that close to each other all the time was a dangerous endeavour to hold back their feelings toward one another.

'The realisation came that they must part and he must find his way back home. Over the course of a few months he sought the help of wizards and witches in order to restore his memory of how he came to be on the beach that fateful day. All the while he learned of the magic of the land and became skilled in wielding it to help others. He kept to the shadows and sought no reward nor recognition, however tales of a far away traveler, come to rid the town of evil, soon spread throughout the town.

'The man would find shelter wherever he could and resorted to theft from the house which had helped him. Having been there for a period of time he knew how to get in and out undetected and took only what he needed. While he took the risk to see the woman he loved she never saw him. It was safer that way, for both of them.

'He eventually regained his memory of the past and with it, once again knew how to get home. The man visited his love one more time before he left, to say goodbye, and the next day he returned home. While he did return a few times to the strange world he had come to know, he never returned to the village and the woman that had saved him and cared for him. It would have caused them both too much pain to part again. In time he settled back home for good and found another whom he loved very much and started his own family.

'And with that I think it's time for bed, Matthew.' George stood up and gave himself another stretch. 'Don't forget you've got work early tomorrow.'

'How could I possibly forget when you go and get updated on my roster from Alaska every other day,' said Matthew, with a somewhat sarcastic tone.

'Where else would I go for a good meal and coffee? I'm not going to get it at those burger and pizza places you kids go to all the time. It's also nice to go somewhere I can have a bit of a conversation,' George said, taking his cup to the kitchen to wash it up.

'We can't all afford those boutique cafe prices, Grandad,' quipped Matthew as he once again started flicking cards with each hand at random objects around the room.

'That would be true if Alaska didn't treat you like her own son. You could have anything you want before and after work.'

'Yeah, but I need that grease.'

George shook his head and put his clean cup away. 'Matthew, tomorrow I'll be going away for one or two weeks so you'll have to look after yourself for a little while.'

'Where are you going?' enquired Matthew.

'Just going to see a few old friends. We're all getting old so there won't be many more opportunities.' He coughed a couple of times and filled a nearby glass with water.

'Are you alright Grandad?'

'Yes, yes. I'm fine. Just old age catching up… As I said, I'll be gone for a little while. There shouldn't be any bills coming in so you don't need to worry about that. Just make sure you keep the house clean and please don't break anything. Oh, and please pick up all those cards you've thrown around the place. I'll be taking them with me.'

'Grandad, are you ever gonna tell me what all the symbols mean on the cards?'

The cards that Matthew had been flicking at objects with incredible accuracy were not a standard deck of cards. They had no numbers or suits and there were a few more than could be found in a deck of cards. There were symbols that did repeat across different cards but Matthew had no idea what games could be played with them. All of them had a symbol in the middle, some an eye, some a lightning strike, some a strange arrow and many more which Matthew could not discern. They were surrounded by shapes. Circles, triangles, rectangles. Then all the cards had a symbol repeated in all four corners. Matthew liked to think they came from some obscure culture that George had come across while travelling in the navy.

'Maybe someday you'll learn what they are for,' answered George. 'But not until you're ready.'

'Ready? Why aren't I ready now?'

'Life is a journey Matthew. Some answers are only available to you when the time is right. Alas, now is not that time.'

The down side to George's amazing ability to tell stories, as far as Matthew was concerned, was that he could find new and inventive ways of being infuriatingly cryptic.

Matthew woke the next morning and slowly rolled out of bed. Another restless sleep was endured. A nightmare which so often frequented his mind once again made an unwelcome appearance.

He was unsure whether this was a memory or just pieces put together from the stories he had been told. In the nightmare he was a small child. Given he was three years old when the accident occurred in which he lost his parents, this made sense.

They were driving down a road in the darkness of night, dense bush either side of the road. The radio was playing old songs from the 1980's. Matthew's father was driving and his mother was in the front passenger seat, both of them jovially singing along. Occasionally his mother would turn and reach back to tickle his stomach, making him giggle. From the car booster seat Matthew could see the trees rush past. He was unsure where they were going but the road definitely felt unfamiliar to him.

'What's that up ahead?' his father asked.

'I can't see anything, Daniel,' she replied, slightly leaning forward in her seat.

'There it is again. There's an orange light that keeps flashing. Can't you see it?' he asked again, pointing forward, out the windscreen.

'Yes, I saw it that time. There aren't any houses out this way. I wonder what it is?'

They continued to drive, his mother and father taking guesses as to what the light could be. Suddenly an orange light filled the car. Matthew's mother turned toward him, fear written over her face.

He could hear his father shout. 'Matthew! Hold on TIGHT!'

Flames embraced the outside of the car. The front of the car shot up into the air. Time seemed to slow as the car rolled to the right. His mother screamed as she stretched her arm out to hold him. As they were upside down the car came down again. He felt unimaginable fear and cried out as the roof met the road.

That was how the nightmare always ended. He wasn't exactly sure what had happened that night. He had asked his Grandad many times and was told that there was a fire, his father lost control of the car and they crashed. Apparently somebody had happened upon the scene soon after. They called the authorities and pulled Matthew from the wreckage, unconscious but still clinging to life. Somehow the rear half of the car was still in good enough condition to not only save Matthew, but allow the rescuer to get through the window and pull him out. The bodies of his mother and father could not be retrieved until the firemen could cut through the wreckage.

It was a mystery as to what had caused the fire which engulfed the car. The surrounding area was charred and embers were still alive on some of the trees when Matthew's saviour arrived at the scene, however there was no indication as to the origin of the fire or why the car had flipped.

Matthew had come to terms with never finding out what actually happened that night and had moved on with just his

Grandad. All of his other grandparents had died before he was born so he was somewhat comforted with the fact that he had stuck around to keep his Grandad company for all those years. He couldn't bare to think what would have happened had George lost all the remaining family he had left.

After steadying himself with a brief wash of his face, Matthew went to the kitchen to get himself some breakfast. George was already dressed and ready to go wherever it was that he was heading, just finishing off the last of his morning cup of tea. He was quite dressed up with a grey three piece suit and a duckbill cap. He also had an old ring which he had been wearing constantly for the past few months. Matthew assumed it was his old wedding ring and he was feeling a bit nostalgic lately. A packed duffle bag was sitting by the front door, ready for the trip.

'Looking good, Grandad,' remarked Matthew, pouring cereal into a bowl. 'These must be some pretty important friends you're meeting.'

'They certainly are Matthew. My oldest remaining friends. A lot of stories over the years…' He trailed off for a second, a look of deep thought on his face. 'I best be off then. Please look after yourself and make sure you keep the place clean, especially if your mates come round.'

'I will. You look after *yourself*. Don't go chasing all the ladies. You might pull a hip.' Matthew laughed and poured some milk onto his cereal.

'Behave yourself, Matthew,' replied George, attempting to scold Matthew while unable to keep a smile from escaping. 'See you soon.'

'See ya, Grandad.'

George picked up his duffle bag and left the house. Matthew set himself up on the couch with his breakfast and switched on the TV. He had enough time to slowly sort himself out before going to work, always one to leave getting ready until the last minute.

Eventually time ran out and Matthew couldn't afford to procrastinate any longer. He quickly showered, clothed in his black jeans and cat t-shirt under a red and black plaid shirt, brushed his teeth and made sure his hair was curated to perfection, despite the shaggy look. With a quick check of his watch and a minor freak out at the time, Matthew ran around the house, picking up his phone, wallet, keys and attempted to put his shoes on while making his way toward the front door. Given the lack of time he'd left himself he decided against taking his skateboard, instead making sure he had his bus pass as he exited the house.

Chapter Two
Full Stop

The nearest bus stop was only a few houses down the road making it an easy option for when Matthew had spent too much time dawdling around the house before work.

Matthew and George lived on one of the last remaining blocks in the area that hadn't been subdivided, fifteen minutes out of town where Matthew worked. It was the house that George and Matthew's grandmother moved into before his mum was born. It was a three bedroom, two bathroom house that had gone through a number of renovations over the years to generally keep up with the times. With the passing of Matthew's mum the garden had regressed to being "easy to maintain", when once it had been home to a myriad of beautifully coloured flowers.

Matthew quickly scrambled down the street as he could see the bus making its way from the other direction. Tagging on, he made his way down to the back of the bus. He plonked himself down on the seat next to a short, slightly stocky, teenager around the same age as Matthew.

'Hey Saf. How you going? Sweet haircut by the way, ' Matthew remarked on his short fade which had been a little more of an afro the previous day.

'I'm OK. You running too late for your board?'

'You know me so well.' They both giggled.

Safiri Bombi had been best friends with Matthew since he arrived with his family from Mozambique when he was nine years old. They had been in the same class growing up through school and remained inseparable despite the vastly different levels of application and results. While Matthew took the more casual approach, coasting through and making sure he was generally liked by everyone, Safiri was pushed by his parents, and his own high expectations and fear of failure, to keep his grades up and get into university.

Following their graduation from school they both took up jobs working at The Floating Star Café. Matthew had no trouble getting a job at the café as the proprietor, Alaska Sinclair, had known Matthew all his life. Alaska was a friend of Matthew's mum and had taken great effort in making sure she could give Matthew as much help and love as she could after his parents had passed away. Matthew, being the charmer he was, found it an easy task to get Safiri employed as well.

They both got off the bus at the closest stop to the café and made their way down the path to work. The café was on a pretty busy strip on the outskirts of town, where business operated from the same small shops erected in the early part of the twentieth century.

As they approached their destination another teenage man bashed between them, smashing their shoulders back.

'Watch where you're going, losers,' he said, followed by a menacing laugh. His two sidekicks walked past Matthew and Safiri and joined him, also finding the situation to be quite humorous.

'What the hell, Brad?' said Matthew, a disgusted look on his face.

'What are you gonna do about it Matthew? Nothing? I thought

so… How about you?' he turned and nodded in Safiri's direction.

Safiri backed up slightly and fixed up his large, thick, black-rimmed glasses which enlarged his already large, round eyes. He said nothing.

'You gonna cry now, you little, fat loser? You're just a couple of pussies,' he continued berating the two startled young men. 'Go run along to your stupid, fairy boss and make some coffees'.

Just then a girl walked out of the café. She was thin, and slightly taller than Safiri. She had shoulder-length, wavy, silver hair with black streaks and dressed in black jeans, a black tight t-shirt and white sneakers. The expression on the faces of Brad and his cronies suddenly became more fearful as a wooden spoon span through the air between Matthew and Safiri, and hit the arm of the cowering Brad.

'WHAT ARE YOU DOING YOU PASTY PSYCHO?!' he shouted as they turned and scurried away.

'If I see you again I'm gonna beat the crap outta ya!' she shouted after them.

Matthew and Safiri turned toward her. 'Thanks Sam,' they both said in unison as Safiri took out his inhaler and took a puff.

'Seriously, you guys need to learn to stand up for yourselves. I can't always save your arses.' Sam walked past both of them and picked up the spoon. 'Are you both gonna just stand there looking like idiots? Come on,' she said as she walked back into The Floating Star Café.

The café doubled up as both a café and a bookstore of the more spiritual variety. Alaska, the owner and operator, was a tall and slim, middle-aged woman who seemed to take a lot of her cues from the swinging sixties. She wore layers of flowing, colourful clothes, hoop earrings and various bangles on her wrists. Her greying, red hair was always kept out of her face by a colourful headband or bandana. Although devoid of makeup, Alaska's red, cat eye glasses were the feature atop the celestial nose on her diamond shaped face.

'Just ignore them, boys. Sticks and stones and all that. The best way to show them is to just be happy and don't let them get to you,' Alaska remarked as they walked through the door, clearly keeping a keen eye on the scene that was unfolding in front of her shop.

'And Sam, you need to watch your temper. It may get you into a lot of trouble one day. Have a little think before you go running off throwing spoons about the place.'

'But they were bullying Safiri and Matthew who, might I add, need to stick up for themselves or it'll keep happening.' Sam's eyebrows raised and body stiffened as she plead her case, unable to understand what it was that she had actually done wrong.

'This is a place of relaxation Sam. I love your passion and desire to help but we can't go around shouting and throwing things.'

Sam clenched her fists and stormed into the coolroom at the back of the kitchen to calm down.

'Sorry, Alaska. We should've just come straight into the shop and ignored them,' Matthew conceded as he and Safiri started organising themselves and preparing tables.

Matthew's more carefree, happy-go-lucky attitude to life had come about from spending so much time with Alaska whilst growing up. The café was like a second home so it made sense he would take the opportunity to get paid for being there. He and Safiri were very well liked by customers of The Floating Star. Both were very well mannered and dealt with every situation in the calm, relaxed way that the café sold itself on. Safiri was quiet but knowledgeable on everything anyone asked of him, and also dressed very nicely in either a white or black v-neck tee (on this occasion it was white) and jeans with business shoes. While Matthew charmed his way into everyone's good books and kept them smiling. Sam Walker, on the other hand, was quite fiery, but nobody made a better (or quicker) tea and coffee in the area. It was like all the emotion she had was channelled into the task at hand and made them all a perfect team.

'Safiri?' called Alaska.

'Yes, ma'am,' he replied while setting out cutlery.

'When do you start uni? I need to start looking for another casual to take up the shifts.'

Matthew couldn't waste the opportunity to start a little banter. 'Be careful Alaska. In a couple of years Mr Businessman over here will have bought this place and turned it into a chain.'

'Oh behave yourself, Matthew.'

Sam also couldn't resist herself. 'How long until we're all sailing around the islands on your giant yacht, Saf?'

'Guys, come on. I'm not doing anything special. I might not even be able to finish my degree.' Safiri turned his round face away from the rest of the staff and awkwardly kept setting up tables, trying to pretend he wasn't the center of attention.

'That's rubbish. Nobody coming out of school knows the ins and outs of government forms and accounting like you do. There's definitely nobody who could tell me how those forms changed throughout history. You're like a vacuum for governmental knowledge,' said Matthew.

This was generally how any conversation went that was related to Safiri. Matthew and Sam would tease him a little. Safiri would be very awkward about it and denigrate himself. Then Matthew would build him up again as the greatest high school graduate who ever lived. To be fair to Matthew, Safiri was extremely smart and helped his parents deal with all their immigration matters, even from a young child.

'Speaking of yachts, Sam, can't your rich, surgeon mum already afford a yacht.' Matthew now started to turn the banter onto Sam.

'I need a bigger yacht than that, Matthew,' she replied, very sarcastically, which was met with laughter from the staff of The Floating Star Café.

'Grandad is going away for a little while if you guys wanna hang out at my place?' asked Matthew, keen to keep some sort of company in the house.

'I'm in,' confirmed Sam.

'I'll talk to my parents and make sure they don't need me for anything,' said Safiri. This was his response every time plans were being made despite him rarely being unavailable. Matthew really didn't mind. For him, he would love to have a family to get in the way of his free time on occasion so he was loath to bear ill will toward Safiri for at least being kind enough to check with them.

The next few weeks flew by with Matthew, Safiri and Sam living the easy life. Other than working at the café they had no other plans and just lived day to day. Their free time was filled with junk food, movies, hanging out at the lake near Matthew's house and generally trying to avoid Brad and his gang who seemed to love nothing more than belittling Matthew and his friends. It was still a month until Safiri started university so they didn't have a care in the world.

When George returned home from wherever it was that he had gone, he found that Matthew didn't quite keep his promise of keeping the house clean. While it certainly could have been worse, there were plenty of packets of chips and lollies on the dining and coffee tables and some empty pizza boxes sitting on the kitchen bench. It was about the level of cleanliness that George had expected on arriving home without giving Matthew any notice.

Rather than clean it all up, George waited until Matthew and his friends came home and gave them a bit of a scare, pretending to be furious with the state of the house. After a well earned laugh at the state of shock on their faces (as they had never seen George so angry) he ordered them around from the comfort of his armchair while they gave the house a good clean.

As they were almost finished, a few rubbish bags sitting by the front door ready to be taken out, George began to groan.

'Are you OK?' called Matthew from the kitchen, as he washed a cloth in the sink.

George groaned again.

'Grandad! What's wrong?' Matthew ran to George. Safiri and Sam appeared from the hallway. They were packing up and getting ready to go back to their parent's houses. George was clearly in pain and struggling to breathe.

'I'll call the ambulance!' Sam immediately pulled out her phone from her pocket and dialed for help. Safiri went to the kitchen and filled a glass of water to bring to George.

As they awaited the arrival of the ambulance, Matthew, Safiri and Sam tried to comfort George, however he did not tell them what was wrong with him or where the pain was. After fifteen minutes of trying not to break out into a full panic the ambulance arrived. The paramedics carefully moved George onto the gurney, gave him some medication for the pain and wheeled him out of the house, into the ambulance and left. As Sam was the only one of the three with a driver's license and a car they quickly jumped in and followed as closely as they could to the hospital.

Sam dropped Matthew at emergency and went to park the car. Matthew ran inside and headed straight to reception.

'Hi, I need to know what happened to George Sampson. He was just brought in.'

'What is your name and relationship?' asked the nurse.

'My name is Matthew Parlour and he's my grandad.'

'OK, Matthew. The doctor is with him now and I'll let her know you are here. Please take a seat and she'll come and give you an update when she's finished with your grandad.'

Safiri and Sam joined Matthew in the waiting area after calling their parents to update them on what had happened. Safiri also called Alaska to update her and get someone to cover Matthew's shift the next day.

They nervously waited in silence for the next forty-five minutes until the doctor came out to summon Matthew.

'Hi Matthew, I'm Doctor Stewart and I've been looking after you grandfather for the last few months. Please come with me.'

Matthew followed the doctor down corridors and up the elevator all the while wondering why she had been looking after his grandad. He hadn't mentioned anything about going to the hospital. They stopped outside a room and Matthew could see his grandad through the open door, hooked up to a number of devices and tubes.

'It's good to finally meet you Matthew, although I didn't want it to be under these circumstances. George talked about you every time he came in. He loves you very much and wanted to keep looking after you but unfortunately we all knew this time would come-'

Matthew cut her off. 'What time? Why has he been coming to see you?'

The doctor was taken aback. 'George told me he had talked to you about this. I'm so sorry Matthew but he's been battling pancreatic cancer. He doesn't have much time left.'

'Why wouldn't he have told me?'

'I don't know. As I said I had been informed that you knew. Did you notice any changes with him? Deterioration in his appearance or lack of appetite?' she asked.

'No. He wasn't a big eater and he didn't look any different.' replied Matthew.

'Are you sure? How often did you see him?'

'He's been away the last couple of weeks but usually I see him every day. We live in the same house. How much longer does he have?'

'Maybe hours. A day at most. I'm so sorry you've had to find out like this.'

'Can I see him?'

'I've given him something for the pain and he's sleeping right now but he should wake up soon. He made sure to tell me that he needs to speak to you regardless of his condition. It might be a good idea to go back down to reception and get a drink and call whoever needs to know.'

Matthew made his way back to reception. His friends asked him what happened but Matthew didn't hear them. In fact he couldn't hear anything beyond his own thoughts, wondering why his grandad wouldn't tell him something like this, especially given he has no other family. What was he going to do now? He had never even contemplated life without his grandad. Really he should have known this wasn't too far away. Maybe he just refused to see it. All these thoughts swirled around in his head. He walked straight past Safiri and Sam and outside, around a corner where it looked like he would be alone and broke down in tears.

Safiri and Sam chased him outside, having no idea what was happening and found Matthew, crouched out of view by a wall with his head in his hands, crying. Matthew had always been the calm one of the group, keeping them all relaxed. They froze for a second, not knowing what to do, then walked over to Matthew, sat with him and embraced him. Despite not knowing the details of what was happening they both also had tears running down their cheeks.

Finally Matthew collected himself enough to get some words out. 'It's cancer. He's got a day at most.' All three cried uncontrollably.

***

When they collected themselves enough to go back into the hospital Alaska was waiting for them. She didn't say anything, she just wrapped her arms around Matthew. After a few moments she let go and put her hands on his cheeks.

'When you're ready you can tell me what's happening. Just know that I'm here for you whatever you want to do.'

'Thanks, Alaska.'

They were all allowed to wait in the room for George to wake up. Nobody spoke as two hours went by. George looked ten years older. His hair looked thinner, the lines in his face even more defined. Nothing made sense. There was nothing wrong with him when they came home from work earlier in the day.

George opened his eyes. 'Hello everyone. Are we ready to get out of here and get some dinner?'

Alaska smiled at George and ushered Safiri and Sam out of the room.

'Why didn't you tell me?' asked Matthew, his voice breaking as he held back more tears.

'Don't be sad Matthew,' George replied, trying to smile. 'Every man's time comes for him eventually. This isn't the end, just a transition.'

'You never talked about religion before.'

'Who's talking about religion? There's so much you don't know. I was hoping I would be around when you discovered it. None of us know all the secrets of the universe, but I know more than most in this world.'

'What are you talking about Grandad? And you still haven't explained why you didn't tell me about the cancer. You were fine a few hours ago.'

'I didn't tell you because you didn't need to know. You've been through so much in your life already and you have so much more ahead of you. I had some affairs to get in order. Would you have let me go if I had told you?'

'Probably not, but I deserved to know.'

'Yes, you deserved to know,' George was unrelenting at projecting positivity in his voice. 'But we don't always get what we deserve and what we think we deserve isn't always what is right. And what is right is how you will go on from this. Everything I've tried to teach you through your life is just a small part of what you will become and if I'm right you will become something great. All you need to do is let yourself go. Let go of your comfort zone and let go of the fear of getting things wrong. You'll get things wrong but you'll get so much more right. I didn't tell you what was happening because it will get in the way of what you'll discover once I'm gone. If I told you everything you wouldn't truly learn and grow.

'As for me being fine, I haven't been fine for some time. I've been able to hide certain things. I'm very good at keeping secrets, you know... I suppose you wouldn't, that's how good I am at keeping them. In time you'll understand how and why I did all this. You just open yourself up to everything. It's OK to believe what you believe, but be open to those beliefs being challenged and to change. All the stories I told you growing up, don't discount them as made up fantasy. Most stories come from some degree of truth. A lot of them are distorted memories passed down through time. I may have embellished some things from time to time, but for the most part, they are true, as hard as that is to believe.'

'How can they be true? They're full of magic and strange creatures.' Matthew's heart was pounding. For a brief moment he forgot that his grandad was near death. Was this his intention? He thought. To distract him from the reality of the situation?

'Magic is but a word, Matthew, given to what cannot be explained, or what just is. There are many things you haven't seen but know to be true. In time your world and knowledge will expand. Maybe I'll be watching you make your own stories to tell your children and your grandchildren. I love you so much and I'm so proud of who you are and what you will do. I'm sure your mum and dad are just as proud. You can and will do great things, just let go.'

Those last words brought Matthew crashing back to what was inevitable. 'I love you too Grandad. How can I go on without you? I won't have anyone left.' Tears once again fell down Matthew's cheeks as he leaned over the bed and hugged George.'

'Rubbish, Matthew. You have your friends. You have Alaska. You'll have a lifetime of people who will join you and love you. Your heart is so big. There's enough room for everyone. I'll be there with you, in your heart, just like your parents. Just let go.'

And with that George closed his eyes and drifted away as Matthew cried on his shoulder.

Chapter Three
Trinkets For The Lad

The following couple of weeks after George's death were mostly a numbing blur to Matthew. As it happened, George spent some of his weeks away making arrangements for his death so that Matthew didn't have to. Even if arrangements hadn't been made, Alaska, the Bombi's and the Walkers were there for Matthew every step of the way, whatever he needed. It was a comfort to Matthew, not just that they were there, but that George was right when he had told Matthew that they would be.

Every last detail regarding the funeral was taken care of. The funeral directors were in touch with Matthew, usually through Alaska, explaining everything that was to be done on the day, where everybody needed to be and when. It was a funeral fitting for a naval officer and many people from the community and George's life, past and present, were in attendance paying their respects. It was a beautiful sunny day with birds singing in the trees, a reflection of how everybody regarded George. Happy and pleasant with everybody that he came across. Matthew gave a short speech about how George had raised him and how good a man he was, all while holding back tears, a strength and courage that many had never before seen in Matthew.

There were a few retired officers from the navy who approached Matthew at the wake after the service, which was hosted at The Floating Star. They introduced themselves as men who had served with George many years before. They had lunch with George recently where he informed them of his condition, however he spent most of the time talking about Matthew and how he was destined for great things. The men chatted for a short while with Matthew about how George was back in their younger days and how George was actually quite the arrogant ladies man when he was younger. A far cry from the man he eventually became. Despite the depressing situation Matthew did enjoy hearing stories about his grandad which he had never heard before.

Matthew didn't work during that period. Safiri and Sam still had their shifts to work and Alaska needed to be there to manage the store. When Matthew couldn't bear to be alone any longer he would make his way down to The Floating Star in an effort to distract himself with the company he could find there. People would often sit down with Matthew to see how he was coping and his plans going forward, and to chat about George. There was also a box left at the counter where people would leave heartfelt messages of support for Matthew or share their own stories.

He was so young when his parents died and did not know his other grandparents so he had never had to deal with a situation like this before. As for George's desire for Matthew to let go and open himself to everything, he felt more lost and directionless than ever. Where before his direction was mostly to just enjoy himself and work to meet those ends, he no longer found enjoyment in anything. He felt no desire to do anything and was essentially going to the café in the hope that it would change.

George's lawyer, Mr. Aldridge, had scheduled two meetings with Matthew. The first was immediately following George's death and the second was a week after the funeral. Alaska joined Matthew on both occasions for both support and to help with anything Matthew didn't understand. The first meeting was to sort through all the immediate affairs, mostly to do with ownership of the house and all the accounts associated with it. George had sorted and signed everything necessary for everything to go over to Matthew. At the time he was so numb to everything that it really didn't register with him that he had inherited the old family home, despite the inevitability that it would one day happen.

The second meeting, taking place at Matthew's house, was more personal as this one regarded all of George's other personal possessions and final wishes. After exchanging pleasantries Alaska made them all tea and Mr. Aldridge began.

'Matthew, I have a letter here that George wished me to read you after he had passed.'

Dear Matthew,

I am so sorry that I have left you. I'm sure you feel all alone, however that is far from the truth. You have people around you that love you and will be there for you whenever you need them. Others will also come and go throughout your life. Everything that was mine is now yours. Everything that I have given to others has already been delivered. Some of your new possessions, however, will only be found if you choose to look for them. If you don't look for them you will have no use for them anyway. It is entirely up to you if you choose to let go.

Forever looking over you,
George Sampson (Grandad)

'George instructed me to also give you this envelope and this deck of cards. He did not disclose to me what was in the envelope as it is for your eyes only. Do you have any questions for me?'

'Do you know what he means when he talks about possessions that can only be found if I look for them?' asked Matthew, looking very confused.

'Unfortunately George did not give me any information about these items. I have known George for a long time. He was a very nice man but also very precise and calculated. He never left out any details unless he purposely intended to leave them out. Do you have any other questions?'

'No,' Matthew said softly, his head lowered looking at the envelope and cards.

'Well if you think of anything else, please do not hesitate to contact me. Again, I'm so sorry for your loss Matthew. George and I saw each other quite often outside of work, usually running into each other at the pub. We would sit down and talk about all sorts of things. He was quite a brilliant man and I'll miss sitting down to chat with him. I'll leave you to it and again, contact me if you have any other questions.'

'Thank you, Mr. Aldridge,' said Matthew.

'I'll see you out Mr. Aldridge,' added Alaska, trying to remain as upbeat and positive as she could on this sombre occasion.

When Alaska came back Matthew hadn't moved at all. He was still trying to process everything that was happening and the letter that George had left him.

'Would you like anything, Matthew?' she asked.

'No thanks, Alaska,' Matthew replied.

'OK. Well Safiri and Sam should have closed up the café by now and will be on their way. I'll leave you all to do whatever you want to do once they get here and get out of your hair.'

'We all like having you around Alaska.'

'I know, but you kids could do with unwinding a little and I've got some things I can get on with at home.'

After sitting in silence for ten minutes, Alaska's arm around Matthew's shoulders and his head resting on hers, Safiri and Sam sent a message to say they'll be at the door in a couple of minutes. They arrived with bags of chips, lollies, pizza, nachos and ginger beer. All the comfort food Matthew loved.

'I'll leave you all to it then,' said Alaska as she picked up her bag. 'Please call me if you need anything.'

'Thanks, Alaska. For everything.' replied Matthew.

'It's no trouble at all, Matthew. Bye now'.

'Bye, Alaska,' they all said in unison as she left through the front door.

'You want anything else Matthew?' Sam asked. 'A drinks run maybe? Any other food?'

'No thanks. This is good. We'll all be sick tomorrow, though.' replied Matthew.

For the next couple of hours the trio gorged on the buffet that had been arranged on the dining table. Safiri and Sam tried to keep the conversation light and try to elevate the mood from what it had been since George had passed. They shared jokes and stupid stories allowing Matthew to finally relax and find some joy, to a small degree, for the first time in a while. The food coma's set in as they attempted to watch a movie and resulted in all three falling asleep on the couch.

The next morning they awoke to an almighty mess. Wrappers, food scraps and leftovers were scattered from the kitchen to the lounge. Attempts to bend their bodies to pick up any rubbish proved fruitless with the torturous state of their stomachs. They did, however, have a couple of hours to clean up and sort themselves before Safiri and Sam left for work, their morning shifts being covered that day.

After they had left and Matthew was alone he decided to open the envelope given to him by Mr. Aldridge the previous day. Despite how close he was to his friends he didn't want to run the risk of breaking down in front of them again. Given the nature of the final talk Matthew had with his grandad, there was also no telling what may be in there and it may be better viewed by Matthew alone.

Matthew went to his room and picked up the envelope from his bedside table. He had placed it there the previous night, quickly after the arrival of his friends, so as not to be tempted to open it while they were there and risk it being the sole topic of the night. Walking to the lounge he gave the envelope a small shake to see if it gave any hint to its contents. It seemed everything was pretty well packed and nothing moved.

Matthew sat on the couch and opened the envelope, removing the contents one by one. Within the envelope there had been three items, each individually wrapped in tissue paper, and another letter. All the items were wrapped in a way to make them all the same size. Matthew opened up the letter and began to read:

Dear Matthew,

I have written you this additional letter as I did not feel it appropriate for anyone else's eyes but yours. I am sure by now I have given you a little hint of the wider universe, unknown to but a few people. I am sure you have many questions and are probably frustrated, if not a little angry at me for being so cryptic in what I have said. I am sorry but you will need to make a decision on whether or not to find the answers, both for yourself to grow and for the safety of everyone. Should you choose to find the answers you will then be custodian to the doorways that will be open and will understand, fully, why I could not risk telling you everything or writing it down.

Within this package you will find three items. You will also have received the deck of cards that you know I always kept with me. They will all be valuable tools for you going forward, should you choose that life. I have also hidden another item within the house that I could not allow anyone, even Mr. Aldridge, to see lest they begin to ask questions.

Unfortunately I cannot tell you any more. The journey of discovery is as important as the answers themselves, for you and everybody else. I wish I could have been there to see you grow to your full potential but alas, time comes for everyone. The love from all your family will be with you always.

Always with you,
Grandad

The emotions arose again inside Matthew as he read, knowing he will never see his grandad again, although this time these feelings were mixed with a little more sense of determination within him to find out what these answers were, as well as what the questions were besides *what the hell is going on?* This also meant the frustration was still there albeit slightly alleviated by the knowledge that there was at least a reason for not being told.

Matthew was hopeful that the items he had in front of him could possibly enlighten him, or at least give him a starting point. He picked up the first of the three items and carefully unwrapped it. The contents appeared to be the same ring that George had been wearing for a few months prior to his death. There was nothing remarkable about the ring other than being aesthetically pleasing. It was a gold band with three sections cut into it. The top and bottom were simply the standard yellow gold band. Sitting just inside each was a thin section of white gold pieces placed to give the appearance of rope. In the middle was a thick section of alternating yellow and rose gold pieces which were made to look like they were interlaced. There was nothing engraved on the ring nor any note attached to give any indication of what it could mean other than just being a ring which George used to wear.

Having given up trying to derive meaning from the ring Matthew put it down and moved onto opening the next item. Again he carefully unwrapped it. Inside was a silver medallion. It was somewhat weathered, however all markings on it were still clearly visible. Both sides depicted a shield encasing a tree with stars above. Matthew thought it might be some kind of old family crest. Again, there was no note attached to give any further information as to what it was or where it came from. At the very least the symbols would give him a starting point for something to look for.

Finally Matthew picked up the last of the three items left to him within the envelope. Unwrapping this revealed a bronze chain holding a pendant. The pendant was also bronze and consisted of an outer ring with a diamond shape at the top. The diamond had a loop at the back through which the chain threaded. Within the outer ring was a coin. Each side was split in half with the top being a lighter tone with an embossed, four-pointed star and the lower half being a darker tone with an engraved star. The coin was held within the ring and could be flipped on a small bar going across the ring from one side to the other. The coin was held in place by a small pin at the bottom of the pendant. Try as he might Matthew couldn't pull the pin out and assumed it had been stuck in place over time. The necklace did look quite old. If Matthew had received it in any other way than what he had, he would have assumed it was some old, useless necklace of very little value. However, Matthew now knew better.

Matthew sat for a short while contemplating what everything meant.

'You couldn't have given me something a bit clearer, Grandad?' said Matthew quietly to himself. 'A ring, a giant-arse coin, a necklace and more cryptic messages. Ugh. Why couldn't he have just made it easy? I guess this is what he always wanted 'cause I was "coasting through life"... Ah well, got nothing better to do.'.

Matthew remembered that the letter had mentioned another item hidden somewhere in the house. 'Where could it be?'

Matthew put the necklace around his neck and the ring on one of his fingers. He picked up the medallion, held it above his head and shouted, 'Grandad! POINT ME TO YOUR STUFF!'

Nothing happened.

'I SAID GRANDAD! POINT ME TO YOUR STUFF!' and thrust his hand in the air again.

He put his hand down and looked around sheepishly, as if people were watching.

'Well that was a stupid idea,' he said and giggled to himself.

Matthew put down the medallion and took off the ring, thinking of where to look for this mystery item that he knew nothing about, besides its existence. The most logical place, Matthew decided, was to start in George's bedroom. The door to the room hadn't been opened since George passed and Matthew was very apprehensive about even touching the door, let alone entering the room.

As Matthew put his hand on the doorknob he took two slow, deep breaths. His heartbeat accelerated.

'It's only a room,' he told himself. 'There's nothing in there that's any different than it was before.'

Slowly he turned the knob and opened the door. Walking through, his chest tightened and his heart was pounding. He looked around the room. Nothing had changed from the last time he had seen it. George always kept his room extremely tidy so it was no surprise that there was nothing out of place.

'Calm down, you idiot,' he scolded himself. 'You had to come in here at some point.'

Matthew started searching the room looking for anything slightly out of place. With George being an elderly navy veteran of simple tastes this wasn't an overly difficult task. His philosophy was always that a bedroom was for sleeping so the bedroom was a bed, a small bedside table with a lamp atop it, a chest of drawers and a small, built-in wardrobe.

Matthew tried to disturb it as little as possible as he carefully shifted the contents of the room. He quickly discarded the bed, bedside table and chest of drawers as having anything which may be of use to him in any way going forward. By now he had calmed himself down and purely focused on finding whatever it was that he was supposed to find. He opened the wardrobe to find it also quite simple. There was a rack of clothes with a shelf above for a small amount of storage. The rack of clothes consisted of a few suits, one grey, one black and one beige; a few nice button-up shirts, all white; and a few jackets of varying lengths to match the suits.

Despite Matthew's tall, lanky frame, the shelf was too high for a thorough search. He took a chair from the dining room, brought it back into George's bedroom and placed it in front of the wardrobe.

The first thing he found was a box about the same size as a shoebox. *Surely this must be it*, he thought.

Matthew jumped down from the chair and sat on the bed, throwing off the lid as he did so. Unfortunately the box was filled with old Birthday and Christmas cards, some of them dating back decades. Matthew put the box to one side, doubting that there would be anything in any of the cards that would be useful, and climbed back onto the chair to investigate the shelf once again.

The next thing Matthew came across were two old photo albums. He took them both down from the shelf and once again moved to the bed to have a look through them. Putting one down on the bed and looking at the cover of the other album, Matthew immediately welled up. The photo placed into the cover was a family portrait of Matthew as a baby, his parents and George. As he flicked through the pages tears streamed down his cheeks as an overwhelming feeling of loneliness overcame him. Despite his friends and how much they had helped him, Matthew couldn't help but feel like he had no family. The album covered from the time his parents got together until a photo of Matthew and George taken on Matthew's eighteenth birthday.

Matthew finished looking through the album and took a few moments to collect himself before picking up the other album. The front of this one had an old photo of George in his navy uniform. Matthew hadn't really seen too many pictures of his grandad from his younger years. He couldn't help but notice how buff he was back in the day. A very handsome man with a look of confidence, bordering on arrogance. Very different from the man that Matthew grew up with. Turning through the pages gave a glimpse of George's travels with the navy. Some of the photos featured George's old friends whom Matthew had met after the funeral. This album had a much more calming effect on Matthew and he enjoyed a laugh at some of the silly photos taken of George during those times.

Matthew came to a set of photos of George and his mates on shore leave at a beach. He noticed something familiar and quickly flicked through to find the closest photo of George. Taking a very close look, Matthew could see that George had the necklace he inherited around his neck. Despite never seeing the necklace before unwrapping it earlier, Matthew at least now knew that his grandad had it in his possession for a very long time. The rest of the album didn't shed any more light on any of the items although it did have a lot of photos of George's wedding and Matthew's mother growing up with her parents. There were also some very strange Halloween photos. Matthew had no idea that George was into dress ups.

Having taken up the better part of an hour looking through the albums Matthew was back to business and back on the chair looking through the contents of the shelf. He pulled out a couple of old hats, some old receipts and a documents folder containing birth certificates, marriage certificates and other documents that George had kept hold of over time. Matthew was starting to get very frustrated that he couldn't find anything else.

'Where else would he have put things?' Matthew said through gritted teeth, hitting his fist on the wall next to the wardrobe. His expression suddenly changed. He hit the wall on the other side of the wardrobe. The sound was different. He went back again to the side he originally hit which was a few inches wide to the corner of the room. He began hitting up and down this strip of wall noticing where the sound changed. Where the wall matched the shelf space he could hear a hollow sound.

Quickly, Matthew jumped down and sprinted to his bedroom to get his torch. Scrambling back onto the chair Matthew shone his torch from side to side above the shelf. There was no visible difference on either side. He lightly tapped the wall with his torch and could hear the same hollow sound. Leaning in as far as he could, Matthew took a close look to try and find a way of getting through to the space behind. The wall appeared as solid as all the other walls. There were no handles or cracks to give the indication that there was a door or hatch of any kind. For a few seconds he scrunched up his face in deep concentration as to what to do next.

'Sorry Grandad… this is kinda your fault though.'

Matthew smashed the butt end of the torch into the wall and punched through to the other side with a crack. The false wall was a thin plank which has been plastered over. Matthew continued to bash through to expose the space. Having cleared out half the false wall he shone his torch through. Inside was a box. The removal of a little more of the wall allowed Matthew to pull the box out.

What Matthew now held was an intricately carved wooden box, stained to a dark red hue. On each surface of the box were deep carvings, about a centimetre deep, in patterns of curves and points as if vines were pushing out from the surface. The top, or what Matthew assumed was the top, contained a carving of the same crest that Matthew had found on the medallion earlier in the day. The shield, the tree and the stars.

'This must be it!' he exclaimed, turning the box around in his hands. 'Where the hell does it open?'

Matthew continued to turn the box, checking each side to find the opening. There did not seem to even be the slightest crack on any of the sides let alone a way of unlocking it.

'OK. I guess I need to break it open.'

Matthew threw the box onto the ground as hard as he could. It bounced a couple of times and rolled like a dice, coming to stop, still in one piece. He picked the box up and inspected it. Not so much as a mark upon it.

'Dammit!' he said crinkling his face in frustrated confusion.

Matthew took the box to the kitchen and picked up the biggest, sharpest knife he could find. He stabbed at the box again and again yet still no mark upon it.

'What the hell kind of wood is this?'

Next stop was the garden shed. Matthew walked in with purpose, switched on the light and set the box up in the vice on his grandad's old workbench. Finding a chisel and a mallet, he attempted to chip away from every angle, on every surface of the box to no avail.

Now at peak frustration Matthew dropped the chisel, gripped the mallet with both hands, held it above his head and swung down as hard as he could. As the mallet head met the box, Matthew swore he saw something strange come from the box. Again he lifted the mallet and swung down to strike again, making sure to keep a close eye on the point of contact. With the low light inside the shed from the single small bulb, Matthew saw a blue glowing cloud emanate from the point of contact and quickly disappear. He hit the box again to confirm again what he had seen. There could be no doubt this time that his eyes did not deceive him.

Chapter Four
An Investigation To Be Had

Matthew loosened the vice, pulled out the box and ran back into the house. He quickly stuffed the box into his backpack and put on some clothes and shoes. Half way out the front door Matthew realised he hadn't showered and decided to take stock of his current odour. Unsurprisingly he smelled disgusting and immediately turned around. A quick brush of the teeth and spray of deodorant later, he was out the door, running to the bus stop.

While sitting on the bus Matthew felt a strange feeling on his chest. It disappeared as soon as it arrived and Matthew thought nothing of it. A couple of minutes later he felt it again. It was a vibration on his chest. Looking down into his shirt Matthew saw that he still had the necklace on that George had left him. He grabbed the pendant on the necklace. It was indeed vibrating in his hand and once again dissipated. Matthew spent the rest of the bus ride looking closely at the pendant, although it did not vibrate again.

Finally he arrived at his stop. Matthew jumped off the bus and ran to The Floating Star. Barging through the door, Matthew bypassed the queue at the counter and started rambling to Safiri whilst attempting to catch his breath.

'You won't believe… what I just-'

'Hey!' shouted the first customer in line. 'Get to the back of the queue!'

Alaska poked her head up from stacking some books on a bookshelf. 'Matthew! Out back now!' she said sternly, about as angry as she gets.

'Sorry… sorry, everyone!' Matthew apologised as he walked through the storeroom and out to the courtyard at the back of the cafe. The area was a small, paved area filled with potted plants. It was used by employees on break and occasionally by Alaska for meetings.

'Sit down, Matthew,' said Alaska. 'I'll make you some tea.'

It was rare that anyone was privy to Alaska's special stash of herbal tea. She said it healed the spirit and calmed the mind. Matthew thought it tasted like regular tea of which he wasn't a huge fan anyway.

'Why are you here, Matthew? Why did you run in, carrying on?' her voice was now back to the calm, motherly tone.

'I just had to show Safiri and Sam something. I know I shouldn't have run in and interrupted customers. I'm sorry.'

'It's OK, Matthew. Did you open the letter George left you? Was it something to do with that?'

'I opened it,' he replied, not wishing to give too much away about George's secrets, even to the person who he thought of most as a mother. 'I went into his room-'

'Oh dear. Are you OK? I'm sure it was very difficult for you.'

'Yeah. I haven't been in there since…'

'It must have been difficult seeing all his belongings in there.'

'It was. I also found some old photo albums. There were photos of me… with Mum and Dad… And some of Grandad when he was younger… in the navy.' Matthew's eyes started to well up slightly. 'I should've been there for him more… near the end. I should have known what was happening. I should've helped him more.'

Despite all the help Alaska had been giving Matthew since George had passed away this was the first time that Matthew really opened up to her. She always told him he could talk to her when he was ready and never pushed him. Maybe there was something in the tea that was making him speak more freely, or maybe he just realised he needed to release the valve a little.

'You can't blame yourself. There's nothing that you could've done. None of us knew and I'm sure George had his reasons for keeping it a secret. I'm sure he just didn't want to worry you.'

'You knew him longer than me,' said Matthew. 'Was he always keeping secrets from people? Did he like making people work for things?'

'What do you mean? As far as I know he didn't keep any secrets from me other than things that weren't any of my business. As far as working for things he always believed people should put in an honest day's work, wasn't one for freeloaders.'

'That's not really what I mean. Grandad... left me things but didn't tell me what they were.'

'What kind of things?' asked Alaska.

'I dunno. Family heirlooms maybe. He had a necklace which I saw him wearing in one of his old navy photos.'

Matthew pulled the necklace out from his shirt. He also took out the ring and medallion. Given the lengths his grandad went to hide the box and what had happened when he struck it, Matthew decided that it was probably best to leave it in the bag.

'Have you ever seen these before?' he asked.

'The ring I've seen him wearing lately. The others, no. Did you find them in his room?'

'No. These were in the envelope that Mr. Aldridge gave me, along with a letter. The letter didn't tell me what they were. He made a point of telling me that I need to find the answers for myself, like some scavenger hunt.'

Matthew took a few breaths and a sip of tea as Alaska took a closer look at the three items presented to her.

'Is the ring his old wedding ring?' Matthew asked.

'Oh, no. His wedding ring was a plain band. I'm not sure why he was suddenly wearing this ring. What are you going to do now?'

'Not sure. I don't know what else to do.'

'Maybe he's trying to bring back the curiosity you had as a child.'

'What do you mean?' asked Matthew, his nose crinkled and one eyebrow raised.

'Don't you remember? You used to come in here with your grandad and he would sit you down with a science book, or a history book, or some magical adventure novel. You were always reading and asking questions. Maybe he didn't want you spending your life working here, as much as I would love to have you around forever. Maybe he wanted you to have an adventure and this was his way of getting you out and helping you find your place in the world,' Alaska was beginning to look excited.

'Well he didn't give me any clues at all. I have no idea where to start.'

'There was a reason you were rambling excitedly when you came in, Matthew. Maybe talk to Sam and Safiri and see if they can help. In the meantime, go home and try to relax. Take your mind off it and maybe something will come to you.'

'OK. Thanks, Alaska. I do want to come back to work tomorrow, though. Still gotta pay them bills.'

'In that case, come in the morning and I'll fix you up a nice breakfast before you start. Now get out of here,' she joked.

'Thanks,' said Matthew as he stood up, putting everything back in his bag and the necklace around his neck.

As he walked out past the counter he called out. 'See you guys at mine when you finish?'

'Yep. No probs,' said Sam.

'See you then,' added Safiri.

Later that afternoon Safiri and Sam walked through the front door of Matthew's house. Matthew had left it unlocked knowing what time they would finish.

''Sup guys!' said Matthew as they put their bags down.

'You're cheery. You find out George was royalty or something?' joked Sam.

'Maybe something better.' Matthew paused his video and walked over to the dining table, putting down his laptop. 'Follow me.'

Matthew took his friends out to the shed where he had already tightened the box into the vice.

'What's going on, Matthew?' asked Safiri.

'Well… Grandad left me a few things with a letter. I'll show you that stuff later. He also said there was something hidden in the house. I looked for ages and found a false wall in the wardrobe. Hidden in the wall was this,' he pointed to the box.

'Nice!', exclaimed Sam.

'Now, stand back,' Matthew picked up the mallet.

Safiri's face went from excited to worried.

'Matthew, what are you doing? That looks kind of expensive.'

'Just keep your eyes on the box. Don't blink.'

Matthew lifted his hands with the mallet, as he had done earlier in the day, and brought them down as hard as he could, hitting the box. The blue, glowing cloud blasted out from where the mallet hit the box.

'You guys see that?' Matthew asked.

'I'm not sure,' said Safiri.

'Was there some blue stuff fly out of it?' asked Sam.

'Yep,' replied Matthew and hit the box again.

'What the hell was that?' Safiri and Sam both asked at the same time.

'No idea… but it's pretty cool, right?' Matthew loosened the vice and removed the box. 'Not a scratch on it. Crazy!'

'I dunno, Matthew,' Safiri said, crouching to take a closer look at the box and poking it with a piece of wood he found lying next to the bench. 'To discharge energy like that… might be dangerous.'

'What are you, a scientist now? What do you think, Sam?'

'Other than bashing it to make a fuzzy glow do we know anything else about?'

'I know it's unbreakable and doesn't open. It's also got something to do with another thing that Grandad left me. Other than that, I got nothing.' Matthew removed the box from the vice. 'I'll show you the other stuff.'

Matthew and his friends left the shed and walked back into the house. They sat at the dining table and Matthew went through each of the items left to him in the envelope, one by one. He showed them the old photos of George wearing the necklace from his time in the navy and how the crest on the box matched the one found on the medallion. After tossing with the idea of sharing the letter with them he decided that he couldn't possibly go any further without their help.

'Man, this is some weird, cryptic stuff. Maybe he was really a spy or went on crazy adventures like Indiana Jones,' said Sam excitedly.

'He did like to tell stories,' added Safiri, 'where he was pretty vague on the details of who the characters were.'

'I dunno,' said Matthew. 'It's not like he went away on trips and that kind of stuff would make a few enemies. No one shifty has ever come around here asking about him.'

Safiri rubbed his chin, assessing everything laid before him.

'They're strange old artefacts. A medallion with a crest none of us recognise; an old ring that George only recently started wearing; a necklace that he wore a long time ago with a broken pin that won't open; and an indestructible box that shares the crest of the medallion, has no distinguishable opening and behaves strangely when hit really hard.'

Matthew and Sam looked at each other, grinning, then looked back to Safiri.

'What?' Safiri asked.

Sam leaned across the table, pinched Safiri's cheek and gave it a wiggle.

'Our little boy is all excited at having a puzzle to solve.'

'We knew you'd come around,' added Matthew, still grinning from ear to ear.

Safiri swatted Sam's hand away in embarrassment. 'Come on guys. We've not got a lot to work with here. We need to concentrate. But if this starts to get dangerous, I'm out.'

'Fine,' conceded Matthew. 'We all agree we're gonna find out what this stuff means until the point that Saf chickens out?'

'Yes,' Safiri and Sam declared in unison.

Sam was straight back on task. 'George said they're all tools that you can use if you choose a certain life. What the hell does that mean?'

'I'm not sure,' replied Safiri. 'They must have some use beyond just looking pretty or possibly being valuable. With the weird properties of the box it could mean anything. The way George is saying it in the letter he makes it seem like the secrets are pretty epic, although he could also just be telling a good story like we're in an escape room. I think the easiest starting point is to find out what this crest is.'

All three took out their laptops and began searching databases of crests and symbols, starting with George's family name and then his father's.

After a few hours painstakingly searching family crests in an attempt to find even the smallest clue as to what the medallion crest meant, or where it came from, they were no closer to answers than when they began.

Sam had fallen asleep on her keyboard and Matthew had taken to flicking his grandad's cards at the TV, which he had initially turned on just for some background noise. Occasionally Safiri had said that a card looked familiar as he took a break from his screen, however that was only because some resembled lightning, snowflakes or other elements, as opposed to finding a connection to anything he was researching.

As Matthew flicked a card at a particularly strange looking plump man flogging his services Matthew stopped and slowly began to stand.

'What is it?' Safiri asked.

'I might have seen something,' mumbled Matthew as he walked over to the TV remote and paused it on the strange advertisement that was playing.

Safiri nudged Sam awake who gave a hard push of her own in retaliation for being woken up.

Matthew made his way to the TV and picked up the card he had just thrown. This particular card contained what looked like an eye surrounded by a curve which made it look like an alien cyclops head. That was then surrounded by a rectangle with a line intersecting the center at the top of the rectangle. In each corner was a cross.

'Take a look at the symbol in the middle. Just the alien head. You think it looks kinda like the symbol that weird guy has in the ad.' Matthew pointed to the TV.

Placed in the top left corner of the TV was the logo for the company in the advertisement. Above the words *The Eye of Dusk* was a hexagon. Inside that hexagon was a symbol very similar to that in the middle of the card Matthew was holding.

Safiri and Sam immediately jumped out of their chairs and ran to the TV to take a closer look.

'No way!' yelled Sam.

'It looks real close to the card, Matthew,' added Safiri.

After a few more minutes of close inspection and confirmation between the three of them they were all in consensus that it was the same symbol.

'I think we've got our first lead, team,' Matthew gushed. 'How about we check it out after work tomorrow?'

'Let's do it!' yelled Sam.

'Hold up,' Safiri interrupted the moment of victory. 'We don't know anything about this guy. Rewind the ad and we'll see what he's about.'

Matthew, still holding the remote, rewound the ad to the start and pressed play. It didn't take long to realise what they were dealing with.

'Ugh,' Matthew sighed as his head dropped. 'A sleazy, weirdo psychic. Just what we need.'

Chapter Five
Antiquities & Extractions

At the end of the morning shift, after a quick bite to eat, the three friends ran to Sam's car full of excitement, Safiri a little more apprehension, at what they might find at The Eye of Dusk. Whilst driving as quick (and legally) as possible, the speculation of what was about to occur escalated to more ridiculous proportions the closer they got to their destination.

'Maybe he knows George and they've set up this weird scavenger hunt to get you out and doing something instead of staying home all the time,' Safiri theorised.

'Maybe he's part of a secret society and this will lead us to some long lost treasure,' added Sam. 'It could be that George learned about it years ago and got too old to finish the job, leaving you to brave the wilds in search of your fortune.'

Matthew added his two cents worth of absurdity into the conversation. 'Maybe this guy's an alien. The first wave of an invading force and Grandad needs us to create a team to defend the world from being taken over.'

'If we were about to be attacked wouldn't your grandad have taken this info to someone with a bit more authority than us? Or at the very least give you all the info he had instead of making us look for it?' Safiri keen not to get too far beyond logic.

'I never said there were no holes in my idea,' insisted Matthew. 'Just putting it out there. Mull it over and get back to me.'

All three laughed.

'Seriously, though. What the hell are we gonna ask this guy?' Matthew asked.

'Just treat him like one of our crazier customers,' Sam answered. 'You're good at making them like you and getting them to talk about all kinds of rubbish.'

'Fair enough. I'll do that.'

The Eye of Dusk was a twenty minute drive from The Floating Star, on the other side of town. Parking the car a short distance down the road, the trio walked along the path to a relatively large storefront given the nature of the business. The windows spanned six large panes of glass with double glass doors for entry.

A sign dropping down from the awning, as well as the two glass doors, had printed *The Eye of Dusk* along with the hexagon containing the symbol which they all now referred to as *the alien cyclops*. On the doors were also printed the words *Psychic, Medium & Seer*.

Very little could be gauged from peering through the windows as the store appeared to be quite dark inside.

An old bell rung, which had been affixed above the door, as they opened to enter. Strangely old-tech given the modern appearance of the store from the outside. Inside resembled more of an antique shop than anything else. Despite the extensive width of the store it was only about ten metres deep.

Shelves surrounded the inner walls housing all manner of random items, seemingly in no particular order. Intricate boxes, strangely shaped musical instruments, bowls, bags, hats, pins, strange constructions of which their use could not be determined, all made up a small part of the random arrangement of antiquities. Some pieces of jewellery and sculptures were displayed on scattered tables and pedestals.

Wooden floors complimented the antique feel of the store, as did an old wooden counter at the back of the store which resembled a saloon bar frequented by cowboys in the wild west.

A round table and four chairs, wooden again, sat in an open area to the left of the counter, in front of a door which Matthew assumed led to a back office.

The door opened and out walked the plump man from the TV. He wore a large, ill-fitting grey suit with a white shirt buttoned down a few buttons further than was comfortable for anybody looking at him. This was to expose a few gold chains hanging around his neck. The man's face looked strangely swollen. A sleazy looking goatee sat above his double chin and thin-framed round glasses rested upon his small, bulbous nose. Despite being inside the man wore a grey fedora upon his shoulder-length ratty black hair.

'Why, hello there. My name is Finnigan Fisk. How are you this fine day?' his voice was overly cheerful, bordering on patronising, occasionally breaking like a teenager going through puberty. 'Would you like a reading? Maybe you would like to connect with somebody you lost? Or perhaps you are here to purchase one of these artefacts you see around you? They are a conduit to the other side so the spirits can protect you, you know?'

'Protect us from what?' enquired Sam.

'Well, anything that might do you harm or bring you bad luck. You can never be too careful, can you? Come, take a seat,' he motioned toward the table and chairs that were sitting between them.

Matthew sat down opposite Finnigan thinking that maybe Sam's theory about the treasure was on point with words like *artefacts* being thrown around.

Safiri and Sam walked around the store, pretending to look at the various artefacts on offer whilst keeping an ear on what was being discussed.

Finnigan put his hands on the table and fidgeted with a bronze ring, a fake smile across his face.

'I sense that you've come here for more than your usual reading.'

'What makes you say that?' asked Matthew.

'My ability as a psychic, my boy,' Finnigan's tone suddenly became more serious and controlled as he once again fiddled with the ring. 'You have a specific question you wish me to answer.'

Finnigan's eyes narrowed and his lips pursed. He held his face like this for a few moments as Matthew lowered his eyebrows in confusion. As if switching personality, Finnigan returned to his overly jovial disposition.

'Unfortunately I cannot be of any help to you. Now I must ask you to leave. The store is closing.'

'But we haven't even asked you anything yet… and it's only two in the afternoon.'

Finnigan stood and motioned his arm toward the door. 'I'm sorry but I cannot be of assistance. Please, if you could make your way to the exit.'

'What? No!' Matthew stood up from his chair and leaned on the table.

Finnigan started moving toward Matthew, the fake cheerful expression still on his face, however beginning to look very strained. He continued to motion toward the door, almost shooing them out.

'Come on Matthew,' sighed Safiri. 'Let's go.'

'NO!' shouted Matthew. 'I came here for answers. Tell me what it is you think I want to know. Why won't you tell me and why do you keep fiddling with that ring?' Matthew, fists down on the table, was now trembling as the anger swelled up inside him.

Finnigan quickly put his hands down by his side. 'I don't have to tell you anything. You're not even a paying customer. You're trespassing on my property. Now, get out!'

Matthew walked to the nearest shelf and picked up a, giant, white and brown snail shell with five buttons on the top like a trumpet. He held the shell up in the air.

'This looks expensive. Wouldn't want it to break.'

'Matthew, what are you doing?' gasped Sam.

'No, no, no, no!' pleaded Finnigan. He raised his hands as if positioning to catch the shell should Matthew throw it.

'Tell me what I want to know!' demanded Matthew.

'Fine! Fine. Just put the shell down… please.'

Matthew lowered the shell but did not return it to the shelf, instead holding onto it as leverage, should Finnigan decide to once again become unwilling to cooperate.

'You want to know about the symbol… the one in my logo.' he mumbled.

Matthew was taken aback, not expecting Finnigan to actually know what it was that he was going to ask. He placed the shell on the table and both he and Finnigan return to their seats.

'Tell me about the symbol,' Matthew demanded.

'It's the mind rune... from Dusk,' Finnigan responded, timidly.

'And what does it mean… what is Dusk?'

Finnigan sat up slightly, controlling his voice a little more. 'No. Now I get to ask you a question. If you want to ask me more then we take it in turns.'

'Fine,' Matthew conceded.

'Why do you want to know specifically about that symbol?' Finnigan asked, becoming more comfortable that things were starting to go more in his favour than it had been moments earlier.

'You're the psychic. Shouldn't you already know?'

'That's not how it works. I can only see what the subject is willing to tell. So I'll ask again. Why do you want to specifically know about that symbol?'

Matthew reached into his pocket, pulled out the card depicting the alien cyclops and slowly laid it on the table.

'Interesting,' Finnigan said with curiosity, reaching across the table to pick up the card.

Matthew, reluctant to hand over the card, continued to push down on the card, forcing Finnigan to pull the card, with an air of annoyance, from under Matthew's fingers.

Finnigan examined the card closely and mumbled to himself, 'I haven't seen another one of these in this world.' Facing Matthew again and speaking more directly he asked, 'Where did you get this card?'

'It's none of your business where I got the card,' Matthew stated. 'My question now. What did you mean by "this world"?'

Stumbling over his words, Finnigan waved away the question. 'No-no-nothing. I just meant this industry.'

'You're lying,' Matthew accused the plump man, now clearly rattled. 'Your industry should all know about something called *the mind rune.*'

'How dare you acc-'

'Why are you lying to me?!' Matthew fumed, beginning to tremble again. 'What is the mind rune? What is Dusk? And what do you mean by this world?!'

Finnigan stood up abruptly. 'Who do you think you are! How dare you come into my-'

Sam picked up a yellow, translucent, glass sphere that was sitting on a small pedestal on a shelf next to where she was standing. 'Answer him!' she demanded.

Safiri, in an effort to display solidarity within the group, picked up a solid, jagged horn, similar to ivory, however with a dark red colouring. He held the horn above his head and tried his hardest to put on a threatening expression whilst hiding his panic.

'No! Put them down!' Finnigan wailed.

Attempting to move away from the table, he stumbled on the chair which he had failed to push away as he stood up. As he began to fall he tried to hold onto the table to keep himself up, his hair caught between his hand and the table. Pushing himself up again his hair, which was now revealed to be a wig, stayed behind and fell to the floor with the fedora. Finnigan screeched with despair as Matthew, Safiri and Sam gasped in horror.

Drooping down from the back of Finnigan's head were a number of thick, fleshy tendrils, like short dreadlocks hanging from the back of a bald man's head.

Finnigan dropped to his knees and began to sob. He scrambled to pick up his hat, with attached wig, and push it haphazardly back onto his head. Despite the hat being relatively straight, the wig was no longer covering the tendrils hovering just above his shoulders.

'What the hell are you?' Matthew gawped. 'What world are you talking about? Are you from another world? Is Dusk the other world? Grandad… the stories… he said they're true. How can they be true?'

'I DON'T KNOW ANYTHING ABOUT YOUR STUPID STORIES!' Finnigan screamed. 'Get out! You've ruined everything!' a modicum of control returning to his voice.

'Not until you tell me the truth,' demanded Matthew. 'Then we'll go.'

Finnigan reluctantly nodded.

Matthew, deciding to take a more kindhearted approach, knelt down to Finnigan's level, 'Please, tell me what you are, what is Dusk and how did you get to Earth.'

'Earth?! I said this world, not this planet, you stupid child!' Finnigan barked, 'I'm from a WORLD called Dusk! Good luck running off and telling everybody. They'll throw you into the asylum. HA! I came to Dawn through a rift that's closed now so you can't prove anything.'

'So our world is Dawn and yours is Dusk? How many worlds are there?' Matthew inquired.

'I don't know. I wasn't sure if there were any others until I came here. I had only heard old stories about Dusk and Dawn.'

Finnigan stood up and walked over to the counter. From a cupboard he retrieved a steel goblet and a bottle containing a purple liquid, which he opened and proceeded to pour.

Matthew picked up his card, which had fallen to the floor as Finnigan stumbled over the chair. He stood and remained at the table, a safe distance from the counter. 'How did you know what I was going to ask you when we first came in? Is it something you… Duskers… can do?'

'Duskers?' Finnigan scoffed. 'I am a Squaar. Oppressed for too long before I came here. Good thing I had my ring with me. You stupid humans are ready to spill about anything and everything at a moment's notice. Will pay big money to anyone who tells them what they want to hear.' He took a sip from his goblet and continued. 'My ring has the mind rune. At least it can still do something. Not like all these other useless artefacts. Your world sucked every last bit of power from them.'

'So you're a fraud?' Sam snapped.

'Fraud?' Finnigan again scoffed at the accusation. 'Girl, there are no rules on how one can read a mind with which to level such insults.'

'Except you also claim to be a medium and a seer,' she retorted, refusing to accept that this was an honest business.

'Oh, please.' He said sarcastically. 'I don't tell them anything they don't want to hear. It's all just sitting there, at the edge of their mind, waiting to be extracted. I provide a service of hope for those with too much money to use it responsibly. They leave happy and I get to live comfortably in the capitalism that is Dawn.' He smugly took another sip of the purple liquid.

Safiri had heard enough, a rare outburst escaped his lips. 'However you want to justify it, you exploit people for profit. It's disgusting.'

'It's *your* world. I just play by its rules. Anyway, I've answered your questions and as agreed it is now time for you to take your leave.'

'Let's get out of here,' suggested Safiri and started making his way to the door. Sam and Matthew turned and followed Safiri.

As Matthew was half way out the door, he turned back to Finnigan and asked, 'Why did you answer the questions?'

'You were about to destroy my stock. What was I supposed to do?'

Matthew clarified his question, 'I mean, why so much detail? You could have just given the bare minimum.'

'To be honest, it was actually cathartic to talk about it. It's not like you can do anything with the information anyway. You'll get locked up if you seriously try and tell anyone.'

'We'll see,' Matthew teased, with a wry smile on his face. He walked out and let the door close behind him as the arrogant grin on Finnigan's face slowly dissipated.

Safiri and Sam were waiting for Matthew outside the adjacent store, keen to get back to the car as quickly as possible.

'Let's debrief at the lake,' Matthew suggested.

Safiri and Sam nodded in agreement and they all walked away from The Eye of Dusk at a brisk pace.

Silence encapsulated the drive back to the lake as all three processed what had just happened. Nobody looked at another. They simply looked out of the nearest window, contemplating this new version of the universe they were now faced with, or in Sam's case, trying to not let it distract her from driving.

With the car parked on the road, they quickly made their way to the nearest park bench under a tree.

'What the hell just happened?' Sam blurted out as soon as they had reached the bench. She slapped herself in the face a few times just to confirm that she was awake. 'He was taking the piss, right? That can't be true.'

Matthew and Safiri sat on the bench as Sam continued to pace back and forth in front of them, trying to make sense of everything.

Safiri chimed in, logic first as always. 'He must have been lying. Good storyteller though, almost as good as George.'

'I don't know guys,' added Matthew. 'I think he was telling the truth.'

'You can't be serious, Matthew,' Safiri scoffed. 'He's a conman. You heard him. He's got no shame. Tell any lie for money.'

'What exactly was he getting off us, though?' Matthew retorted. 'He wasn't getting any money from us. What reason would he have to lie about it?'

'Maybe he lies so much that it's second nature to him. He just can't help himself,' Sam deciding it was too outrageous to consider as truth.

'He knew what I was going to ask. None of us gave any indication of what we wanted from him. I doubt anyone else goes in there wanting to know what we did. We also caught him out in a lie. Why go back to making up some random story?'

'Maybe he was baiting us?' suggested Safiri.

'Maybe, but that's a lot of effort to go to just to tell us some over-the-top story. One more thing, Grandad told me the stories were true. So either they both just happen to be taking the piss; they're in on it together, which seems a bit too cold for Grandad; or they're both telling the truth. We all saw the box. It's wood and hollow but couldn't be broken. Nothing is that strong. And the blue glowing stuff that flew off it when I hit it. There's nothing logical about anything that's happened since Grandad died. Even his cancer made no sense. He looked perfectly fine right until we had to take him to the hospital. It's like he aged in the ambulance.'

'Wait. What do you mean his stories are true?' inquired Sam.

'He literally said to me, in the hospital, that the stories he told were true, at least for the most part. He said that he knows secrets of the universe that nobody else knows. Why would his last words to me be lies? That's not him... Don't know about you guys but I feel like the stories are pretty consistent with what Finnigan said. Artefacts, magic, strange worlds.'

'Sorry, Matthew,' Safiri continued to doubt. 'There's not enough evidence to make me believe something that crazy.'

'We're forgetting about those weird tendril things coming out the back of his head.' Sam added, 'and the weird purple drink.'

'That drink could be anything, Sam, and the tentacles could just be prosthetics for movies and stuff,' Safiri continued to reject the narrative, still very skeptical. 'There was also nothing that he said that gets us any closer to whatever it is we're looking for. Even if he was telling the truth, the rift, as he called it, is apparently closed now so what are we looking for?'

'I dunno guys. I don't have an answer,' Matthew conceded. 'We're in an even worse position than when we started. We've got a whole heap of questions and no idea where to go next.'

'Let's get out of here. Go and watch a movie or something,' Sam suggested.

'You guys go. I'm gonna take a walk. Try and relax a bit and clear my head.'

'You sure?' asked Safiri.

'Yeah. I'll catch you guys tomorrow at work.'

'OK. See ya,' said Safiri.

'Catch ya later,' added Sam.

Chapter Six

Just a Normal Doorway

As Safiri and Sam made their way back to Sam's car, Matthew walked toward a dirt path which ran between the main lake and a smaller one. The two lakes were connected by streams which flowed through dense brush and trees. The path followed along the banks of the smaller lake with small bridges crossing over streams.

A small, one metre strip of grass flanked the path on either side with a few trees and reeds protruding from the edge of the lake and the banks on one side, and an impenetrable barrier of plants blocking access to the main lake. The streams connecting the two lakes also had a small strip of grass on either side, however it was barely wide enough to walk down and the steep embankments meant that it would be a difficult task to return to dry land should one fall in.

The lakes and streams were home to numerous types of water birds. Ducks and swans could usually be seen riding the winding streams with their young, diving for food. A number of other birds nested in the surrounding trees, singing their songs to all who pass by.

Matthew regularly took this route to get away from the noise of cars and people and just leave himself with the serene tones of nature. Any time things weren't going right for him, or he just wanted a little peace and quiet he would spend some time strolling between the lakes, letting the ambiance take his worries away.

As he walked along the path he began to feel the necklace vibrate, like it had done when he was on the bus. It continued to intensify as he continued walking across a small bridge that crossed a stream. The vibration then began to dissipate slightly as he continued to walk on down the path.

"What the hell is going on with this necklace?" Matthew whispered to himself.

He stopped and pulled the necklace out from inside his shirt. The vibration continued. Turning around, he began to walk back where he had come from. The vibration intensified once again. Matthew crossed the bridge and walked down the path at which time the vibration decreased.

Again, he turned and walked toward the bridge. This time, as he reached the bridge, Matthew stopped. Looking down, he noticed that the necklace was slightly pulling to his right, down the stream toward the main lake. Matthew moved onto the bridge and faced the stream. The necklace continued to pull toward the stream, now pulling slightly away from his body.

'Do you want me to go down the stream?' he asked. 'Why am I talking to a necklace?'

Matthew rotated his body left and right to make sure that the necklace continued to pull in the exact same direction, no matter which way he was facing.

'Fine. I'll walk down the stream. But if I fall in you're gonna be in trouble.'

Matthew walked off the bridge and stared toward where the necklace wanted him to go. Taking in two deep breaths he slowly stepped onto the grass which lined the thin channel of water before him. The dense trees grew over the entire area leaving everything in shadow. The grass was a few inches long and, being on an angled embankment, quite slippery. Branches pushed out at differing heights along the strip forcing Matthew to duck and climb in order to pass through.

The proportions of his body proving to be both a curse and a blessing as there was no easy path through the obstacle course of trees. A constant state of concentration was required to keep from slipping on the moist grass and tumbling into the stream. He did, however, have the lanky flexibility to contort his body through the tightest of spaces, and reach to ensure he was always holding onto something. His backpack, proving to be another challenge altogether, regularly getting caught on anything even slightly protruding from the branches into his path.

The further he pushed through into the unknown the more eery the surroundings became. As the stream took slight turns left and right, sight of the dirt path became impossible. The hint of civilisation which could be heard from the path was now gone. Even the volume of the stream seemed to have reduced to a mere trickle. The silence only occasionally broken from the tweet of a nesting bird high in a tree or the flapping of wings overhead.

As Matthew crept along the bank of the stream he stopped dead at the sound of movement in the bushes next to him. He turned his head, the intensity of his heart quickening. Remaining as still as possible while his feet spanned the gap between two large branches, Matthew attempted to scan the dense bushes where the noise originated. The sporadic crack of a twig or the rustle of leaves seemed to be moving in his direction.

Movement a few metres further up the path could now be heard. The same slow crack and rustle heading slowly toward him. Matthew tried as hard as he could to remain still, quiet and slow his breathing, which had rapidly accelerated with his heart. As both potential threats converged on his position he started to panic, looking around for a potential quick escape.

It was too late. With the rapid crunch of foliage from two directions, Matthew's left foot slipped off the branch. Falling sideways, he crashed down onto the branch which had previously been a relatively steady foothold, his shoulder colliding painfully with the wood. He bounced off the tree and onto the grass between the branches, sliding down the steep embankment.

Matthew reached out his right hand in a last desperate attempt to save himself. Gripping his hand as tightly as he could onto the only branch within reach, he managed to stop sliding and stabilise himself. Quickly, Matthew took hold of the same branch with his free hand and pulled himself up. As he did the source of his terror revealed itself from the shrubs. Two swamp hens emerged from a scuffle, pecking at the ground, to the humiliation of Matthew.

'You idiot!' he scolded himself. 'Crapping yourself over a couple of birds.'

Collecting himself, he lifted his body and stood upon the branch which saved him before continuing on alongside the stream. The branches reaching across now becoming more sparse as more clear grass became walkable on the flat surface. Although he hadn't gone too far as the crow flies, it had taken him a good twenty minutes of traversing trees to get to where it was now much easier to walk.

Matthew also noticed that the necklace was now pulling with more ferocity below his shirt. He pulled it out and saw that it was now at a forty five degree angle from his body, urging him to continue along the banks of the stream. He put the necklace back and continued on.

As the more pleasant walk continiued, Matthew could see that he was approaching where the stream merged into the large lake. Trees shot out from the banks at the mouth of the stream with the grass trail veering left into a relatively large clearing. The water surrounded three quarters of this round clearing with trees running along the bank, blocking any view out over the lake.

In the middle of the clearing sat an old park bench upon a small rectangle of red pavers. As Matthew entered the clearing the necklace stopped pulling and dropped flat against his chest. Matthew looked down and saw a bright, white light glowing, pulsing through his black t-shirt where the pendant rested. The shade from the trees enclosing the clearing made the pulsing glow that much brighter.

Matthew slowly stepped forward, fists clenched, trying with all his might to be mentally prepared for anything. If the seemingly sentient necklace pulling him wasn't causing him enough anxiety, the change in its behaviour upon reaching its desired destination put him firmly on edge.

Slowly he crept toward the bench. As he drew near he noticed nothing out of the ordinary. The bench was cast iron with wooden slats on the seat and the back. The arms were made to look like a series of layered iron leaves. The frame on the back branched across the center of the wood paneling to hold a ring. Within the ring was large bronze disc, moulded to depict the same design as that which was shown on the pendant, the two halves of different tones with a star in each.

Matthew's breath quickened.

'This is it,' he told himself. 'This is what Grandad wanted me to find. This bench… which does what exactly? Maybe I need to sit on it?'

He sat down very slowly, shutting hit eyes, bracing himself for whatever happened when he touched down.

Matthew opened his eyes again, not knowing what to expect. He looked from side to side.

'Nothing. Nothing happened. Am I supposed to take this bench home? Is it the long lost treasure I'm supposed to find? Who the hell am I even talking to? Grandad! What do I need to do now?!'

he asked in a commanding tone.

Matthew waited a moment just in case somehow he received an answer. He stood up and walked around the bench, inspecting it from multiple angles in case there was some clue or secret he was missing. There were no other markings on the bench other than the disc.

Throwing himself onto the bench in defeat, Matthew put his head in his hands, going through everything in his mind that had occurred since George had passed, hoping for an epiphany. Still nothing came to him.

Matthew removed the necklace from his shirt and stared at it. Despite the brightness of the light it did not cause him any pain to look directly at it. Strangely the pin wasn't behaving in the same manner as the rest of the pendant. While the ring and coin pulsed white, the pin did not pulse at all. Instead it emanated a blue glowing cloud in the same way the box did when Matthew hit it. On closer inspection, the cloud seemed to be made up of thousands of tiny sparks falling from the pin like a tiny blue sparkler.

Matthew moved his finger to the pin and touched it. Contrary to expectation there was no heat. The sparks provided a slight tingling in his finger, however he felt no pain at all. Deciding to take a chance on something that was impossible last time he had tried it, Matthew gripped the pin with his thumb and index finger and pulled.

To his surprise the pin released with very little effort. In shock, Matthew let go of the necklace as the coin within the ring began to spin on the axis. The pendant did not drop, however, it remained in mid air for a second until the pin snapped back into place and the pendant fell to his chest, no longer pulsing but remaining a white glow, along with the pin.

Matthew looked up. Mere meters ahead of him stood the

outline of a rectangle in white light, akin to light reaching through the sides and top of a doorway around a closed door. Slowly he stood up from the bench and picked up a nearby stick from the ground. Creeping toward the light he poked the stick through the middle with no effect. Swinging the stick, he cut through the center of the white outline. This briefly broke the light like wisps of smoke before returning to its straight form. The stick was also unaffected by its contact with the light.

Matthew dropped the stick and, step by step, moved to within touching distance of the strange phenomenon before him. Looking closely at the light, it proved to be exactly the same as the pin had been prior to being pulled. Tiny, glowing, white sparks appeared and fell throughout where the white appeared, giving the impression of a solid, white light when viewed from a longer distance.

Matthew raised his hand slowly pushed it through the sparks. As with the pin there was nothing more than a tingling in his fingers as they passed through.

Matthew moved across until he was directly in front of the outline. As he did the outline spun around him and a blinding white flash embraced him, forcing Matthew to close and shield his eyes. The light disappeared as quickly as it had come.

Matthew opened his eyes as white sparks fell and faded away into nothing around him. It was now much darker than it had been when Matthew walked into the outline. He now knew for sure what it was and everything was now starting to click into place. Matthew had walked into a doorway to another world. *This must be Dusk*, he thought to himself.

Matthew was now standing behind a building at the end of what looked like an alleyway. He was surrounded by red brick walls which reached up into the air three or four stories high. The ground was paved with large grey slabs. A massive container, which Matthew guessed was for rubbish, was sitting in the back corner, although it didn't seem to exude any kind of odour.

Beside him was a bench which looked exactly the same as the bench in the clearing except the disc now had the dark half at the top and the light half at the bottom. Matthew quickly grabbed the necklace and looked at the coin in the middle of the ring. Just like the bench, the coin had now flipped with the dark half at the top and the light half at the bottom, although it was once again pulsing as it had done before the pin had been pulled.

Looking up there were no clouds, however the light was similar to that of an overcast late-afternoon. This was no ordinary sky, though. It seemed to glow with a green tinge, feathered with ribbons of lighter green flowing through it, like an aurora.

Matthew could hear the sound of hard-soled shoes on a path or road echoing down the alleyway. He could also see the outer reaches of an orange light illuminating what seemed to be his only exit. The wall to his right ended about ten metres ahead of him with the alley continuing around the building.

Matthew slowly crept along the wall and peeked around the corner. The alleyway was nothing different than what he could find back home between some old heritage listed buildings. Old, red brick walls, a back door on each and windows on the higher levels, beautifully framed with light grey arches and carvings.

For a few minutes he stood, hidden by the wall, and watched everything that crossed the space between the buildings. Despite lengthy periods of staring out into an empty street there were a few cars that quickly passed between the two buildings as well as the occasional pedestrian strolling past. Due to Matthew's attempts to hide himself as much as possible, as well as the dull light, it was difficult for him to really make out any details beyond everybody being very nicely dressed. Like everyone was going to the opera.

After a few false attempts to emerge from his cover, Matthew decided that the street was now quiet enough to finally creep into the open while avoiding being seen. Unfortunately for him there was no other cover in the alley with which to break up the journey to the street and take a closer look, only a couple of stacks of small metal crates which would do very little to hide him from view. It was all or nothing.

As Matthew continued to move down the alley the necklace ceased pulsing and returned to a vibration, which reduced the further away he walked from the point that he entered Dusk. Where the alley met the street stood an old street lamp with six glass panels. The actual post was made from a strange, bottle green metal which Matthew had never seen before.

There didn't seem to be a globe inside the frame, instead it was something now familiar to Matthew. The light was made of a massive swarm of the same magical sparks that Matthew had seen in the doorway, this time gold, floating out of the lamp as if the glass was not even there, and bathing the surrounding area in a warm, orange light. Despite the sparks thinning out, some lingered and floated some distance from the lamp like tiny, weightless snowflakes catching the sunlight.

The street was made of cobblestones of varying grey tones. Looking back, Matthew could see the front facade of the buildings. He decided it was probably a good idea to take out his phone and take some photos. The buildings surrounding him all seemed to be of Georgian architecture. Mostly red brick with light grey window framings, arches and parapets. Further down the street were some buildings which were cream or white, however they were too far away and the light was too dull for Matthew to be sure.

Turning back, Matthew took some photos of the street lamp. He continued to stare for a moment, transfixed on the lamp and the beautiful light emanating from it. So distracted was he of his surroundings that he didn't hear someone walk up beside him.

'Hello? What are you doing there?' came a girl's voice.

Matthew turned toward the voice and shrieked. Standing before him, like any other person, was a cat. She stood bipedal, a short, stumpy body, long waving tail and covered head to toe in blue-grey fur. She had small white patches just under her eyes, going onto her cheeks. Strangely, at least to Matthew, she was wearing a white, flared dress, with a light blue coat over the top. She also had black framed glasses, similar to Matthew's.

Matthew's shriek very much startled her and she let out a loud scream.

'Oi! What you two doing over there!', shouted a man, in full London Bobby garb, from down the street. He immediately began to run in Matthew's direction, retrieving an object from his belt.

Matthew would have been scared to death if this had happened in Dawn, let alone in Dusk. He had no idea what could happen to him if he were arrested, no matter how civilised Dusk seemed from his brief visit so far.

In his fear Matthew turned and dashed back into the alleyway. The necklace around his neck once again increased its vibration and pulled him toward the site of the doorway. Taking a look back he bashed into a stack of crates which bundled over, but luckily did not overly impede his getaway. Once he reached the corner of the building and the alley turned, the necklace pulsed white.

The officer chasing Matthew was now sprinting down the alley after Matthew.

'Come back here, boy!', he shouted.

Matthew took hold of the necklace, mid-stride, and pulled the pin. After a few quick flips of the coin it stopped and the pin clicked back into place. The spark-lit doorway appeared out of nothing in front of Matthew, a few metres away.

Not missing a step, Matthew ran through the doorway, which

spun around him and everything turned a bright white once again.

Opening his eyes, and still running, Matthew had to jump up and over the bench in the clearing to avoid falling over. He looked back, heart pounding in his chest, trying to catch his breath. Nobody else was in the clearing with him. He had escaped.

Matthew sat on the bench for a few moments to collect himself, the adrenaline still pumping through his body.

'It's OK. I'm back home,' Matthew quietly told himself, dealing with the fear of being chased by the law before even contemplating everything else he had just discovered.

Looking up Matthew could see through the trees that the sun was starting to get low and knowing the difficulty in negotiating the obstacles along the stream, decided that it was a good time to get back to the safety of his house.

Once safely back on the familiar dirt path Matthew took his phone out of his pocket and sent a message to Safiri and Sam. *Guys, my place. Now!*

Chapter Seven

A Science Experiment

Matthew paced the lounge waiting for his friends, turning over in his head what he had seen and trying to make sense of it.

Safiri and Sam took no time at all in getting to Matthew's house, both of them still being together having gone for a burger. Opening the front door they entered to see a pacing Matthew with a herbal tea sitting on the dining table.

'What's wrong?' asked Sam with concern. 'You never drink tea.'

Matthew had never been one for tea. Generally he had drinks that amped him up, usually coffee.

'Alaska gave me a little bit of her stash,' Matthew retorted. 'I need something to calm me down. You guys will want some too once I tell you what happened.'

'Matthew, what happened? Look at your arm!' Sam almost shouted at him as she pointed to his arm and ran over.

'I hadn't even noticed,' Matthew remarked as he looked down at the scratches on his elbow and running down his forearm. The adrenaline kept him from feeling the pain.

'Come on. We'll patch that up and then you need to tell us what's going on.' Matthew and Safiri had never seen Sam so motherly.

After a quick cleaning and covering of the scratches they all sat down. Safiri made some more tea while Sam was patching up Matthew.

'So what's all this about?' asked Safiri.

'I found it,' replied Matthew.

'Found what?'

'Dusk,' a small smirk beginning to appear on Matthew's face.

'You mean that crazy story that weird guy was telling us? Very funny Matthew. We came rushing here thinking something had happened and you're here just drinking and mucking around. You've been into George's whisky collection, haven't you?' Safiri scrunched his face up, not appreciating the apparent con that Matthew was trying to pull.

'I haven't had anything to drink. Just the tea. I'm serious. I found Dusk.'

'Prove it,' demanded Sam.

'OK. Well after you guys left I went for a walk,' Matthew recounted the story of what had happened. No detail was spared.

'That's not proof, Matthew,' Sam wasn't convinced and judging by the lack of change in Safiri's expression, neither was he.

'Fine,' Matthew took out his phone and showed them the pictures he had taken of the buildings.

'Just stock photos of old buildings. This isn't funny, Matthew,' Safiri was getting even more agitated.

Matthew continued scrolling past the photos of the buildings and came to the lamp.

'This is the stuff… the sparks. It seems to be a massive power source. It makes the necklace glow, the doorway appear, it lights their lamps. It appears out of nothing and floats around,' Matthew explaining again the mysterious substance he had discovered.

Reaching the last photo taken, Matthew gasped. Safiri and Sam leaned in closer and their expressions now changed to bewilderment.

'This is her! The cat-girl! I must have accidentally taken a photo when she came up behind me.'

The strange angle of the photo was testament to how unintentional the photo was.

'This can't be real,' doubted Safiri.

'She looks so cute,' added Sam. 'Look at those hands! It's like half way between a human and a cat. Short, stumpy fingers and thumbs with little pads on them. Beautiful colouring. Would cost a fortune to get a cat that colour. How do her glasses stay on? She doesn't exactly have a human shaped face with ears to hang them off.'

'I dunno. I wasn't exactly in a conversation... or have time for an extensive look. *I* freaked out, *she* freaked out, then the cop came running and I legged it as fast as I could. I must have scratched my arm when I ran into the crates.'

'This still doesn't prove anything, Matthew. You could've gotten these photos from anywhere,' Safiri still wasn't budging despite a glimmer of hope when he first saw the photo of the cat-girl.

'OK. Everyone get your things. We're going now. I'm gonna prove this was all real,' Matthew declared, not willing to let them doubt any longer.

'It's night, Matthew,' Sam pointed out.

'I've got torches in the shed. We need to take a few more things as well. I've got some experiments I wanna do to see what this doorway is capable of.'

Standing up, Matthew grabbed his backpack and marched to the shed, his friends scrambling after him. He took a torch for each of them as well as a radio each, a few ropes and whatever planks of wood they could carry. Going back inside he put on a hoodie for a bit of added protection and shoved his skateboard in his backpack, the top poking out being far too long to actually fit.

'OK. Let's go!' he commanded.

'What are the planks for?' asked Sam.

'It'll make getting to the doorway a lot easier. We can lay them between branches to walk across instead of having to climb over them.'

Matthew led Safiri and Sam to the dirt track and then to the bridge where the necklace vibrated the most. Taking it out from his hoodie, Safiri and Sam were astonished at how the necklace pulled away from his body.

'I just thought of something else,' Matthew announced. 'This wasn't the first place I felt the necklace vibrate. I felt it happen on the bus on the way to work. You know what that means?'

'What?' enquired Safiri.

'It means there's other doorways,' a huge grin spanning Matthew's face. 'Now let's get going.'

Matthew pushed the group alongside the stream with conviction, keen to prove that this wasn't just a story. Moving with confidence, Matthew placed the planks where they needed to go and passed through the dense trees in a fraction of the time it took him the first time he negotiated his way through, even with the time taken creating makeshift platforms to walk across.

Upon reaching the clearing, Matthew made sure to show his friends the change in the severity of the necklace's pull.

'Keep watching the necklace,' Matthew advised.

As he stepped into the clearing the necklace dropped and pulsed. He held the necklace up for his friends to closely inspect its change in state, especially the pin where the blue sparks materialised and floated down before fading out of existence again.

'Believe me now?' Matthew grinned, a little smugly.

Safiri moved in close and poked the pendant with his finger. 'It just tingles a little, but otherwise it's like there's nothing there.'

'So what's the plan?' asked Sam.

'We are gonna do a few experiments and test this baby out,' he replied.

'How very cavalier of you, Matthew. You're not worried about us, you know, getting killed?' she retorted.

'I've been through it once. I just wanna test the boundaries a bit so we know exactly what we're dealing with.'

Safiri opened his mouth to protest and was immediately cut off by Matthew.

'We know, Saf. Your job is to keep it from going too far… Now, keep your eyes on the coin.'

Matthew pulled the pin on the pendant and, to the shock of Sam and Safiri, the coin began to spin on its own, stopping with the pin clicking into place. Safiri and Sam's mouths agape.

In front of the three friends appeared the doorway, although not in the same place it had done last time. This time it had appeared on the other side of the bench, close to where they were standing.

'Strange,' remarked Matthew.

'You think?' added Sam.

'Not the doorway, although I guess it's more strange for you guys. I mean where it is. It was over there last time,' Matthew pointed to the other side of the bench. 'Maybe it appears based on where the necklace is.'

'Can you close it and reopen it again?' Safiri asked.

'Maybe. I didn't think about closing it last time. I'll try and pull the pin again.'

Matthew did so. The coin spun once and clicked into place. As hypothesised, the doorway faded into nothing and the pendant returned to a pulse.

'Experiment number one complete,' Matthew put forth. 'The doorway can be closed without going through it. Let's see where it opens if I move over here.'

Matthew walked to the opposite side of the clearing, Safiri and Sam remaining closely by his side, and opened the doorway. This time it opened a few metres in front of them again.

'I guess that settles that question,' Safiri professed. 'The doorway opens an equal distance in front of the necklace every time.'

As Matthew began to unpack his bag, Safiri and Sam began experimenting in the same manner that Matthew had the first time the doorway had appeared. They picked up sticks to poke at the light, waved various body parts through it and inspected the tiny, falling sparks closely.

'I'm impressed, Matthew.' said Sam. 'I didn't think you had it in you to push through the bug filled trees and discover all of this, especially on your own.'

Matthew had chosen not to disclose the situation with the birds when he told the story initially and was very happy with that decision.

'I can't believe this is real,' Safiri whispered as he took a puff from his inhaler.

'OK. Let's see where this goes,' Sam cried out as she took a few quick steps before jumping through the doorway. 'Looks exactly the same.'

Sam turned around to see Safiri staring at her, wide eyed, mouth open.

'I guess we just finished our next experiment,' Matthew snorted as he burst out laughing. 'No going through the doorway without the necklace.'

Safiri and Sam then joined in the laughter.

Matthew picked up one end of a long piece of rope and tied it around his waist.

'Grab a radio each. We gonna start to get real now.' Matthew commanded.

'I think it's been real enough, Matthew,' Safiri retorted.

After each of them picked up a radio and gave them a quick test Matthew tied the other end of the rope to the bench and walked over to the doorway.

'Someone record this on your phone so we can keep track of what happens. We all have to promise this doesn't go beyond us, though. Grandad kept this secret for a reason.'

Safiri removed his phone from his pocket as he and Sam sat on the bench. Matthew did the same to record what happened on his end.

'When I get through I'll try to talk to you on the radio and you guys do the same… You guys ready?' he asked.

'Ready,' confirmed Safiri.

Matthew took the remaining few steps, holding his phone in front of him to record, and entered the doorway. The light spun around him and disappeared, along with Matthew. The rope fell to the ground, severed where the light passed through it.

Immediately Sam picked up her radio and tried to contact Matthew. No response came. She then tried to call him on his phone and it went straight through to voicemail without ringing.

A few seconds later the light appeared again in mid-spin, disappearing with a fading of sparks and Matthew had returned.

Safiri and Sam jumped up from the bench and ran over to Matthew.

'What happened on your end?' Safiri asked. 'The rope got cut by the light and we tried to call you on the radio and your phone.'

'Seems like when the doorway spins then anything in the way will get sliced. I tried the radio too and got nothing. There's no phone reception there. Let's take a look at the videos. I kinda shut my eyes with the flash so I'm not sure what happens when I get transported.'

They first look at Safiri's footage of the doorway. Nothing in it surprised Matthew after having already discovered the potential danger in flailing limbs while the doorway spun.

Next they reviewed Matthew's footage as he walked into the doorway. As expected there was a quick explosion of white light followed by falling, fading sparks and the reveal of another world. As the video wobbled around Safiri noticed something.

'Wasn't the sky green last time?' he asked.

'Yeah,' Sam added. 'It's purple now and everything's darker than it was in the photos.'

'It was definitely darker,' Matthew confirmed. 'Last time I went it was still daytime here. The sky was green and the light was about what you would get when the sun is blocked.'

'Or when the sun goes away… as in dusk,' Safiri concluded.

'Now that it's night here it's more like night there. So purple is night and green is day. I'll confirm that the more I go.'

'You're going to keep going?' Safiri asked.

'Yeah. This is what Grandad wanted me to find. I can't just stop now.'

'Can I go through and see it?' asked Sam.

'You want to go as well?!' Safiri fumed.

'Just for a minute. Then we'll come straight back. Are you worried about me, Safiri?' Sam mocked.

'Worried you guys will get stuck and I have to explain to everyone what happened. They'll lock me up for sure.'

'We'll be fine. Be back in a minute,' Matthew assured him as he opened the doorway once again. 'Grab a walkie, Sam and we'll test them on that side.'

Matthew and Sam walked up to the doorway as Safiri returned to the bench.

'We don't have much space here. How do you wanna do it?' Matthew asked.

'Hold me, Matthew,' joked Sam. 'Seriously though, I don't think there's another option.'

Matthew and Sam embraced each other in an effort to take up as little space as they could and avoid losing a limb.

'Enjoying yourself?' she mocked as she winked at Safiri.

'I… er…what?' Matthew stammered.

'Hahahaha! Calm yourself, Matthew. I'm just kidding around.'

Together, they slowly crab-walked into the doorway, holding each other as closely as possible.

As they crossed, Safiri held his breath and put his face in his hands.

The light spun around Matthew and Sam and in a flash, they were gone.

Safiri pulled his hands down and ran to the spot where his friends had been moments before. Giving a sigh of relief, he could find no trace of body parts severed by the light of the doorway as it spun around. He returned to the bench and awaited their return, hoping for it to be quick.

Matthew and Sam emerged from the bright flash, into the alleyway in Dusk.

'Whoa!' exclaimed Sam.

'OK. We go to the corner and peek around but nothing more,' Matthew commanded.

'Just let me look around for a while, Matthew.'

'No. I didn't see anyone that looked like us here last time and we promised Saf we'd go straight back. If something happens and we get held up, he'll freak out.'

'Fine. We'll take a look from the corner.'

As they reached the corner and looked around Sam scurried over to the crates Matthew had knocked over. Quickly stacking a few, she took her phone from her pocket, started to record and crouched behind the crates. She quickly realised that they really didn't offer any cover at all.

'Sam, come back!' Matthew hissed. He put the walkie to his mouth and repeated the command.

'Just chill,' came the reply from Sam.

People of all different shapes and sizes were walking past the alleyway. Far more than had been there when Matthew had visited Dusk the first time. One of them, seemingly floating an inch off the ground and garbed in a hooded cloak, stopped and turned.

Matthew pulled back and Sam made herself as small as possible against a wall where she could find a small bit of cover, holding her breath. After a few brief moments the mysterious, floating figure turned back to the path and carried on their way.

Sam immediately stood and ran back to Matthew.

'What were you -'

'Sorry. Sorry. I just wanted to see. I shouldn't have gone.'

'We're going back now.' Matthew barked.

'Yeah. I'm sorry, Matthew.'

Matthew summoned the doorway and he and Sam returned to Dawn the same way they had left it, with a crab walk into the doorway.

'That wasn't a minute!' Safiri admonished his two friends.

'Sorry, Safiri. Got a little carried away. I think that's enough adventure for tonight.' Matthew apologised, Sam looking a little sheepish. 'On the plus side the walkies still work over there.'

'No. I've decided I want to go and see Dusk.' Safiri tried to put on a brave face.

'Really?' asked Sam.

'Yeah. Why? Anything happen that I should know about?' Safiri asked.

'No,' replied Sam. 'Just stick to the corner and don't expose yourself. Just in case.'

Matthew gave her a glance, knowing Safiri didn't need to be told twice to follow the instructions.

'OK. Let's quickly go and take a look.'

Once again the doorway was opened to Dusk. Matthew and Safiri walked over to the doorway and put their arms around each other.

'Looking good, boys! Got the video going!' joked Sam.

'Enough out of you, Sam.' Matthew responded, a slight bit of venom in his voice.

They began to crab walk to the doorway, Safiri breathing more and more heavily the closer they got to the light.

As they were about to cross, Safiri caught hit foot on a tree root which was protruding from the ground. Falling, his body pushed Matthew forward who also began to fall. Sam stood up and shrieked as Safiri, wide-eyed, stared into Matthew's eyes, paralysed with fear.

'No!' Matthew shouted as he fell, Safiri holding his leg, through the doorway of light.

The doorway spun and flashed white.

Matthew opened his eyes in Dusk. Laying on the floor as if he'd dived through a portal, He looked back, bringing himself to terms with the horror that would momentarily meet his eyes. He could still feel Safiri's hand gripping his leg.

'Matthew,' came Safiri's voice. 'I'm OK! I didn't get cut in half!'

Matthew jumped to his feet and pulled Safiri up with him, embracing his best friend whom he thought he had killed.

'What the hell happened?!' Matthew asked.

'I have no idea,' Safiri replied, 'but I won't question it.'

'Do you still want to take a look or do you want to go straight back?'

'I'll take a look. I don't think I'll ever come back. Scared the crap out of me.'

'I think plenty of crap was scared out of us,' Matthew replied as he took Safiri to the corner of the building to look out toward the street.

'Wow! This architecture is beautiful. Georgian, or as close to it as another world could be.'

'Trust you to arrive in another world with all kinds of strange looking people and check out the architecture.'

'Oh HA-HA, Matthew. Real funny. There's more to other civilisations than just the physical people. They would have their own government and finances. Everything could, and probably is, different.'

'I'll make you a deal. I'll document as much as I can when I come here and you can study it all when I get back.'

'Deal. Now let's go home.'

Matthew and Safiri emerged from the white light to find Sam kneeling on the ground crying. Looking up and seeing both Matthew and Safiri alive and whole, she lept up and embraced them both.

'I'm OK Sam,' Safiri comforted her.

'I thought you were dead,' she sobbed. 'I didn't know what happened. I was looking for body parts on the ground.'

'Did you record us going through?' Matthew asked.

'Yeah. My phone's still on the bench.'

'Let's take a look at the video and see how the hell no damage was done.'

They slowly walked over to the bench, Sam still in shock after what had just transpired.

Pouring over the video for a few minutes none of them could work out what had happened.

'I think we need a bigger screen,' suggested Matthew. 'Let's get out of here and plug this in at home.'

Safiri and Sam both agreed. They quickly packed up their belongings and set off back to Matthew's house to have a more detailed review of the incident.

Once on the TV it was much easier for them to more closely inspect how Safiri's body was still in one piece.

'Let's take this frame by frame,' suggested Safiri.

Matthew stood up close to the TV while Safiri and Sam sat on the couch. Sam controlled the video through her phone.

'So here's where you start to fall onto me... and here's where I start to fall through the doorway... OK... let's slow it down... the light gets more intense here... and now it's starting to move... aaaand stop!'

Sam stopped scrolling forward as instructed.

'Look at the doorway here,' Matthew's finger touching the screen to make his point. 'It's growing to fit us both into the doorway. Go forward a couple more frames... Stop! That's definitely grown. There's no way that's the same size as it was.'

'But why would it grow?' asked Sam. 'When I first jumped through it nothing happened. It only spins for the necklace.'

'If it only spins for the necklace then how would the wearer fit. Maybe the necklace is sentient. It knows how big the wearer is and adjusts to fit.'

'That doesn't account for me still being here,' Safiri pointed out. 'One hypothesis is that it resizes to allow for its wearer and any person, or living being, touching the wearer. Kinda like a chain. Or it may be that the wearer is the key and the necklace knows what they want. You wanted me to come through with you so it adjusted for both.'

'Either way, no more hugs required,' Sam added. A welcome lightening of the mood was met by giggles from the group.

'Well let's just say that everyone who needs to go through has to be touching the wearer, just to be sure,' Matthew decided. 'Although I don't want to put you guys in that situation again. You've got families and it's not fair on them.'

'You're part of our family, Matthew,' Safiri corrected. 'You may not be blood but us three are a family and the Bombi family loves you anyway.'

'Still, it's probably better if I go alone from now on. At least you guys know the truth behind all this now.'

'You're talking about going back, Matthew, but what's the actual plan?' Sam enquired.

'I guess I'll resign from work and tell everyone I'm going travelling. I'll give it a week to get everything ready. I want you guys to move in here and look after the place while I'm gone. Rent free, of course.' Matthew gave them a slight grin.

'Are you sure?' asked Safiri. 'This is all happening pretty quickly. Maybe take some time to think about it.'

'I think I need to do this, Safiri. Grandad was right. I don't have any direction. This is the first time I've ever felt the need to not take the safe option… like deep inside me… it's hard to explain.'

'Are you sure it's not just part of grieving? It hasn't been long since George died. You really want to do this?'

'Maybe it is grief. Or maybe it's the push I needed. This isn't just some tiny thing, though. Our whole world changed today. Our universe, even. This is huge. Grandad set me on this path for a reason. He obviously knew more than what he told me. I need answers. About Dusk and everything else that he left me. We only know about the necklace at the moment.'

'Fair enough,' Sam accepted. 'George wasn't stupid. He always wanted the best for you and I don't think he would've exposed you to all of this if he didn't think you could deal with it.'

Safiri finally succumbed. 'Fine. But I'll only let you go on one condition. I'm coming with you. There's no way I can let you go there and get into all kinds of trouble.'

Sam's eyes shot open. 'Well if you're going, Saf, then I'm going as well. If I don't go you won't get into enough trouble. You'll never even leave the alleyway.'

'OK. New plan. You guys can come but it'll just be a scouting mission. Keep it short and safe. Outside the alleyway, Safiri. We'll tell Alaska we're all taking a camping trip.'

'We're gonna need a codeword for the group,' suggested Sam. 'Something cool and niche so that it's obvious to us.'

'Everything there is probably going to be niche, Sam.'

'How about just *Humans*?' Safiri offered.

'Lame!' Sam joked. 'Let's go with *World Jumpers* or *Dusk Invasion Squad*!'

'Nah. A bit long and will probably draw too much attention… I got it. *Dawn Crew*!' Matthew declared.

'Sounds good,' agreed Safiri.

'All good with me,' Sam confirmed.

Chapter Eight
Into Dusk

The next morning the three friends, now known to each other as Dawn Crew, met with Alaska to inform her of their plans to take a holiday. They reached an agreement to work the rest of the week before taking two weeks off. As far as Alaska and the crew's respective families were concerned they would take Sam's car and drive to different, currently undetermined, locations to camp. This story gave them the flexibility they needed to take whatever time they needed in Dusk.

Over the course of the week they spent some of their free time driving around town, mapping the areas which made the necklace vibrate. Unfortunately every location they found was far too exposed for them to risk opening the doorway, or completely inaccessible. Still, the decision was made that keeping track of where these doorways were located could be useful should they return via a different location. As far as Safiri was concerned it would be an interesting experiment, if he were to be able to duplicate the process in Dusk, to see how the positioning and distances between doorways corresponded with those in Dawn.

The rest of their time was spent working out exactly what they would need to take with them. It was impossible to know which items would even work once they were in Dusk so they decided to keep it as light as possible, each member of the crew sticking to one medium sized backpack each. The crew each packed a torch; a compass; their radio; spare batteries; whatever extra clothing or personal items they wanted to take; and a selection of snacks to keep them going in case food was hard to come by.

They also knew that at least some of the population of Dusk, the ones the crew had seen, looked nothing like the humans of Dawn. For this reason they were quite selective of the clothing they were going to wear, or take with them if they were packing extra. Every effort was made to hide their appearance as much as possible while still allowing freedom of movement to hide or flee if required.

Finally the day had arrived for the Dawn Crew to begin their scouting mission into Dusk. The crew all spent the night at Matthew's house to make sure they were all packed and ready to go, with Sam's car hidden in the garage. There was a mix of nervousness and anticipation, fear and excitement over what they were possibly heading into. The only knowledge they had of the foreign world was that the architecture was similar to Dawn and there were people that luckily, and strangely, spoke their language.

The quiet, tense, morning atmosphere was slightly alleviated by Matthew playing uplifting music and attempting to joke around with the others.

'Do you have enough black makeup?' he asked Sam, elbowing her in the side.

'You think my pasty skin won't reflect something and give us away?' she responded. 'Not all of us have the luxury of having beautifully tanned, olive or dark skin. Without this makeup I could be a liability.'

'There's nothing wrong with your skin colour, Sam. I like our diversity,' Safiri apparently missed the joke.

'Oh Safiri, such a romantic,' Sam mocked.

'What? I-I-I didn't mean-'

'Relax, Saf. We're just joking around.'

It didn't take them all long to get ready. For once there was no procrastination. No relaxing, watching videos until the last minute, then scrub up and scramble to throw on whatever was in reach in as little time as possible. This time they all had everything they needed ready to go. All of them went through their personal grooming process with an expectation that they wouldn't get the opportunity to shower again for a while. Their clothes were ready and their bags were almost completely packed.

All wore black jeans which had a bit of stretchiness to them. Matthew and Safiri wore sneakers while Sam wore black boots. Nothing out of the ordinary for any of them. Each of them also wore a hoodie, giving them a quick option to hide their heads and, to a lesser degree, their faces should they need to. Sam was, as usual, in black, Safiri in navy blue and Matthew in dark green.

Matthew made the crew a full breakfast with bacon, sausages and scrambled eggs with truffle oil, his favourite. It went down well, everyone savouring what could be their last good meal for a while. After finishing and washing up they packed the last items into their bags, which was mainly the snacks they had pre-packed. Matthew also packed the deck of cards, box, ring and medallion.

'All set to go, guys?' Matthew asked as he slipped on his backpack.

'All set,' replied Sam.

Safiri gave a nervous nod.

'OK. Let's get this show on the road.' Matthew opened the door and allowed his friends to exit the house as he took one last look back into the living area of his family home before walking out and locking up the house.

The walk to the doorway was quiet and tense. They passed a few people on the way, most of them walking their dogs, giving a courtesy nod as they passed.

Immediately upon arriving at the clearing Matthew pulled the pin holding the coin in place and summoned the doorway.

'Let's keep this slow and safe. We've got our phones to document what we see but be subtle about it. We don't want to draw attention and have people ask us questions.'

'Agreed,' said Safiri.

'That was quick,' Sam joked.

'Alright. Let's go.'

Matthew turned and walked toward the doorway, stopping a few steps short. Sam and Safiri flanked him on either side and each took hold of one of his hands. Matthew glanced each way at his friends and walked forward, Sam and Safiri following suit. Passing through the middle of the doorway it spun around them and flashed white, transporting the Dawn Crew into Dusk to begin their journey into the unknown.

White sparks fell and faded away as the three friends opened their eyes. The green tinged sky giving a dull light in the alleyway as the day turned to night.

The Dawn Crew walked to the corner of the building, as they had on every previous visit, and peeked around to the street. A moderate amount of traffic flowed past the alleyway.

'Hood up, guys. Hopefully we can blend into the crowd.'

'What's the plan, Matthew?' Safiri asked.

'I think at this point we just walk around a bit and try to pick up as much as we can from looking and listening. We need to work out how money works, what people eat, how they dress. We also need to look out for anything that might give any clues about Grandad's stuff.'

Stepping out from their cover the Dawn Crew lifted their hoods over their heads and walked, as calmly as possible, toward the street.

'I'm crapping myself,' Safiri pointed out.

'I think we all are,' Matthew responded.

'Confirmed,' said Sam.

As they walked out into the street they stopped at the lamp, taking in their first real exposure to the life of Dusk.

Safiri turned to Sam and Matthew and whispered, 'It's like watching a period movie with aliens.'

'Didn't know you were into that kind of thing?' Sam replied, immediately looking around to see if she spoke too loudly and drew attention.

'Grandad loved watching that stuff,' said Matthew. 'Well… period dramas and stuff. Not so much the aliens. Look at the way they're all dressed… and the cars. The fashion's all over the place, though. Take a look around. Dudes look like they're in the 1800's but the women look like they're fashion is a bit later. None of those puffy dresses. Car's definitely look like they're from the 1920's, right? Guys?'

Matthew caught both Safiri and Sam staring at the feet of a passer by. It wasn't the elegant, white heeled shoes that caught their eye, but the large white claw that protruded from the back of each of their ankles, down the rear of the shoe.

Matthew gave them both a nudge. 'Tone it down on the staring guys.'

He could see, as he was looking at the faces of the people walking past, that this particular individual was staring, disapprovingly, back at Sam and Safiri as they walked, not appreciating the type of attention they were getting.

There was a small resemblance, to Matthew, of the man he had an altercation with at The Eye of Dusk, Finnigan Fisk. This person, however, was not a plump, sleazy looking person, but elegant, radiant and almost aquatic.

The similarities were in the fleshy tendrils that fell, like dreadlocks, from the head. Unlike Finnigan, who's tentacles were short and falling from the back of the head, these tendrils were long, thin, more plentiful, and began at the forehead. They also fell half-way down their back, over the white fur coat that covered a white formal dress.

Their skin was also more grey than Finnigan, almost dolphin-like, making this person seem far more aquatic and definitely more pleasant to look at. The long, diamond-shaped face with large, round eyes and sleek, thin nose were also far more aesthetically pleasing than Finnigan's pudgy face with goatee and bulbous nose.

As they turned their head away from the Dawn Crew, Matthew quietly said to the others, 'I think that person was the same race as Finnigan, or at least to some degree the same.'

Safiri added his observations of the people they had seen so far, 'Everyone looks to be humanoid… maybe mixed with some animal, like the cat-girl you saw. Bipedal with no extra limbs.'

'I haven't seen many cat-people so far,' said Sam. 'Since everyone is dressed so nice and driving swanky cars, this might be the rich side of town. Maybe most of the cat-people don't come around these parts.'

'These are some damn nice cars,' Matthew agreed.

There was a steady stream of traffic travelling down the cobbled roads. Beautiful classic 1920's cars, most of them soft-top convertibles. All with large, exaggerated front grills and massive curved fenders covering the tires. They came in a varied combination of colours from black, white, cream, maroon, bottle green and navy blue. The occasional car even rolled by in bright yellow.

'You know what's strange about them?' Safiri quizzed the others.

'You can't hear them at all.'

'You're right,' confirmed Sam. 'With this cobbled road they should be making a lot of noise. Can't hear an engine either.'

'Don't think they're running off the same engines as we have,' Matthew pointed out. 'Look at the hood on all of them. There's a slight blue glow coming out of the vents. Wouldn't be surprised if it's those sparks that seem to power everything around here.'

A shout came from someone nearby 'What are you kids standing around here for. Move along!'

Startled, all three turned to see a man at the open front door of one of the buildings next to the alley. His skin, especially around his face was rolled and sagging like a hairless Shar-Pei and his ears were long and floppy. In contrast to the high fashion of everyone around them, this man was dressed in very rugged trousers, boots, button-up shirt, gloves and a thick, leather, brown apron.

'Get out of here!' he shouted again, waving his hand to shoo them away.

'Apologies, sir. We're going,' Matthew forced a response before taking Sam and Safiri by the elbows and pulling them away, disapproving glances coming from passers-by. Some were tendril people, some saggy-skinned people, a couple of cat people. It was clear that none of them looked like the Dawn Crew.

After taking a few deep breaths to calm his heart rate he said, 'Probably best if we don't stay in one place too long, attracting attention.'

'Probs need a change of clothes, too. We're way too conspicuous,' added Sam.

As they walked down the street they realised they were in some kind of restaurant precinct. They passed by some upscale bars and restaurants with alfresco dining. As much as they all wanted to know what it was that people ate in Dusk they determined it was far too risky to stop and look at what people had on their plates. It didn't smell any different to what they were used to back home but that wasn't necessarily an indicator that it was tasty, or safe for that matter.

They could see in the distance the silhouettes of much larger buildings, most likely more of a commercial district, however what really caught their attention was much closer, about fifty metres down the road.

Trees lined the road on either side unlike anything the Dawn Crew had ever seen before. From a distance it seemed like just normal trees surrounded by fairy lights winding around the trunk and branches.

'Is that light coming from the trees?' Matthew asked.

'I think it is,' Sam replied as she quickly jogged up to have a closer inspection of the trees. Safiri and Matthew quickly followed suit.

'It's like there are pulsing arteries of glowing orange light flowing up the trunk, all the way to the leaves,' she continued.

'I'll assume they're sparkling like everything else?' Matthew asked with the hint of mockery in his tone, as he and Safiri joined her at the tree.

Sam glared at him. 'You bored of this already?'

'No. Was just joking.'

'It changes colour to purple further up the road,' said Safiri. 'Would be interesting to find out if there's any difference between the different colours of the sparks. The trees all generally look the same.'

'So pretty,' Sam remarked.

Matthew and Safiri were stunned.

'Since when did you like anything pretty?' Safiri asked.

'Since when did you ever ask?' she retorted.

'You wear black all the time. I've never seen you wear anything colourful or even say the word pretty,' Matthew pointed out.

'Well we're all complex beings. Maybe you guys don't really know me at all.'

'Clearly,' Matthew replied. 'Now there's an even more interesting tree.' Matthew pointed up the road. Clearly visible against the backdrop of the green ribboned sky, far in the distance, they could see a massive, blue, glowing tree.

'That seems quite far away and we can see it even above most of the buildings around here. Must be gigantic!' Safiri remarked. 'The trunk must take up at least a block by itself. How far away do you think it is?'

'I'd say it has to be at least five kilometres away. I've never seen a tree that massive.'

Taking his gaze across to the other side of the road Matthew noticed a small, but dense garden of various sized plants and trees. Some of them glowed, some didn't. They also contained a vast array of different flowers, varying in colour and size.

Within the dense foliage was a grey stone temple. It was double story and very plain, other than some glass domes on the roof. At the top of a short stairway was a large, arched, double, wooden door. Above the door was an unmistakable carving of the same tree as depicted on the medallion that Matthew had inherited. *Finally, Something we can work with!* Matthew thought.

Walking up the steps to the door was a tall girl in a short, dark green, hooded dress, dark brown trousers and boots the same green as the dress.

'Hey!' Matthew shouted to her and began to run across the street.

'Matthew, wait!' Safiri called after him.

The girl, either not hearing Matthew, or ignoring him, continued up the stairs and into the temple.

'Hey you! Scavenger! Stop right there!'

Reaching the other side of the road, Matthew turned to his right and saw the same police officer that had chased him the first time he had traveled to Dusk.

'Don't even try to run. You won't get far,' the officer said menacingly.

Now having a closer inspection of the police officer, as he didn't turn and sprint off this time, Matthew could see that he was of the same race of saggy skinned people as the man that had shouted at the Dawn Crew earlier. *Grouchy bunch of people*. Matthew thought to himself.

'What are you doing here, son? This area isn't for your kind.'

Any hopes Matthew had of charming himself out of the situation soon disappeared, 'I-I-I-'

'Come on. Spit it out, boy.'

Matthew's mind was blank. The only thing he could think of was to not look toward his friends and give them away.

'Why did you run from me the other day? What are you doing here again?'

Matthew had no idea what he could possibly say in a world he knew nothing about. Trying to explain that he's from another world probably wouldn't have gone down too well.

'Lost your voice now? Maybe a night in the lock up will jog your memory? Or maybe I take you straight to The Authority and let them deal with a stray Scavenger.'

A voice came from a little further down the street, 'Officer! Officer! Sorry, sir. He's with me. He's a bit simple, you know.'

The cat-girl who Matthew had startled ran up to Matthew and the police officer.

'Ahh, Miss Moon. He's with you, you say? That's funny, you didn't seem to know him before,' the officer inquired.

'Just a misunderstanding, sir.' Replied the cat-girl. 'He's under my care and I'll take him home at once.'

'Fine, Miss Moon. But if I see him out here again, chasing after people I'll make sure he's locked up. Now get out of here, both of you.' The officer turned and walked back up the street from where he had come from.

Matthew, realising he had been holding his breath, let it out and bent over, putting his hands on his knees. His heart was racing.

'Thank you so much. I don't know what I would've done. Lucky you were walking up this way.'

'Well… to be completely honest I was following you. I've been on the lookout for you since I saw you last.'

'Really? Why?' Matthew asked.

'Firstly, you're a very strange person who clearly needs reminding of how dangerous this area can be for certain types of people. Secondly, you dropped this.' She handed over a button of a sinister looking cat with the words *Evil Cat!* written on it. In all the excitement of the past week, since he had first been to Dawn, he hadn't noticed that it was no longer on his bag.

'What's a *cat*?' she asked.

'Ahh… it's nothing. Where did you find it?'

'Over by the crates you knocked over. I picked it up before Officer Doggery came back from chasing you. I'm Daisy by the way. Daisy Moon.'

'Nice to officially meet you. My name's Matthew,' he said as he shook her paw-hand. He was unsure whether to describe it as paws with elongated fingers or furry hands with stubby fingers.

Knowing it was now as safe as it was going to be, he motioned for his friends to join them.

'This is Sam and Safiri,' he said as they walked across the road.

'Hiya. I'm Daisy,' she introduced herself to the rest of the crew.

'I like you clothes,' Sam commented, taking a sideward glance at Matthew.

Daisy was wearing dark blue overalls over a white blouse this time as opposed to the white dress with blue coat she had on last time Matthew had his brief interaction with her.

'Thanks, Sam. I spend a lot of time in the Scavenger District, but I've never seen you before, or anyone who looks like you. You all dress funny.'

'We're trying out some new types of clothes, seeing what trends.'

Matthew decided to add to the story, 'We generally keep to ourselves, thinking up new things. We're kind of entrepreneurs. Trying to get our products out into the market first. See what sticks. Might be able to make our way up in the world.'

'Good for you. I've always hated how Scavengers get trodden on. There's so many good people down there that don't get the opportunity to do anything more. Denied basic things that everyone else gets. I'm on my way there now to help my friend, Kyrral Kass, at the medical station. You know him?'

'No. Must be from another part of town,' Matthew responded.

'You all want to walk with me since I'm going that way?'

'Yeah, sure.'

'What's the deal with this guy?' Daisy pointed her thumb in Safiri's direction, who was still wearing a state of shock on his face at conversing with a cat.

Matthew elbowed Safiri in the stomach. 'Sorry, he's just shy around new people.'

'I understand. Kyrral's the same, bless him. Kind heart, though.'

'You don't happen to know anything about this place here?' Matthew motioned his head toward the temple.

'Not really, no. I know that it's run by House Errothin because of the tree above the door, but I'm not sure what they do in there. Probably scheming ways to keep everybody in line.'

Daisy turned and began walking up the street.

'What about the girl who walked in before Officer Doggery came?'

'No, but you'll want to keep your distance from that lot,'

'Why?' asked Matthew.

'You hit your head or something? Or been hitting that wombus juice too hard?'

'I just wanted to hear your perspective on it.'

'Well… we all know the Pure control The Authority, don't we?'

'Do we know that for certain? I mean, can we prove anything?'

'I don't have any evidence, if that's what you're asking, but my dad works in The Office of Magic and says he's seen some strange things, even for him. My mum also hates dealing with them. Anyway, the Pure have all the money and The Authority are full of greedy bureaucrats. Never seen no Pure get into any trouble neither. Makes sense that they're in control.'

'True, true,' Matthew feigned agreement despite having no idea what she was talking about.

Matthew glanced back at Safiri and Sam who were walking behind him. Sam gave him a thumbs up and mouthed *You're doing great!* Safiri still seemed to be in a state of shock at everything that was happening.

'Why are you all out here anyway?' Daisy asked. 'You know it's dangerous for you out here. You almost got caught twice, at least from what I've seen myself.'

'Well, Daisy. You can't innovate without research. If we want to improve, we need to see what all the people have to offer.' Matthew was proud of the way he was able to sound philosophical without really saying anything at all. He was especially proud of not giving away that they had no idea about the people they were purporting to be.

Daisy's tail, which protruded from her overalls, was waving around quite a lot. Matthew guessed that she enjoyed being able to openly chat about the intricacies of Dusk society and he was more than willing to let her ramble on as much as she wanted. It was all very useful information.

For the first time since they had begun walking Matthew realised that they were continuing toward the giant tree. While he was excited that they had a guide to Dusk, albeit unwitting, the fact that they were moving away from the only known doorway was also adding to his anxiety. *Grow up*, he told himself, *gotta stop trying to take the easy way*.

Chapter Nine
That's a Big Cave

As Daisy and the Dawn Crew walked closer to the Scavenger District, the architecture ceased and a sprawling park lay ahead of them. Apart from some brick paths, dotted occasionally with street lamps, the park was acres of flora.

The grass was the same as any that could be found in Dawn, green and lush. The trees were a mix of those that lined the roads, as well as tall, thick-trunked trees similar to beech trees. The leaves of these trees, however, were an electric indigo with blue vines hanging down. A soft song emanated from them while they all swung in unison, as if sentient.

'Wouldn't get too close,' Daisy advised as Sam began to wander off the path.

'Why? Are they going to grab me and suck the life out of me?' Sam asked, her face becoming more fearful as the words left her mouth.

Daisy giggled. 'No. They won't kill you, silly, but they will grab you and have a play around. They tend to get a bit rough.'

Sam quickly returned to the path, careful not to stray again.

Protruding from the centre of the expanse they had entered was the blue behemoth that could be seen from the street near the doorway. Now that they were closer they could see that the tree was actually a drastically enlarged version of what they were already familiar with lining the streets. Blue sparks flowed up through the trunk. The apparent lifeblood of the tree pulsing up to the canopy where it escaped the leaves, showering down like a light rain to create a blue mist of floating, fading sparks.

The crew took a right turn onto another path which lead them to a small road along a river. A black iron fence separated the road from a ten metre drop to the slow flowing water. Periodically they passed a bridge which crossed to streets lined with white townhouses.

'Who lives over there?' Matthew asked.

'Some of the slightly more wealthy non-Pure people.'

'And where do the most wealthy live?'

'Why? Are you looking to break in and steal something? Are you really thieves?'

'No. Definitely not thieves. Just getting my geography right.'

'You think this one is stealing anything?' Sam added, pointing at Safiri.

'Hey! I could be thief if I wanted,' Safiri argued.

'Sure you could, Saf,' said Matthew as they all laughed.

Matthew walked over to the river to take a closer look. A school of small, pink, glowing fish shone through the water, like a twisting and stretching ball.

'Does everything bloody glow around here?' asked Sam as she and Safiri joined Matthew and Daisy at the fence.

'The lifeblood tends to do that, doesn't it?'

'Yeah, I guess.' Sam gave a quick shrug in Matthew's direction.

'What are your thoughts on the lifeblood, Daisy?' asked Matthew.

'That's a strange question. What do you mean?'

Matthew was starting to enter panic mode, trying to find a way of extracting information from Daisy regarding common knowledge in Dusk. *Keep it vague,* he thought to himself. 'I mean, what are your thoughts about where it comes from and what it does?'

'It's mined from under the Gift Giver and powers everything. Can you be more specific?' she asked.

'I guess what I'm asking is where exactly are the mines and how is it converted to a power source?'

'Gift Giver-' Daisy pointed at the massive tree. 'Under,' she moved her arm down to the base of the trunk. 'As for how it powers things, I don't know. I'm not a magineer. You'd probably know more about that. You lot down there are pretty good at jerry-rigging things... But you aren't from the Scavenger District are you, Matthew.'

'I'm not sure what you mean, Daisy.'

'Come on. I'm not stupid, you know. You three look like Pure with the tips of your ears cut off, you dress strange, you keep asking about things you should know. So who are you really? Are you from beyond the wall?'

'Let's just say we're from very far away,' said Matthew, still unwilling to give too much away.

'And how did you get over the wall?'

'Ahhh... we bypassed it. It's a long story.'

'And if you're not Pure, Fenlis, Lorrai, Squaar, Stroen or Taerith then what are you?'

'We're human.'

'Hu-man?'

'Yep.'

'And what can hu-mans do?'

'I dunno. Move around and talk and stuff, like everyone else.'

'OK. So nothing like Pure. That's good.'

'And what are you?' Matthew asked.

'I'm Fenlis.'

'Cool. So Cat-people are Fenlis.'

'Cat? Like that thing you dropped?'

'Yeah, except cats are more like small pets that can't talk.'

'How absurd.'

After a few moments of slightly awkward silence a dark shadow thrust itself through the school of fish like a knife, splitting the enthralling dance of fish in two.

'Damn crinlers!' Daisy exclaimed.

Not wanting to ask any questions and receive more in return, Matthew decided to was best to not ask about *crinlers* and just assumed it was a large fish. 'Maybe keep the whole human thing on the down-low, you know, for security reasons.'

'Don't worry. I won't say anything. I've seen enough to know you won't do nothing. Probably best we get moving on now.' Daisy turned from the river, Matthew, Safiri and Sam followed suit and the group continued along down the road.

After another fifteen minutes of walking along the river, at the crossing of a bridge, the road forked. One side continued on following the river. The other, which is the direction they followed, sloped down toward the water.

At the bottom of the ramp was a small area carved into the stone wall, which hid, from the view above, a double sized iron door. Daisy casually walked up to the ominous looking door and knocked as loudly as she could manage.

A small window slid open exposing two large eyes.

'Who's there?' a gruff voice asked from the other side of the door.

'Hi, Ganlin. It's Daisy.'

After a number of clicks and the occasional scrape of metal sliding on metal, the large, and apparently very heavy, door was pulled open.

'Hello Daisy. It's been a while.'

Ganlin, the owner of the gruff voice, was a very large man, at least four feet taller than Matthew and twice as wide. He seemed to be extremely solidly built. His features were very similar to the lady the Dawn Crew were staring at in the street earlier in the day. Long tendrils extending from the forehead and going down the back, although his were much thicker. Slightly darker slick, grey skin and large eyes. Ganlin's face was very square with a somewhat well maintained short, black beard and prominent nose.

His clothing, however, was in stark contrast to that of the woman. Where she was elegant and beautiful, Ganlin was rough and tattered. He wore dirty, heavy, brown trousers and boots, a greasy white shirt and a thick, brown hide trench coat with the occasional un-mended hole.

Inside the door was a small stone room, clearly not made for a gathering of people. The room contained only a table, a couple of wooden chairs and a stretcher upon which sat a dirty pillow and blanket.

'Who's this you brought with you Daisy? They look a bit off. You know we don't like strangers around here.'

'They're OK. They've come to help. You know how short we are of volunteers, especially with the paranoia going around about missing people. This is Matthew, Safiri and Sam.'

'Nice to meet you, sir,' said the Dawn Crew in unison.

'Well, if you vouch for them then that's OK with me. Just don't be starting no trouble or I'll be throwing you out real quick.'

'You won't get any trouble from us, sir,' said Sam, smiling and wide-eyed to seem as innocent as possible.

Ganlin turned back to Daisy. 'So how have you been? I haven't seen you in ages.'

'I've been OK,' replied Daisy. 'Dad's been on me not to come down here because of the missing people.'

'Yeah, that is a bit worrying innit. I'm sure they'll turn up somewhere. Maybe they took a stroll outside the wall.'

'Don't be silly, Ganlin.'

'Well, just make sure you stay safe. If it means not coming around here for a while then so be it.'

'I'll be fine, Ganlin. Stop worrying.'

Daisy smiled at Ganlin then walked over to the table. Upon it sat a metal bar, which Matthew assumed was a crude weapon, a few bottles, some small boxes and some plain black lanterns with a glass panel on each of the four sides.

As Daisy picked up one of the lanterns, Sam leaned over to Safiri and whispered, 'Bet you anything it sparkles.'

Engraved into the base of the lantern was a small symbol of an upside-down diamond. Daisy touched the symbol. Seemingly out of nothing, orange sparks began to emanate from the middle of the lantern, much like the street lamps.

'Told you,' Sam said smugly to Safiri.

'Lifeblood?' Matthew asked Daisy.

'Lifeblood,' she replied and began to walk to the other end of the room.

The Dawn Crew followed as Daisy led them through a relatively thin tunnel, fitting no more than four abreast. Small lamps were dotted throughout the tunnel although none provided as much light as the lantern.

'So that engraving you touched, how does that work?' Matthew asked.

'I'm not one hundred percent sure on how it all works. Again, not a magineer. All I know is that when you touch it, it'll turn the lantern on. It's the way most lights work. This is a fire rune,' Daisy pointed to the engraving. 'My Dad told me. His job is Historian of Artefacts and Magical Entities at The Office of Magic so he tries to talk to me about magic all the time.'

'That sounds like a great job,' Safiri said.

'He loves it. Wouldn't wanna do anything else. Not for me, though. I prefer working with people.'

'Fair enough. I like to know the details of how things fit together and work,' said Safiri.

'And Ganlin,' said Matthew, 'he's a...?'

'He's a Squaar.'

After a long walk through the tunnel, which seemed to have an almost constant curve to the right and a slight downward slope, Daisy led the crew to a doorway very similar to the one being guarded by Ganlin. This doorway was already open, was a little wider and higher and consisted of two thinner doors as opposed to one large door at the entrance.

As they passed through, Daisy said hello to a guard sitting on a stool beside the doorway who smiled and nodded in return.

'Are you cozy with all the guards around here?' asked Matthew.

'They appreciate any help they get from the surface. It doesn't come around too much and it's generally always the same few. They're good people who don't deserve the way they're treated.'

'We've seen plenty of that where we're from. It sucks,' said Matthew.

Daisy turned off the lantern and placed it on a table next to the guard.

The tunnel opened into a massive cavern so large that they could barely see the other side despite the abundance of light. Matthew guessed it was probably eight or nine storeys high from the ground to the roof.

Where they stood was about a third of the way up, on a wide ledge that ran around the wall of the cavern from where they were, at the doorway, to six man-made platforms housing hundreds of tents and small cabins.

In the centre of the cavern was a massive tree trunk that protruded from the ground and continued through the roof.

'Is that the Gift Giver?' asked Matthew.

'Yep. It gives a bit of light but not enough to really see properly.'

Matthew could see that the light in the cavern came from the orange of the lamps as opposed to the blue of the tree.

They walked forward to a large set of stairs that had been carved into the wall of the ledge they were standing on. On the ground were rows and rows of tents and canopies split by laneways packed full of people.

'This is the marketplace here. When I'm not helping out I like to walk around here and watch the people and the things they make and sell. They do a lot with what they have. Over there,' she pointed at the platforms, 'is where most people live although a lot of the stall owners have stretchers here and some people just pass out wherever they've had their last drink. Most of the bars and taverns are around the Gift Giver and there's an amphitheater on the other side where they do all kinds of shows.'

'What's that over there?' Sam asked as she pointed to the right at what looked like a BMX track.

'That's the local mageball racing track. It's not much but lots of people enjoy it and lose their money, or other belongings, betting. It's all too stressful for me.'

'Can we take a look?' asked Matthew.

'OK, but only for a few minutes or we'll be late.'

After reaching the bottom of the stairs they entered the marketplace on their way to the mageball racetrack. The Dawn Crew followed Daisy closely through the masses of people.

All kinds of food, animals, clothing and other items were being sold. Noodles of all different colours and thickness, root vegetables, meats, sausages, grains, spices. Grills, hotplates, ovens and pots over fire, or the Dusk sparkling equivalent of it, cooked all kinds of street food that the vendors were shouting over each other to sell. The melange of scents from the cooked food and spices pushed through Matthew's nostrils, making him hungry.

The animals, like some of the people, appeared to be a mix of different animals that could be found in Dawn. Dogs with eagle beaks or tails which seemed to be on fire, snakes with wings, birds with spikes protruding from their backs and scaly tails.

Despite all the strangeness of this new world each of the Dawn Crew found some familiarity in the smells and atmosphere of being in the market. Although all of them no longer frequented markets it brought each of them back to their youth.

Everybody in the Scavenger District dressed in a similar fashion to Ganlin. Rugged, sturdy and mostly quite dirty. The majority of people were due for a good scrub. Matthew was fully aware, however that the chances any of them would be fortunate enough for a bath or shower were very slim.

As the crew exited the market and neared the mageball racing track the concentration of people rapidly decreased. With the lack of activity on the track Matthew assumed a race wouldn't be coming up any time soon giving no reason for anybody to congregate there.

'How often do they have races?' Matthew asked.

'I think it's every few days,' Daisy replied. 'You'll know when it's time for a race because the market will be much quieter. The stand will be full and there will be a lot of people around most of the track.'

A relatively small, and somewhat unsafe looking, wooden stand stood in front of the start line. The stand, which consisted of around ten rows of benches, was raised above what was essentially the pit area. The area was lined by a number of curtains that were currently open. A couple of people were having a discussion over some equipment which Matthew assumed was whatever was used for the race.

'OK. Let me know what's going on here,' said Matthew.

'Well, it's pretty simple really. Racers clip the grav-boots onto their shoes,' explained Daisy. 'They then grab the mageball and use it to move around while balancing with their feet. They go around a bunch of times and someone wins.'

'Cool. How does the mageball work?'

'I'm not exactly sure. I never really watch it. I like doing more relaxing activities.'

'Like what?' asked Sam.

'Reading, watching the trees pulse in the park, playing with Misty, my feilin.'

'And a feilin is?'

'An animal. Misty is the family pet. She's furry and cute and flies into my arms whenever I get home.'

'Nice.'

'Someone's going onto the track,' Matthew said as he pointed to the start line.

They walked up to the wooden fence just before the first corner to take a closer look. The track was relatively small. A few hills and some large banked curves. The ground was compacted dirt.

The racer was fully covered, wearing black boots; baggy grey trousers; a dirty long-sleeve shirt; a thick khaki vest over the top; a grey, leather helmet similar to what racing drivers wore in the old days; large goggles; and a grey bandana around their nose and mouth.

They floated out to the starting line, hovering a few inches above the ground, slowly moving toward what looked like sprinters blocks with a pole sticking up just in front of them.

'Why are they called grav-boots?' asked Safiri.

'What are you talking about?' Sam questioned him.

'I mean, they're anti-gravitational, making the racer hover. They should be anti-grav-boots, not grav-boots. They're not even boots either…'

'I dunno,' admitted Daisy. 'Maybe they just shortened it. Maybe they used to be boots.'

The grav-boots were like an extra metal sole on the bottom of the boots which were then braced around the ankles.

'That's the mageball there in their hand,' Daisy pointed at the racer.

The mageball looked like a steel kettlebell. The racer's hand was down by their side. A blue glow came and went from various small holes around the ball.

'It looks like the glow is that flame stuff,' Safiri deduced. 'It must change in intensity to push the racer in a certain direction so they must be able to control it somehow. Look how the glow is coming mostly from the holes facing back and they're all making small adjustments.'

'Sounds like we've got a magineer on our hands,' Daisy teased Safiri. The group laughed.

The racer held onto the pole and set up their feet in the blocks. Once set they extended the mageball out in front of them and nodded to a old ginger Fenlis standing on the inside of the track at the start line. The Fenlis opened a large, wooden box. From the box rose a large, red, glowing orb that floated over to the racer and hovered in front of them. Just like the rest of the lifeblood, the orb emitted sparks which floated around and faded away.

The orb began to pulse and changed colour to yellow, sending out a small explosion of sparks. After a few more pulses it changed to purple and exploded again. A few more pulses and it exploded a light blue and shot up into the air.

The racer's mageball blasted blue flames out the back, over the handle and the racer's hand. The racer pushed off the blocks and flew about a metre in the air, shooting forward, and landing back down on the track with a puff of dust pushing out from the grav-boots. As the racer charged forward a trail of dust streamed in their wake.

As they quickly flew toward the first left corner, which banked up quite considerably, the racer moved their right foot forward and shifted to the right side of the track. As they hit the top of the bank they changed their weight to the left foot, moving it forward and tilted the mageball, pushing it slightly across their body, allowing them to shoot down the curve and onto the next straight.

In the middle of the straight was a hill. The racer increased the intensity of the mageball and accelerated up the hill, flying superman-style, twenty metres down the track before landing in an explosion of dust and continuing around the track.

Daisy gave a screech of terror and covered her eyes as the racer flew through the air while the Dawn Crew all watched, mouths open, not believing what they were seeing.

As the racer finished their first lap of the track the mageball adjusted to shoot flames out the front as they leaned back and slowed down.

'Great lap!' shouted the old Fenlis. By now the orb had hovered back into the wooden box.

The racer zig-zagged a little down the straight before turning and heading back to the pit. Matthew jogged over toward the pits to take a closer look. Coming to a stop the racer seemed to play around with their arm before dropping the mageball. Matthew hadn't noticed a thick glove that had been on the hand of the racer when holding the mageball. They also unclipped the grav-boots, stepping out and back onto solid ground. As they stepped out of each boot it switched off and also fell to the ground.

'Still not getting enough power on the start,' came the voice of what sounded like a young girl.

'I'll tinker with it and see if I can get any more out of it. Ain't got any money for an upgrade,' said the old man.

As the racer removed their goggles and helmet the Dawn Crew were surprised to see that the racer was a small Fenlis girl. Her tail had been hidden in the baggy trousers. This Fenlis was very different to Daisy. She was ginger, making Matthew assume that the old man was her father, smaller and much slimmer.

Daisy suddenly shrieked, 'We're late!' Come on, quickly!' and rushed the Dawn Crew away from the mageball racetrack.

'Late for what?' Matthew asked as they rushed back into the crowd.

'Late to meet Kyrral and help at the medical station!'

Chapter Ten
Finding My People

Daisy turned and bolted back into the market, taking Matthew's hand in the process. Safiri and Sam followed close behind. Zigzagging through the hoards of people, they ran toward the trunk of the Gift Giver, trying not to knock over anyone or anything.

Surrounding the gigantic tree was a large plaza. Unlike most of the Scavenger District, this part of the cavern was paved. Bars and taverns lined the area with small sweets vendors also popping up.

Music was pouring from each of the bars, some from bands and some simply a drunken singalong. There were also some street musicians out on the paving, around the tree.

They played instruments that were mostly similar to those found in Dawn. Buckets and pots of various sizes were being used as drums. Shells were being used as trumpets and flutes. There was one instrument, however, which was unlike anything the Dawn Crew had ever seen before. A small girl with crusty skin sat on the ground in front of a box. Ten streaks of light shot out from the top of the box in two rows of five. The light stopped a little less than a metre above the top of the box. The girl touched each stream of light as if plucking a string, with the pitch of the sound changing depending where she touched it. As with the doorway, a wisp of sparks broke away from the light at the point of contact. She created beautiful music which sounded like a mix between a keyboard, violin and a choir.

A group of small children danced and giggled in front of the band as they played. The adults either danced around them or stood and watched a little further back.

Rounding the Gift Giver, the crew came to the medical station which was situated in a large tent next to an open tavern.

Standing at the entrance to the tent was a large, bulky man with rough, blue, stoney skin, shaggy black hair and some light stubble. Daisy ran up to him, jumped and threw her arms around his neck.

'Kyrral! I haven't seen you for ages!' shouted Daisy.

Much like the rest of the people in the Scavenger district, Kyrral was dressed in a dirty, white, button-up shirt with the sleeves rolled up. Black suspenders held up dark brown, baggy leather trousers and black boots finished his ensemble.

Daisy turned to each of the Dawn Crew. 'Kyrral, meet Matthew, Safiri and Sam.'

They each shook his hand although Kyrral seemed to do his best to avoid eye contact.

'Nice to meet you,' said Kyrral in a deep, yet quiet voice.

'Likewise, sir,' Matthew responded.

Kyrral turned back to Daisy. 'You're late,' he said as they both turned and entered the tent.

'Sorry, Kyrral. I found these guys getting into a bit of Authority trouble and helped them out.' As Daisy said this she elbowed Matthew lightly in the gut.

'I was worried you weren't coming again,' Kyrral said, looking quite somber.

'Sorry. It's been a lot harder trying to get down here lately. My parents aren't exactly enthusiastic about what I do in my spare time with everything that's been going on with the missing people.'

'Well, at least you're here now,' Kyrral said as a smile finally started to appear.

The medical tent had a small reception area with a desk and a few benches for those waiting for attention. Behind the desk were rows of stretchers, some were curtained off. Most of the stretchers were empty, however those that weren't were being monitored regularly by a small batch of nurses in white gowns.

'Hi Daisy,' called the nurse at the reception desk. 'I've got some packages I need you to deliver. It's very important that they get to the right people. Who's this here with you?'

'These are my friends. They've come to help out today,' Daisy replied.

'Well in that case I'll give you two trollies.' The nurse handed two pieces of paper to Daisy. 'Here's where everything needs to be delivered and here are your pointers.' The nurse gave them each a leather wrist band with a thimble connected to it.

The Dawn Crew waited and watched while Daisy and Kyrral strapped the pointers to their wrist and placed the thimble on their index finger. Looking simple enough they followed suit. The connecting piece of leather from the wrist to the thimble seemed to tighten over their hands once the thimble was on and adjusted, like elastic, to the movement of their hand and finger.

Kyrral and Safiri each took charge of a trolley and wheeled them outside.

'So what's the go, here?' asked Matthew.

'It's simple,' Daisy replied. 'Each of these packages needs to be delivered. This sheet,' which she held up, 'tells us who each package needs to go to and the pointer will point the way to where they live. Kyrral, the first package please.'

Kyrral retrieved a package from the trolley.

'Now, this one needs to go to Sarai in the purple tent on level four, row eight,' Daisy read from her sheet.

She touched a symbol on the side of the package with the thimble which then lit up with a dull, orange, sparkly light. Each of them then touched the symbol with their own thimble to activate it.

'Does anyone else see a trail of lifeblood going around the tent there, coming from my pointer?' Matthew asked.

'I can see one from mine but not from yours,' replied Sam.

'You'll only be able to see your own pointer path,' Daisy pointed out to the rest of the crew. 'OK. Let's go. There's lots of packages to deliver.'

Daisy and Kyrral set off following their pointer paths, zig-zagging between tents and stalls toward the platforms. As they approached, Matthew could see they were made of a mix of wood and metal in a manner that suggested they had been extended as needed using whatever materials they had available at the time. Each platform was connected to the next by a number of ramps and ladders dotted along the outer side and each platform had twelve to fifteen rows of five to eight tents and cabins.

The crew followed their pointer paths up to level four. Where Kyrral was easily pushing his trolley up each ramp, it was quite a struggle for Matthew, Safiri and Sam to push theirs, despite their joint effort.

As they approached row eight Daisy stopped and turned to face them. 'Sam and I will take the lead on this. You guys hold back a little. Some people feel quite vulnerable and anxious and can spook easily.'

They slowly walked down the row of tents until they reached the purple one. It was no bigger than a four person tent Matthew had when he had gone camping with George. Daisy and Sam approached the entrance to the tent.

'Sarai? I'm Daisy. I have a package for you from the medical tent.'

A Fenlis woman poked her head out of the tent. She was a soft, ginger colour. Despite wearing a hood Matthew could see that her face was much more slender than Daisy's and looked a little malnourished.

'Daisy, you say?' she asked.

Daisy nodded and replied 'This is Sam.'

Sam smiled and waved politely to Sarai.

'Thank you, Daisy. You have no idea how much we need this.'

Opening the tent more to take the package, Daisy and Sam's expression changed to shock and sadness, although Matthew couldn't see why from where he stood with Kyrral and Safiri.

'I'm so sorry, Sarai. Is there anyone else who can help you? Do you have Fenlisten?'

'No. Everybody else is gone.'

Matthew turned to Kyrral. 'What's Fenlisten?'

Kyrral glanced sideways at Matthew with a quizzical look and didn't answer. He quickly realised that Kyrral wasn't in the loop on who they were and where they were from.

'We'll do what we can to help both of you,' assured Daisy.

'Thank you and bless you Daisy and Sam.' And with that she returned to her tent and Daisy and Sam made their way back, looking quite upset.

'She has a child in there,' said Sam. 'He doesn't look in good condition at all.'

'What's Fenlisten?' Matthew asked Daisy.

'It's a Fenlis pack. It could be family but it could also be more.'

'Is it common around here? What Sarai is going through?'

'Unfortunately it is and it's getting worse. The Authority is willing to give less and less help to the Scavengers and with the recent disappearances, people down here are starting to hoard instead of looking out for others. It's probably what The Authority want. For everyone to turn on each other. Means there will be less for them to deal with. Anyway, we've got more packages to deliver.'

Daisy wiped a tear from her eye as she picked up the next package.

As they continued on to the next delivery, Matthew was keen to get a bit more information about the issues facing the Scavengers.

'How has it come to this? Why doesn't anyone help? Why don't the Scavengers just leg it out of this place?'

'It's not that simple, Matthew. The Authority uses The Decree to make sure nothing changes, to keep the Scavengers down here where they can't cause trouble and have any real power for themselves.'

'So who are the Authority and The Decree? Officer Doggery threatened to take me to The Authority.'

'The Authority controls everything. They're a massive, some would say very corrupt, organisation that governs everyone and everything… well, except the Pure who really pull the strings. Anyway, The Authority is split into The Treasury, who control the money, business, trade; The Decree, which is the law and whatever cronies are enforcing it; and The Office of Magic, which is in charge of all artefacts, rune licenses and anything else that has to do with magic. Most people usually call the constabulary The Authority, I guess because people see them as the face of The Authority. '

'OK. Cool, cool, cool. So all they care about is making sure they keep the poor from having a better life so they can hang onto their comfortable, wealthy lives 'cause they're a bunch of douchebags? The Authority has no interest is creating a bit of equality between everyone?'

'Well when you put it that way it is quite simple. But there's nothing we can do about it. Every time anyone has tried to do anything it's ended badly for them.'

'How badly?'

'Beaten, resources taken away from the whole community. That's why there are guards at all the doors. To keep people from doing anything stupid.'

Sam kept Kyrral occupied, chatting about anything she could point to and make comment at, hoping that he wouldn't catch any of the conversation between Matthew and Daisy. Safiri wheeled his trolley in the middle of the group to create a little distance.

'Officer Doggery, he's obviously not Fenlis, Pure or Squaar so what is he? And Kyrral for that matter?' Matthew asked.

'Officer Doggery is Lorrai and Kyrral is Stroen. Don't you have any of them where you come from?'

'No. Where we're from everybody looks like us.'

As they continued on through their deliveries, all the recipients were either sick or malnourished, it was obvious to them all how dire the state of the Scavenger District was.

Matthew continued his enquiries about the way of life in the district. 'How do people pay for things here? Other than the people in the market, how does anyone make any money?'

'A lot of people work mining lifeblood from caves below the Gift Giver. They don't get much coin for it, though. It's practically slave labour. That money then gets circulated around the district at the markets, although a lot of it goes back out to pay for ingredients or materials to make things. They reuse as much as they can to try and keep the money here. Everyone is pretty resourceful. There are some vegetables and other, technically edible, foods that grow in the caves but they're pretty bland and need to go with other ingredients to really make anything remotely nice. That's why there are a lot of spices being sold. They have to get those from outside, though. Most of the meat is whatever can be caught in the caves. Rangles, wileybirds, spranglesnouts, slythes and winged slingots, although some taverns and market vendors occasionally get their hands on something better through more illegal channels.'

'Sounds appetising.'

After emptying out the trolleys a little more the Dawn Crew

made use of the extra space and removed their backpacks. This was welcome relief for all of them as they had been walking around with them on their backs for hours with very little rest. None of them were in any way seasoned hikers or travellers and were definitely not used to carrying that much weight for such a long period of time.

'Next up,' said Safiri, 'Tran, level seven, row three in the cabin.'

'Mind if I give this one a go?' asked Matthew.

All agreed with the changeup from having Daisy and Sam deliver the package, under the assumption that having a cabin meant the occupants were slightly less vulnerable than the rest.

Matthew knocked on the door. The door was quickly opened, however, only slightly. Only an eye and a sliver of their face could be seen. The person at the door was quite short.

'Hello, are you Tran?' Matthew asked.

'Sorry, not here,' the mystery person replied and promptly closed the door.

Matthew knocked again.

'I told you. Not here. Go away.'

'Do you know how long they'll be? I've got a package for them from the medical station.'

The door quickly swung open. A short, wrinkly, saggy, bald man with floppy ears and grubby clothes stood before Matthew, who he now recognised as being Lorrai, looking similar to Officer Doggery.

'I can take that off your hands,' said the man as he reached out to take the package.

Matthew recoiled, pulling the package away. 'Sorry, it needs to be delivered directly to the person it's addressed to.'

'Come now, boy. It's address to this here cabin. You can just leave it here. I'll make sure it gets to the right person, err… Tan.'

Matthew glanced across to the rest of the crew waiting for him to come back. He moved the package under his right arm and held tight. 'I don't think I'm going to do that, sir. I'll come back later and see if they're back.'

'Just give me the package boy!' The man, anger growing, stepped forward and tried to take the package from Matthew, who turned and pushed him away with his left hand, back through the doorway. After regaining his footing the apparent thief once again attempted to attack Matthew for his prize.

By this time Kyrral had walked up to the doorway and grabbed the man by the shoulder as he reached out again. Anger turned to fear as the grubby thief saw the size of his foe.

'NO!' Kyrral shouted in the man's face as he threw him back into the cabin and closed the door. Matthew scrambled back to his friends while Kyrral angrily walked back behind him.

'Not home. Next package, please… quickly now,' said Matthew pulling the next one out and handing it to Safiri. He took hold of both trolleys and pushed them out of the row and toward the ramp at the end of the platform.

'What happened?' asked Daisy.

'Tran wasn't there. Only this dodgy looking guy who tried to steal the package off me. Is there anyone we can get to look into what's going on there?'

'I'll pass it onto medical when we get back and they'll look into it. Resources are low so I'm not sure anything will be done about it.'

'What about security?' asked Safiri.

'I'm not sure any of them would leave their post without us having more for them to go on.'

'What about the missing people? Tran seems to be missing.'

'I don't think Tran not being there at the precise time we made a delivery will be enough. I'll pass it on and we'll see what happens.'

After finishing off the last couple of deliveries they all made their way back to the medical tent. Zig-zagging their way through the tents and away from the platforms, Matthew felt less anxious about his altercation and started to relax again.

The open tavern next to the medical station was bustling with chatter, singing and drinking as they made their way past the benches. As the crew were entering the tent a large, old, cheerful Stroen man, who had clearly had a few before they had passed, grabbed Matthew by the shoulder and pulled him down onto the bench next to him.

'Have a drink, boy! Celebrate the end of a hard day's labour,' said the man, motioning to a young Squaar waiter to bring another drink.

'Matthew!' shouted Safiri at the entrance to the medical tent.

'It's OK. You guys go in. I'll be there in a minute.'

'That's the spirit, boy,' said the man. He was a darker shade of blue than Kyrral and wore black boots, trousers and tattered waistcoat. His hair was black, short and spiky with a long, pointed goatee.

The drink promptly arrived for Matthew in a well used metal tankard. The man cheersed the group of people sitting around them with Matthew joining in. As the others drank Matthew looked in the tankard to see what the substance was that they were consuming.

'What's the matter, boy? Never had wombus juice before?'

As Matthew looked around at the jovial crowd, waving their drinks around, drops of purple liquid escaped the containment of the tankards. *This must be the same drink Finnigan was drinking,* thought Matthew and took a sip. The wombus juice was thicker than wine, a little sweeter and, after a few seconds, provided a deep warmth in his stomach followed by a burn in his throat, prompting Matthew to cough.

'Hits you hard doesn't it, boy? HAHAHA! Cheers!' and the man clapped his tankard to Matthew's before taking a long drink himself.

For a few minutes Matthew listened to the jokes of the people around him as he finished his wombus juice. Standing up, and taking a second to collect his head and balance, Matthew turned to the old man.

'How much do I owe you for the drink?'

'On me, boy! I see you helping folks out. I thank you for that.'

'Thanks, sir. I'm Matthew by the way.' Matthew extended his hand.

'Rackma is my name. Nice to meet you, Matthew,' he said as he shook Matthew's hand.

'Nice to meet you, Rackma. See you around.'

'You're welcome to join us any time.'

Matthew made his way over to the medical tent to join his friends. Just before reaching the entrance he was grabbed from behind. A very large hand covered his mouth and an arm pinned Matthew's arms to his sides. The unknown assailant dragged Matthew behind some nearby tents.

Waiting for them was the grubby, saggy, little Lorrai who tried to steal the package from Matthew.

'You think you can disrespect me and get away with it? You'll regret laying hands on me, boy!'

He punched Matthew in the gut. Matthew dropped to his knees, trying to catch his breath. He then felt a sudden pain in the back of his head as he was clubbed by the brute that had taken him. Everything went black.

Chapter Eleven
Whip It

Matthew woke, very groggy with a throbbing on the back of his head. His hands and feet tied and mouth gagged. It took a few seconds for his eyes to regain focus and for him to regather his wits.

He was being moved somewhere, laying on his back, wheeled in a large open sack attached to the top of a trolley which Matthew could hear and feel clearly rolling on an uneven surface. The ceiling above him was rocky and not particularly high. There seemed to be plenty of light.

After a couple of minutes of grunts and the trolley wheels struggling, Matthew was pushed through a doorway where the surface became much more even, although the trolley came an abrupt halt very shortly after passing through.

Footsteps away from the trolley were followed by the sound of a key turning in a lock and a heavy door opening. The trolley moved again toward the sound of the door then suddenly tipped forward. Matthew fell hard, out of the sack and onto a dusty, wooden floor. He took most of his body weight on his shoulder and neck, making him wince in pain.

The large man who had initially grabbed Matthew back at the tavern moved the trolley aside and stepping into the small cell which Matthew was now laying in. As he removed a knife from his belt Matthew scrambled back to the far wall of the cell. Matthew kicked out his legs and attempted to shout through his gag. The man laughed at Matthew, pushing his swinging legs aside and grabbing Matthew's hands. He cut the restraints on Matthew's hands and feet and removed the gag.

'Thank you,' said Matthew, trying to display some kindness in an attempt to gain mercy from whatever was going to happen to him.

The man laughed and kicked Matthew in the side, driving the breath from his body once again. He picked up a bucket which was sitting in the corner of the room and threw it at Matthew, continuing to laugh. He then turned and left the cell, closing the door and locking Matthew inside.

Matthew picked up his glasses which had fallen off when Matthew was kicked. He quickly checked in his shirt for the necklace and found it still in place. *Strange that they didn't take this,* Matthew thought although he decided not to question it and just be grateful he still had in his possession the only route home.

Matthew stood up and walked over to the door. 'What the hell is going on?!' He shouted. 'Let me out of here!'

No answer came. Matthew scanned the cell for anything he could possibly use to try and escape, not that he had ever attempted to pick any kind of lock. The cell consisted of four rough, stone walls, stone ceiling and large, metal door. He noticed a hole the size of a brick at the base of the wall on his right as he looked toward the back of the cell. The cell was well lit although the light seemed to be coming from a few bugs flying around the ceiling of the cell.

Matthew started to panic. 'I shouldn't have ever come here. Idiot!' he scolded himself, trying to remember why he thought it was a good idea in the first place. This just made him panic more.

'Why did you listen to Grandad? You're not like him. Should've just stayed where it was safe.'

He started to miss his friends, people back home, his favourite foods, everything he knew. The thought of food reminded Matthew that he hadn't eaten for hours and his stomach started to grumble. For a second he though the men had taken his bag until he remembered it was back in the trolley at the medical station, with his friends.

Matthew banged his fist on the door. 'Hey! Is anybody there?!' he shouted.

'I wouldn't waste my breath if I were you,' came a female voice through the hole in the wall. 'They're not going to answer any of your questions. I've already tried.'

She sounded like she was of a similar age to Matthew.

'Who are you?' he asked.

'I'd rather not say at this time,' she replied. 'I don't know if you were put there to get information out of me.'

'You didn't hear the loud thud when they tipped me out onto the floor or that guy kick me in the ribs?' Matthew asked with a hint of sarcasm.

'Yes, but so would a sack of potensoes. Can easily be staged.'

'You got a lot of experience staging kidnappings?'

No reply came.

'How long have you been here?' he asked. A simple enough question which their captors would already know so she wouldn't be revealing anything of importance.

'A couple of hours I think, although there's no way for me to be sure.'

'I heard some talk around town of missing people. Maybe we were taken by the same people?'

'Maybe,' she replied. 'But then the question is where is everyone else? Maybe this is just a bunch of thugs who think they can extort money from our families.'

'Good luck getting money from no one,' Matthew said and chuckled to himself, although it was filled with pain.

'You have no family?' she asked.

'Nup. Just me. Sucks to be those guys, am I right? Ha!' Matthew made a quite poor attempt to hide his sadness when saying it aloud.

'I'm sorry to hear that. May I ask what happened to them?'

'My parents died when I was a little kid. I was pretty much raised by my Grandad. He died a few weeks ago.' In truth Matthew had forgotten how long it had been since George had passed.

'Weeks?' she asked.

'Not too long ago,' Matthew quickly replied. Apparently they had hours but weeks was a Dawn concept. Matthew was annoyed at himself for slipping. 'He used to tell the most amazing stories,' Matthew moved away from their differing measurements of time.

'That's nice. My mother used to tell me stories when I was younger but not so much anymore. My father would only tell stories if it in some way served his purpose.'

'A bit of a tyrant then?' Matthew asked jokingly.

'Some would say that, I'm sure.'

The door to the room opened and they both fell silent. Footsteps grew louder and someone approached Matthew's cell. The door clicked as it unlocked and swung open.

The large man was again before Matthew, who jumped back to the opposite end of the cell. He was holding a tray with something that looked very much like mouldy bread, some kind of vegetable and a cup. The man set the tray down on the ground. He looked at Matthew with a devilish grin on his face. Matthew could tell by his stoney skin that he was Stroen. He was of a similar build to Kyrral, although he had no hair and his skin had a tinge of green as opposed to the blue of Kyrral.

As he stood up he motioned to Matthew to take the tray. Matthew didn't move.

'Take the food you ungrateful turd!'

Matthew slowly moved toward the tray. The man's smile grew larger and his eyes narrowed. He grabbed Matthew by the hair and punched him in the stomach as the Lorrai had earlier. Matthew fell to his knees, gasping for air.

'HAHAHA! Weak little boy!' The man turned and walked out of the cell, closing and locking the door and leaving the room, never stopping the sadistic laugh at his outsmarting of the inferior boy.

Matthew struggled for a couple of minutes to catch his breath, angry that he had been hit again and that he was even in the situation he found himself in.

'Are you OK?' The girl asked.

'I'll be fine. Don't suppose the food is any better than the service?'

She giggled. 'Not really. I would advise you steer clear of the solids.'

At this point Matthew was desperate for some food and decided to give it a go despite the advice he had just received. Breaking off the least mouldy looking piece of the bread, Matthew put it in his mouth and began to chew. It was sour, far more than sourdough bread. Whether that was the mould or the actual taste of the bread, Matthew had no idea.

Picking up the vegetable, which looked like sweet potato, Matthew took a bite. The burn hit his tongue immediately and he felt his eyes popping out of his head while watering profusely. He spat it out and began coughing. He reached for the cup, taking a swig of what seemed to be sugar water. It wasn't a thirst quencher but it definitely helped relieve the burn in his mouth.

'Well that was disgusting. I'm hungry but not hungry enough for that.'

The girl giggled again. 'I warned you.'

Matthew could sense that he was breaking down the barrier she had put up and decided to try and get her to open up again.

'I'm Matthew by the way. You trust me enough to at least tell me your name now? I did just take yet another punch in the gut.'

'My name is Sarrus.'

'Nice to meet you, Sarrus, although I guess the circumstances could be better.'

'Yes. We're not in the best place right now.'

'I've gotta say you're taking this all really well. You seem to be quite calm about the situation.'

'One of the pluses of a tyrant father, I guess. He was always pushing me to toughen up.'

Matthew stood up and took a closer look at the door.

'Don't suppose you've seen any weakness in this door or happen to have some kind of magical lock pick?' Matthew asked.

'Can't say I have, however I may have something else that I've been working on.'

'Really? A portal? Maybe a potion to walk through walls?'

'I'm going to need you to take what's coming into your cell through the hole, but don't touch the flower.'

Curious, Matthew walked over to the wall with the hole at its base and crouched down. A vine emerged, creeping from the hole in the wall. It looked like a standard vine Matthew could find back in Dawn. At the end of the vine a bud grew from nothing then bloomed into a dark, red flower with several long filaments in the middle and large petals. It was like watching a plant growing in fast-forward.

'The guard will come to collect the tray soon, ' said Sarrus. 'When he does, blow the flower into his face. Understand?'

'Got it,' Matthew replied.

After a few seconds without movement of the plant Sarrus became confused.

'What are you doing. Take the flower.' She demanded.

'Quiet!' said Matthew, sternly.

'What's wrong?'

After a few more seconds of silence, the sound of a liquid hitting the bottom of the bucket could be heard throughout the room.

'Really?!' she shouted.

'Hey, brother's gotta go,' replied Matthew.

'Who's brother? What are you talking about?'

'Wha? I'm the brother… forget it. I've been holding this for ages and I can't hold it no more.'

Once finished Matthew gave a sigh of relief, went back to the plant, took hold of the stem and broke it off, keeping as much distance between the flower and himself as possible.

After a few awkward minutes holding the plant the door to the room opened and the heavy steps of the large man could be heard heading toward Matthew's cell. Matthew turned toward the back of the room, keeping the plant out of sight from the entrance of his cell and listening for the guard.

The lock clicked and the heavy metal door swung open.

'Hey! What you doing!'

Matthew heard the man step into the cell and start approaching him. He quickly turned, bringing the flower up to the level of his face and blew as hard as he could. The flower disintegrated under the force of the air and the resulting red powder flew into the man's face.

He stumbled back, swatting the powder from his face as Matthew crouched in the corner of the cell in an attempt to keep as much distance as possible between himself and the stumbling man.

After a few seconds the man started to slow. His eyes began to droop and his limbs became limp. His legs crumpled awkwardly beneath him and his body dropped hard onto the dusty, wooden floor.

'Is he dead?' Matthew asked, still quite panicked.

'No. Just unconscious. Now get the key and let me out of here, please.'

'On my way.'

Matthew gave the man a quick kick in the stomach and headed toward the door where the key was still hanging in the lock. It was a large, old style key on a large keyring along with a number of other keys. Matthew closed the door behind him and locked it. He hesitated for a second.

'What are you waiting for?' asked Sarrus.

'I just locked this guy in. What he starves to death?'

'He won't starve to death. Either we get caught and he get's released or we escape and The Authority can deal with all of them.'

'Fair enough.'

Matthew scurried over to the other cell. After trying the lock with a few different keys he finally heard the click of the lock and could push the door open.

Shock hit Matthew as he saw before him the girl he had called out to in front of the temple, still in the same green hooded dress and brown trousers she had been wearing earlier. She was the most human looking of anyone Matthew had encountered so far although she had a slightly green tinge to her hair, her skin was slightly bronze and her ears a little pointed. To Matthew she looked a little like a cosplay elf.

'It's you,' he said.

'Do I know you from somewhere?'

'No. I saw you going into a temple earlier today.'

'Were you following me?'

'No… I just happened to be passing by at the time.'

'Is this really important right now?' she asked.

'No, I guess not. I'm gonna check out the room to see if there's anything we can use to help us get out of here.'

'Like what?'

'I don't know. A club or something in case we run into anyone like this guy,' Matthew motioned to the other cell then took a look around. Besides a table and single chair there was nothing else in the room.

'Why don't you just stay behind me, Matthew, and I'll get us out.' Sarrus reached into a pocket in her dress despite there being no visible sign that it was actually there.

'Magic pocket? A girl of many secrets, I see.'

Sarrus gave a wry smile, pulled her hand out of the pocket and put something into her other hand.

'Give me a second,' she said as she closed her eyes and extended her arms down. A look of deep concentration on her face.

Matthew noticed a slight emerald glow emanate from her closed hands. Green stems appeared out of the sides of her fists as a long green vine grew in each of her hands. One end wrapped itself around each of her wrists as the other extended out toward the floor.

'Vine whips. Nice!' Matthew said, a huge, excited smile on his face. Despite everything he had seen since arriving in Dusk, he was still very much amazed at what was happening in front of him.

Sarrus turned toward the door which would take them out of the room.

'Wait!' Matthew demanded.

He scurried back into the cell he had just escaped from and moved the bucket right next to the thug's face, giggling to himself as he admired his brilliant idea.

'I don't think this is the time, Matthew,' Sarrus scolded.

Matthew looked at Sarrus, still smiling and pointed to the bucket.

'When he wakes up he's gonna knock over the bucket. HAHAHA! He's probably gonna get some on him!'

'How old are you, forty?'

'Forty?'

'Ugh! Let's go!'

'Fine.'

They ran to the door and took a quick but careful look at what was on the other side. A short stoney tunnel turned to the left, at which point they couldn't see any further. Lanterns, similar to the one Daisy held as she led them to the massive cavern, were nailed into the walls of the tunnel.

After a few seconds confirming that nobody was coming, Sarrus led Matthew quickly and quietly down the tunnel. Several twists and turns took them to another door which was slightly ajar.

Sarrus slowly opened the door a little more, enough to stick her head in and peek into the room beyond. She quickly pulled her head back.

'There's two men and one woman in the room. One man is sitting at a table and the other two are talking in front of some barrels. There are a few more barrels to the left of the door where we can get some cover. Hopefully we can just slip though without being noticed. The man at the table is slightly larger than the others but nothing we shouldn't be able to take care of if necessary.'

'What are you, a ninja now?'

'Just stay behind me and be quick and silent.'

'Hold up. What are we gonna do if they try and fight us?'

'We fight back.'

'I don't know anything about fighting!'

'You better not let them see you then.'

Panic started to hit Matthew again. This was the type of situation he had avoided his entire life. No confrontations. Keep everyone happy.

Sarrus quietly opened the door and ducked behind the barrels.

Matthew looked down at his shaking hands. He had moved beyond jokes being able to help him cope with the situation. He took a deep breath, slipped into the room and joined Sarrus behind the barrels.

The room seemed to be a store room about four times the size of the room with the cells. The dirt floor of the tunnel became dusty wooden boards. There were quite a few barrels and crates as well as a few rows of shelves.

The man at the table, a peach coloured Squaar with short tendrils tied up behind his head, was sitting on a chair, feet up on the table, arms crossed and seemingly dozing off.

The other two were Lorrai. A man and a woman, Matthew assumed based on their voices, although it was hard to tell since they were both bald with saggy skin and floppy ears. They were both having an intense discussion about which of the barrels were the ones they needed.

Just behind them, in the far corner of the room, Matthew spotted something familiar. Although his view was somewhat obscured by both the barrels and a shelf packed with a number of strange looking items, Matthew could see part of the outline of a doorway like the one the Dawn Crew used to get to Dusk. This one, however was literally an open doorway with the other side clearly visible. There was a blue tinge to everything on the other side of the doorway, like looking through glass into an aquarium.

'Damn liar,' Matthew said under his breath.

'What was that?' Sarrus whispered.

'I'll tell you when we get out of here,' Matthew replied.

Sarrus then nodded and pointed the path for them to take. After Matthew nodded confirmation they crept around their cover and scurried over to another group of barrels just behind the man at the table. They held low and still for a few moments to ensure they hadn't been noticed. The two Lorrai continued their discussion and the Squaar was still dozing on the chair.

Carefully, they crept out from the barrels and slowly moved past the dozing man. They passed the table and reached the rows of shelves which would give them extra cover. They were almost to the door when Matthew stepped on a loose floorboard. A loud creek erupted from under his foot. Matthew's eyes widened and Sarrus turned her head to look at him, her eyes just as wide. Matthew looked back behind him. They held their breaths as the room went silent.

The man on the chair opened his eyes. It took a few second for the Squaar to register what was happening. As soon as he had he stood up and shouted.

'The prisoners!'

The Lorrai came running around the shelves and barrels to join the Squaar.

As Matthew stood he was able to get a good look at the doorway. The other side looked like a warehouse with high industrial shelving. Matthew grabbed the first thing on the shelf next to him. It happened to be a mageball with a black glove. Even though he had no idea how to use it, he could at least use it to hit someone over the head.

The Squaar began to run toward Matthew and Sarrus.

'Run!' Sarrus shouted and pulled Matthew behind her, to the door.

Matthew reached the door, pulled it open and looked back before running though. As the man ran toward Sarrus she brought up the vine in her right hand and whipped him in the face. With the vine in her left hand she grabbed the shelves.

'Daaaaamn,' Matthew said as Sarrus turned and ran to the door, pulling down the shelves. Matthew jumped through the doorway as she ran and slid, pulling the door closed as the shelves crashed down over where she had been, blocking the door.

They both got up and began running down another stoney, dusty tunnel. Up ahead of them was a supply cupboard carved into the stone with a trolley in front of it similar to the one used to wheel Matthew to his cell. Matthew suddenly had an idea.

'You know how to use this thing?' he asked Sarrus, holding up the mageball and putting on the glove.

'Not really… wait… are you going to do what I think you're going to do?'

A mischievous smile appeared on Matthew's face. 'Yep,' he replied.

Once Matthew had finished putting the glove on it seemed to resize to perfectly fit his hand and arm, as well as extending up his forearm to his elbow. Once the process had completed it left what appeared to be a black layer of skin over the top of his own.

While they continued running toward the trolley, Matthew inspected the handle, trying to find a way of turning on the mageball.

'Get in!' he shouted to Sarrus as they reached the trolley.

Sarrus promptly climbed into the sack in the trolley and held onto the front bar which the top of the sack was attached to. Matthew climbed in after her, at the back of the sack, continuing to search for way to switch the mageball on. He also noticed there were no holes in the ball as he had seen at the track.

At the far end of the tunnel, from where they had come, the door finally swung open and the two Lorrai ran toward the escapees.

Sarrus looked back over Matthew at the oncoming Lorrai.

'Better get that thing working, Matthew!' she shouted at him.

While there was no button to be found there was a symbol on each end of the handle.

'Runes! Of course!' Matthew shouted and placed his thumb on the symbol.

Suddenly the mageball hissed and made a sound like a treadmill speeding up.

The Lorrai were now seconds from being within touching distance.

Matthew pointed the mageball out the back of the trolley, closed his eyes and hoped it would fire up and propel them in the right direction.

As the woman reached out to take hold of Matthew, small circles across the ball glowed blue and morphed into holes. Blue, intense flames erupted from the holes facing away from Matthew, scolding the woman's outreached hand as the trolley shot forward. The woman fell to her knees screaming in pain from the burns and cradling her hand.

Matthew and Sarrus held onto the bars surrounding the top of the trolley, trying to keep it balanced as it rolled at an immense speed across the dusty, rocky floor. A trail of dust kicked up behind them, obscuring any sight of the Lorrai and tunnel where they had come from.

'Matthew! The crates!' Screamed Sarrus.

Matthew looked forward to see a stack of crates on the right hand side of the tunnel, coming up fast. He turned back to look at the mageball again, pointing out the back of the trolley. As soon as the thought came into his mind that they needed to turn, the flames on the right hand side of the mageball slightly decreased, while those on the left increased, pushing Matthew's hand to the right and kicking the back of the trolley across, turning them slightly left, passed the boxes. Matthew then though about correcting their path again, so as not to steer the cart into the wall. The mageball seemed to read his thoughts and adjusted to set them back on course.

As they continued through the tunnel it began to widen to become a small cavern. Wooden pillars were placed throughout the cavern presumably to ensure the roof didn't cave in. A wall was quickly approaching.

'Turn off the mageball and hold on tight!' shouted Sarrus.

Matthew touched his thumb onto the rune again and the mageball powered down. He held onto the trolley as tight as he could with one hand and wrapped the other around Sarrus' waist, knowing what she was about to do.

Sarrus held onto the trolley and with the other hand, whipped a vine around one of the pillars in the cavern. The trolley swung three quarters of the way around and Sarrus release the vine from her wrist and hand. The trolley slid ten metres until the sack ripped and both Matthew and Sarrus fell out, rolling until they came to an abrupt stop, crashing into a pile of empty wooden crates and then painfully ending all momentum by colliding with some metal bars.

Matthew turned around to see the face of a giant lizard, a horn at the end of its nose, staring at him like Matthew was its next meal. Matthew scrambled back quickly.

'Sarrus?!'

'I'm OK,' she said as she pushed off debris.

Voices could be heard nearby as their abrupt and noisy entrance seemed to have broken the peace. Matthew and Sarrus quickly got to their feet and ran in the opposite direction of the voices. They ran through a door and found themselves in a cabin.

'Hey! What are you doing in here?! Nyster! Buck! Help!'

It was the grubby Lorrai who kidnapped Matthew. Not having any time to think, Matthew ran up and hit the plump man in the face with the mageball. He fell straight back onto the floor, knocked out. Matthew and Sarrus exited through the cabin door, onto level seven, thugs close behind.

Finally they were somewhere Matthew had seen before. They ran for the end of the platform. Matthew took Sarrus' hand.

'We gotta jump,' he said. 'Hold onto me when we do.'

They reached the edge of the platform and both jumped, Sarrus turning her body to hold onto Matthew. Matthew pointed the mageball up into the air and pressed the rune with his thumb. The mageball took a moment to fire up and in that time Matthew's heart almost stopped as they began to fall. Once it had finally kicked in, Matthew pointed the mageball toward the top of the Gift Giver and with maximum speed they flew across the Scavenger District, people below pointing and shouting.

Matthew could see the medical tent and pointed the mageball in that direction. As they approached he adjusted to point his arm straight up, changing the power of the mageball to take them both slowly down to the ground.

As soon as they touched ground Matthew was nearly tackled by Daisy, but only because she was quicker than the rest. Safiri and Sam also rushed out of the tavern with Daisy. They all grabbed Matthew, asking questions at the same time. Sarrus nimbly jumped out of the way a second before Matthew got swamped.

Kyrral stood with Ganlin and a large group of similarly sized, and dressed, men under the canopy of the tavern.

'Where were you?!' shouted Safiri. 'What happened!'

'We were so worried!' added Daisy.

'We were about to send out a search party,' added Ganlin.

'Calm down guys. We're OK. Water please. Lots of water… and maybe some decent food? Can someone please tell me how to get this damn glove off?' Matthew waived the mageball around. 'Somebody get me my bag… I'm keeping this.'

'I've got it here,' said Sam, holding out the bag.

'This is Sarrus by the way. She was locked up in the cell next to me and we helped each other escape.'

'Locked up?! You need to tell us what happened!' Safiri demanded. 'And isn't she the one you shouted at?'

'Maybe…' Matthew replied.

Ganlin and his men introduced themselves to Sarrus and treated her as royalty.

Kyrral walked up to Matthew and pressed on both the front and back of his wrist. The glove expanded and moved back down his forearm, allowing Matthew to take it off.

'Thanks, bro!'

Kyrral smiled at Matthew and offered them a seat on the bench as Daisy rushed off. She returned with a cup in each hand.

'Here's some water. It's also got a bit of quranroot, bussellweed and bellberry seeds,' she said, trying to catch her breath.

'Thank you,' said Sarrus, giving a courtly nod of the head.

Daisy curtsied in return. As she turned away she rolled her eyes making Safiri, Sam and Kyrral laugh.

After a few sips Matthew felt much more refreshed and everyone had gathered around, watching him intently for an update on what had happened.

'You guys have a bit of a smuggling problem. Food, drink, random stuff… and people as well it seems.' Matthew turned to Daisy 'Remember that douchebag in the cabin that tried to take the package?'

'I don't know what a douchebag is, but yes.'

'Well it seems he's part of an operation to smuggle things out of here,' Matthew continued, careful not to disclose anything about the doorway to Dawn. 'There's a warehouse and a bunch of tunnels behind the cabin, going through the stone. After I had a drink with Rackma some guy grabbed me and dragged me over there,' Matthew pointed behind a nearby tent where he had been taken. 'The plumpy guy punched me in the gut then the other guy hit me in the back of the head. Next thing I know I'm being wheeled down a tunnel in a trolley and chucked in a cell.'

As Matthew finished the sentence a group of thugs rounded the corner of an alleyway, into the open area near the tavern canopy.

'There they are!' one of them shouted and they began to run toward the group.

Ganlin immediately stood up. The would be attackers quickly realised they were both outnumbered and outsized.

'Get 'em, boys!' shouted Ganlin.

Ganlin's men made their move and the smugglers scattered, losing the guards in the swarms of people in the marketplace.

'Which cabin is it?' asked Ganlin.

'Level seven. Row three.' Matthew replied.

'Tran?'

'Yes, although Tran wasn't there, just the douchebag.'

'I fear for what's happened to him if that cabin is the way into their operation. You kids better get out of here and it's probably best you stay away for a little while. We'll scope out Tran's cabin and put an end to all this smuggling business. Sounds like it might be the cause of all the missing people. Sorry you got dragged into all this but your information might just be very valuable, indeed. Kyrral, go with them and make sure they all get back safely. I'll have a couple of my guys accompany you to the surface.'

'No probs. Thanks Ganlin,' said Matthew, handing over the keys he had taken from the guard. 'There's a massive dude locked in one of the cells.'

'We can go to my place,' Daisy offered. 'My parents will be OK with it and will be happy to give you all a good feed and rest.'

'That would be great, thanks,' said Sam.

The adrenaline hadn't fully subsided making Matthew a little agitated. He took his phone out his bag and put it in his pocket, walking around to get a few sneaky photos and some video as everyone got themselves ready to depart.

He was quite proud of himself for how he had dealt with everything following his kidnapping. It went against the way he had lived his entire life up until that point. *Maybe Grandad was right*, he thought. By crossing into Dusk he was making his own story which was far more exciting than his life would have been had he stayed back home, working in The Floating Star.

Chapter Twelve
Cultivating Secrets

Ganlin took some time organising his men and sorting out who was going to escort the Dawn Crew and their Dusk counterparts.

Sam realised that during all the drama of Matthew dropping down from above she hadn't officially introduced herself to Sarrus. Walking over to her, she grabbed her hand and shook it.

'Hi Sarrus, I'm Sam.'

Sarrus had a slightly confused look on her face which did not disappear as Safiri came and also introduced himself, shaking her hand as Sam had done.

Daisy and Kyrral then walked over and introduced themselves officially, Daisy giving an exaggerated curtsy and Kyrral an awkward, deep bow.

'My lady,' he said as he held himself low for what seemed like an unnecessary amount of time.

'There's no need for that,' said Sarrus, giggling. 'I'm not fond of the pageantry many of my fellow Pure insist upon. Just treat me like you would anyone else… please.'

Sam and Safiri looked at each other, realising why Sarrus looked so confused at their introduction and feeling a little embarrassed at not knowing the expected etiquette when in the presence of a Pure.

They did, however understand why Daisy would feel the way she did about them. Just hearing Sarrus call herself Pure seemed quite arrogant to them, despite Sarrus' protestation at the regal greeting she had received.

While Daisy and Kyrral were performing their introductory duties Matthew was standing behind Sarrus giving an extremely exaggerated curtsy, making the others, except Kyrral, laugh.

'He's behind me being stupid isn't he?' asked Sarrus.

Kyrral nodded, eyes wide with shock at Matthew's behaviour.

Sarrus quickly turned and whipped the ground just in front of Matthew with the remaining vine she had in her hand, making Matthew jump and the others all laugh.

'Now that we're all past the awkwardness,' said Matthew, 'how about we get going.'

Ganlin joined the group with two of his guards, also Squaar, although these two were a lot smaller than Ganlin.

'This is Mason and Tark. They'll see you safely back to the surface.'

'Thanks Ganlin. See ya soon,' Daisy said as she ran and gave him a hug.

'Not too soon, I hope. You all need to keep home safe for a while.'

The rest of the group said their goodbyes to Ganlin then headed back into to marketplace, toward the entrance to the Scavenger District. Mason kept to the front and Tark behind with the group keeping tightly together between them. The excitement for exploration had very much diminished as all were keen to get back to the fresh air outside as soon as possible.

There was no conversation at all until they had climbed the stairs to the tunnel which gave them passage out of the Scavenger District. Even then it was slightly awkward. Matthew, Sam and Safiri didn't want to discuss the things that Kyrral and Sarrus would expect them to know. Daisy and Kyrral were silent, having no idea how to have a conversation with a Pure.

The silence did give Matthew an opportunity to process the past few hours. The more he thought about it the more he freaked out about how dangerous the situation actually was.

Once they had made it through the tunnel the group dusted themselves off and made themselves somewhat presentable to the more judgemental people of Dusk. Daisy made sure to fix Kyrral's hair a little and wouldn't allow them to leave until she was done.

Mason and Tark unlocked and opened the door. Tark had a quick check of the surrounding area to ensure there was no immediate danger while Mason guarded the door. After Tark had returned the group was allowed to leave.

'I'll tail you for a little while to make sure nobody follows you,' said Tark. 'You won't see me so I'll say my goodbyes now. Mason will stay here and await my return. Good luck and stay safe.'

'You too. Thanks guys. See ya around.' Matthew responded as everyone said goodbye and walked out onto the path by the river.

It was now much darker with a purple tinge to the sky. *It must be night*, thought Matthew. It was peaceful as they walked up the slope to the bridge, Daisy leading the way as they headed toward her residence. Schools of glowing fish gracefully swam in the river as a light breeze slightly rustled the leaves of the glowing, pulsing trees in the park.

Daisy led the group back the same way they had initially walked to get to the Scavenger District.

The ice was somewhat broken between Daisy and Sarrus in the form of complimenting each other on their clothing. Sarrus explained her father's distain at the plain and common temple dress which happened to be her favourite, much for the same reasons that her father hated seeing her wearing it.

The Dawn Crew walked behind, joking around, trying to bring some familiarity back to their day, which allowed them the opportunity to slightly relax.

Kyrral walked between the two groups, happy to be having a peaceful stroll outside in the fresh air.

Sarrus stopped as they reached the temple.

'I just need to grab a few things from here. Please keep quiet when we're inside.'

'So what is this place?' asked Daisy. 'It looks a bit miserable… forgive me my lady. I didn't mean to-'. Daisy lowered her head in embarrassment.

'It's OK, Daisy. And please just call me Sarrus. The sooner we can do away with the divide between everyone the sooner we can all get along as equals and treat each other properly.'

'Some advice needed for where we're from,' said Matthew.

'Where are you from?' asked Kyrral. Matthew preferred the less curious version of Kyrral.

'All in due course, my tank friend,' Matthew replied, slapping him on the shoulder. 'We'll talk about all that stuff when we get to Daisy's place.'

'You're an Errothin, aren't you?' Daisy asked Sarrus.

'Why, yes I am. But only by blood,' she giggled.

'I noticed the tree on your dress and the temple.'

Matthew hadn't noticed that there was a slightly darker tinge in the shape of a tree on Sarrus' dress, although in his defence he had been slightly preoccupied.

'I do a lot of reading,' Daisy added. 'You're not what I expected, though.'

'What did you expect? What do your books say about me?'

'Nothing… I'm sorry… I didn't mean to offend. I just…' she trailed off.

Sarrus laughed. 'Don't worry, Daisy. I know what's written about us in all the underground books and news that are supposed to be hidden from us. My family and my kind. They're quite accurate. Obviously the books in my house have a different point of view but I like to explore outside what the Pure think about everything.'

Daisy gave a small, nervous smile. Everyone else laughed. Although Daisy was still unsure, the others could see Sarrus was messing with her. Despite all that Sarrus still carried herself with an air of prestige and nobility in the way she talked and her posture. She was quite elegant despite how much she seemed to despise it.

'Shall we go inside?' Sarrus said as she turned and walked up the steps, opening the arched door and walking into the temple.

They entered into a short hallway with floor to ceiling bookshelves which were filled with various sized books and pots with flowers. The hallway led through an arched doorway into the main chamber of the temple. It was all stone blocks, pillars and arches with an open space in the middle. The space spanned two floors to a glass dome ceiling.

This chamber was huge and broke off into three smaller chambers laid out in a similar fashion. Around the perimeter of each room were even more bookcases, filled to the brim with books; some small desks; green, velvet armchairs with the House Errothin crest embroidered in gold; and some plants encased and displayed in glass containers sitting atop wooden pedestals.

Above was a balcony encircling the perimeter, accessed via spiral staircases on each side of the chamber. The balcony was furnished in the same manner with books, chairs, desks and various plants on display.

In the middle, in the open space, were rows of planter boxes with different kinds of plants. In front of each type was a small plaque with the name of the plant engraved on it. Some plants pulsed like the trees outside, some had coloured flowers, some branched out to make strange shapes.

'Please don't touch anything, especially in there,' Sarrus pointed to one of the other chambers. Above the doorway was a sign which said *Dangerous Species*.

A few people dressed in a similar manner to Sarrus walked around, looking at different plants, taking notes. Strangely, whenever they completed writing on a page a new one just appeared above it and they continued writing.

Matthew walked up close to Sarrus. 'So what do you guys do here?' he whispered.

'It's a little hard to explain and I've kept it that way for a reason so please don't go telling anyone. It's a temple, but not in any official capacity as far as The Authority is concerned. As far as they know it's just a hobby of mine which I have opened to a few select people. In essence it's just a greenhouse but to the outside world it's a Temple for the Pure and they need not ask any questions beyond that. The crest of the tree above the door and on my dress is of House Errothin so that's generally all people need to know.'

Matthew perked up a little at this bit of information. It was the crest which was also on the medallion that his grandad had left him. The one that Matthew had been pursuing and had gotten him into so much trouble. On the other hand it had also allowed the Dawn Crew to gain some contacts, even possibly friends, in Dusk. He needed to know more about the crest. Why did his medallion have the crest on it? Who was House Errothin to his grandad? At least he now had confirmation that Sarrus could give him some more answers. He now had to work out how and when to get them.

Sarrus continued. 'As for the purpose if it, you all know we have some kind of magic. Despite our crest nobody in my family has had any magic to do with plants for generations. That was... until me. You've already seen what I can do. Give me any plant seed and

I can make it grow. Sometimes I feel like I can speak to the plants. That is why I had this temple built. It's a place I can go to help me practise my magic. It's also a research facility for plants. That is what the other people do here. They help me research what these plants are, what they can do, and how we can cross species to create new ones with their own unique properties. I also come here just to relax. I generally like being around my plants more than people.'

'Don't worry. We won't tell anyone what's going on here. It's cool that you've got somewhere you can just go and chill when you need to, and if you can be productive at the same time, even better.'

Sarrus smiled and her body relaxed. The trust still wasn't quite there, however it was slowly coming. There was still a noticeable split between Daisy and Kyrral, Sarrus and the Dawn Crew. While they were all being friendly to each other they were also still hesitant.

Sarrus showed everyone around the temple, explaining the properties of some of the more interesting plants that they had been researching. Some were medicinal, some edible, some dangerous and some just strange.

One door led down into a large basement beneath the temple. A glow came from some of the plants in the room, however there was no other natural light. Kyrral was familiar with many of the plants found in the room as they could be found underground and were easily accessible from the Scavenger District.

Continuing down the stairs was a large, extra high storeroom. In the room were floor to ceiling rows of small drawers containing seeds for all the plants. Sarrus pushed ladders up and down each of the rows, taking a selection of seeds from some of the drawers and placing them inside twelve small pouches on a belt she had taken from a rack when they had entered the room.

'These are a contingency for anything that may come up,' Sarrus informed them as she added the seeds to the pouches.

'What do they do?' asked Safiri.

'All different kinds of things. These ones create vines that I can use as rope or whips, as you've already seen. These one's have a flower that can put people to sleep. These form very rigid branches that twist around each other which can be used for a staff. This one creates flowers which react with flowers from these seeds to create fire. This one creates a sap that, when rubbed on the skin, creates bony spines. I've also got a few mild poisons and medicines. Each has their own unique property that is useful, however I can also combine different seeds, or the flowers from the seeds, to create other things. I spend a lot of my time working out how different plants work together. We probably know more about plants here than The Authority does.'

'How long does it take you to grow them?' asked Sam.

Sarrus and Matthew grinned at each other, Matthew knowing the answer already. 'It's extremely quick, usually just a few seconds.'

Sarrus took a seed in her hand. An emerald glow emanated for a second, as it had done previously to create the vine whips. Sarrus opened her hand again to show them a bulb which had grown.

'Everyone stand back,' she instructed and everyone moved behind her.

Sarrus threw the bulb into a large, clear corner of the room. As soon as the bulb hit the ground it exploded with bright green sparks which then dissipated into a small cloud of gas.

'That bulb will burn the skin when it explodes. The gas will then burn from the inside if someone breathes it in.'

'That's pretty dark,' commented Daisy as she emerged from behind Kyrral.

'Don't worry. There are drinks that burn more than this and do more permanent damage. I can let it grow more and that will hurt a bit more. If I grow it too much, though, then the plant grows out of the bulb and its properties completely change. I also wouldn't use it on anyone who didn't really deserve it.'

'I wish I had a power,' said Daisy, lowering her head in disappointment. 'Then I could do a lot more.'

'You do important things Daisy,' Sarrus assured her.

'Yeah,' added Sam. 'All the Scavengers you help could die without you.'

Kyrral nodded in agreement.

Sarrus continued. 'Nobody in this temple can do what I do, but they're just as important in researching what all these plants do and also in preserving all the different types of plants. You're powerful in a different way, Daisy.'

Matthew's stomach grumbled loudly as he sat on a desk. 'Maybe we should get going.'

As the Dawn Crew, along with their new counterparts, ventured past the bars and restaurants in the area around the doorway back to Dawn, audible grumbles could be heard from the stomachs of a portion of the group, namely Matthew and Kyrral. The visual nature of their overwhelming desire for sustenance started to draw attention and the judgmental eyes of nearby patrons.

Daisy and Sarrus made sure to flank Kyrral, as Safiri and Sam did likewise for Matthew, to ensure neither of them gave in to temptation to steal a bite and consequently create a scene. This was, of course, an area frequented by Officer Doggery who, it had become clear, was looking for a reason to drag away anyone who he deemed as unsavoury.

Matthew's thoughts of a feast were snapped as the necklace began to pulse in proximity to the doorway. He quickly checked to make sure any visible sign of the necklace was obscured from anybody who looked his way as they continued past the alleyway and on toward Daisy's house.

Despite all efforts to remain incognito it was impossible for people not to notice, and be intrigued by, the strange mix of individuals in the group. Despite best efforts Kyrral remained barely presentable and stood out like a sore thumb. That, along with a Fenlis, a Pure and three strange travellers with hoods covering their heads, made being discrete an extraordinarily difficult task. The group slowly increased their speed as the following eyes became a little too much to bear.

It had crossed Matthew's mind, however, the question of why they hadn't encountered more inquiries regarding their strange appearance. At this point it had only been Daisy who had confronted the Dawn Crew about it, although she was a very curious person.

Matthew whispered to his friends. 'Has anyone beside Daisy asked you about why we look different? The guards or anyone in the medical tent while I was locked up?'.

'No, no one,' Safiri replied.

'Strange. We don't exactly fit in.'

Matthew decided it was best to leave it for the moment. At some point they would have to tell their story to the others and could get some more clarity when that time came.

As they moved beyond the commercial part of town and back into a more residential area, the Dawn Crew were amazed at how much the architecture still resembled that of Dawn. Despite the more suburban nature of where they grew up, the rows of two and three story attached townhouses wouldn't look out of place in many cities around the world in Dawn. Occasionally the townhouses were broken up by three, four and five storey apartment blocks.

All the buildings were made of beige brick with grey, gabled roofs. Each window was framed in white as were the doorways and stairs which gave access to them.

After a few hundred metres and a number of turns Daisy finally stopped.

'This is us,' she said.

'How happy are your parents really going to be that you brought us all home?' asked Safiri.

'They'll be fine after I talk to them. As soon as we tell them what's going on they'll be happy to help.'

'That didn't sound overly convincing,' whispered Sam in Matthew's direction.

Sarrus also looked back in his direction, clearly skeptical about the situation.

Daisy led them up the steps toward the door.

'I'll go in first, talk to my parents and then come and get you,' Daisy said, a forced smile on her face.

The group huddled together on the small porch, keen to keep out of view. A click from the door indicated it had been unlocked although Matthew didn't notice her produce a key. Daisy opened the door enough for her the squeeze through and shut it again behind her. The others put their ears to the door in an attempt to listen to the reaction she received from her parents.

'Mum? Dad? I'm home!" Daisy shouted.

The rapid thuds of feet running down stairs could be heard.

'Daisy! Where were you! I told you to stay at home until the missing people have been found. You could have been kidnapped!' The voice was clearly from Daisy's father who was not impressed that Daisy had disobeyed his request to not be out walking the streets in the current climate.

'Are you OK? Where did you go?' asked her mother.

'It's OK, I was with Kyrral.'

'You were with Kyrral? In the Scavenger District again?!

Daisy… I told you not to go down there unless someone accompanies you. It could be dangerous down there!'

'I did have someone accompany me.'

'So Ganlin or one of his guards were with you?' asked her mother. 'I doubt that would've gone down well and we would've heard about it from the neighbours.'

'It wasn't Ganlin. It was some other… friends.'

'What friends?'

'Well… I made some friends and they came with me to help out but something happened and we got separated but I was with Kyrral at the time and they turned out OK and we helped people and the missing people is kind of solved and my friends need some help so I brought them here because you guys are the bestest!'

Everyone outside stared at each other, amazed that Daisy managed to get all that out without taking a breath. The intention seemed to be to talk her parents into submission.

'What friends? They're here? Where? Wait… missi-'

Daisy cut off her father mid-question. 'Dad! I'd like you to meet my friends,' she said as she opened the door to the group standing awkwardly bunched up on the porch.

Chapter Thirteen
To The Moon

Those waiting outside stood with guilty faces, like they had been caught trying to break into the house. Matthew stood up straight and took a step forward. Attempting to make a good first impression he tried to turn the charm up to eleven.

'Hello, sir. My name's Matthew, friend of Daisy and new to these parts. I'm so sorry to impose but it is very nice to meet you… and you Mrs Moon.'

An exaggerated smile remained on Matthew's face as he waited for someone else to speak. Mr Moon walked up to Matthew and looked him up and down.

'Hello, Matthew. My name is Lestar Moon and this is my wife, Madonny.'

Daisy's parents looked very much like Daisy although Madonny was slightly darker, a little more grey than blue.

Safiri and Sam stepped forward and waited for Matthew to introduce them.

'These are my companions, Safiri and Sam.'

'Nice to meet you, sir… ma'am,' they each said as they waved at Daisy's parents.

Daisy took Kyrral by the arm and pulled him forward.

'Dad. This is Kyrral,' Daisy said pushing him toward her father.

'Ahhh. This is the mysterious Kyrral I've heard so much about.'

'Good to meet you, sir,' Kyrral kept his head and eyes to the floor as he greeted Lestar.

'Nice to see you again, Kyrral,' said Madonny.

'You too Mrs Moon,' Kyrral replied.

'You two know each other?' Lestar enquired.

'We've met a few times when I've been down with the Scavengers.' Madonny stepped up to Kyrral and gave him a hug. 'Thank you for always looking out for Daisy... even when she shouldn't be down there,' she glared at Daisy for a moment to emphasise the point.

Sarrus gracefully walked through the door and into the hallway. She stopped and gave a low curtsey, putting her arm across her chest then moving it out to her side as she raised. Matthew assumed it was some kind of respectful gesture.

'Good evening Mr and Mrs Moon. My name is Sarrus Errothin of House Errothin. Delighted to make your acquaintance.'

Lestar immediately stiffened then bowed low.

'Miss Errothin... It-it-it's our honour to have you here in our humble abode. Please come in and take a seat, my lady. Can I get anything for you? Whatever you would like. It would be my honour.'

'That isn't necessary, Mr Moon. Please... I'm a guest in your home. The same as everyone else.'

'You're too kind, my lady.'

'Lestar!' whispered Madonny. 'Get a hold of yourself!' She then bowed herself, although in a much more relaxed fashion. 'Please come in... all of you. Leave you coats on the rack here and we'll move through to the kitchen. Lestar, Daisy and I will prepare some food and drink for you.'

Daisy's home seemed to be what the Dawn Crew would call

upper-middle class, however all they could compare it against was the Scavenger District so it was hard to tell for sure.

The decor resembled that of an early twentieth century home albeit with a twist of technological and magical upgrades which seamlessly fit in with the old styling of the furnishings.

The walls were a dark beige with white cornices and ceilings. The floor a polished dark wood.

The light in the house came from chandeliers of differing sizes, depending on the size of the area, with the soft orange sparks of the lifeblood. Where each chandelier attached to the ceiling it was surrounded by decorative ceiling panels of various curved, floral patterns.

As he took off his coat and placed it on the rack Matthew noticed a small hall table with some black and white photos of the Moon family as well as some flowers. As Sarrus walked past the flowers she touched a few that looked a little worse off and quickly brought them to their full, lush beauty.

On the wall were some paintings of various colours which moved and swirled as if they were alive. It was very hypnotic and seemingly random yet never lost its beauty or looked out of control. It was almost as if there was a purpose to its movement despite Matthew having no idea what it was.

On a shelf opposite the hall table sat some globes which contained hologram-like videos of the family.

To the right of the shelf was a lounge. From just a quick glance Matthew could see the window which looked out to the street. There were a couple of cream coloured couches facing a framed, moving painting which took up most of the wall on the far side of the room. This painting was a little more reserved. Matthew guessed this was likely a result of its immense size. To the side of the painting was a gramophone on a pedestal and a large bookcase.

They all walked down the hall toward the back of the house,

past a staircase, which led upstairs, and into a dining area with an open kitchen at the back. A large, circular, wooden dining table and chairs sat in the middle of the room on top of a rug.

The floor in the area consisted of stone tiles of various sizes making it look more like a country cottage than part of the house Matthew had previously seen.

The kitchen looked no different to one from back in Dawn. It had a stove and an oven just like Matthew had, however is was most likely completely different in how it worked. There were a number of wooden cupboards and drawers. Pots, pans and an array of large spoons hung from a rack which dropped from the ceiling above a polished stone island.

The only difference which Matthew could make out was that there didn't seem to be a fridge or anything resembling a microwave. Despite this, the homeliness of the Moon residence did put Matthew at ease. He could see that Safiri and Sam were also far more relaxed now that they were seemingly safe in a comfortable and somewhat familiar setting. He even allowed himself to feel confident that the Dawn Crew could actually be able to make things work in this strange world.

That feeling didn't last long, however, as he quickly realised that the questions would now come thick and fast as to who they were and where they came from. They would also be given food which was completely foreign to them and had no idea how their bodies would react.

While the Dawn Crew were taking in their new surroundings the Moons had moved into the kitchen to whip something up for everyone. Madonny was cutting ingredients and heating a large pot on the stove while Lestar and Daisy returned to the table with a couple of grazing boards of cured meats, bite sized fruits and vegetables and a few items which left Matthew guessing as to what they could possibly be.

'Look who's finally woken up,' Lestar remarked, looking back at the hallway.

'Misty!' screamed Daisy, a smile on her face.

From the hallway a small animal trotted in. It looked very much like a Pomeranian. It's fur was a mixture of ginger and white with hints of black, a black nose and lips. On any other day this would be normal but in Dusk it raised plenty of questions.

Suddenly Misty jumped up, like a cat, onto a buffet against the wall and leaped toward Daisy who was definitely too far away to expect to make the distance. Moving past Matthew he could see that its tail actually consisted of feathers. As it stretched its legs a sheet of skin stretched out the sides of its body, connecting all the way from the ankles of the front legs to the back. The small, dog-like creature was now able to glide through the air and into Daisy's outstretched arms.

'This is my feilin, Misty. Misty, meet my friends,' said Daisy, hugging Misty and twisting from side to side.

'You weren't wrong about her flying into your arms,' Matthew said.

After Misty stopped licking Daisy she turned her head and looked at the strangers in the room. After a few seconds of staring she gave a small bark and wiggled her feathery tail, making it look like a small feather duster.

Everyone settled down once again and took their seats at the table. While Matthew and the rest of the Dawn Crew surveyed the food before them, Lestar returned to the table with a tray of cups for everyone and a couple of bottles of some sort of drink. *Hopefully not wombus juice.* Matthew thought.

'Go ahead. Get stuck into it,' said Lestar as he poured a drink for everyone.

Matthew took a piece of meat from the board closest to him. Safiri and Sam watched Matthew and waited for his reaction before daring to try anything for themselves. The piece of meat that Matthew had taken looked very much like salami although there was no telling what it actually was. Matthew ripped off a small piece from what he had taken and studied it a little more.

'You look like you've never seen food before,' remarked Lestar, now standing behind Safiri.

'It's a little more…' Matthew paused as he tried to find the right word, 'exotic than what we're used to.'

Matthew put the meat to his mouth, preparing himself to finish it and look delighted no matter how it tasted. As he did he glanced at everyone at the table. Safiri and Sam looked like they were watching a car about to crash, Kyrral and Sarrus looked very confused, Daisy was trying extremely hard not to laugh and Lestar seemed like he was just enjoying the company.

Relief washed over Matthew as he finished the small piece of meat. To his surprise it actually tasted exactly like salami. A small smile appeared on his face, his shoulders relaxed and he finished the rest of the meat on his small plate.

'Not bad is it?' asked Lestar, rhetorically, as he slapped Matthew in the back of the shoulder and laughed.

Safiri and Sam immediately took some for themselves now that they knew it was Matthew approved.

Each of them tried everything on offer. Some they liked and some they didn't. Most of the food was like a variation of what they would get in Dawn.

Luckily the drink that Lestar had poured each of them was not wombus juice. Instead it was a very welcome non-alcoholic fruit punch. Very tasty with none of the burn which Matthew had endured last time.

Daisy offered up some small noodles in a little ramekin to each of the Dawn Crew. As they picked them up with a fork they noticed that the noodles began to wriggle. Safiri gave a loud intake of breath. Small creatures which crawled or slid were not overly appetising to any of them, however they all understood it would be rude not to try.

In unison each lifted their forks to their mouths and took the plunge. The initial taste of the oily noodles was unexpectedly sweet. On biting into the wriggling noodles the insides burst and started popping. It was similar to eating popping candy in the form of a wriggling worm and tasted like lollies.

Daisy burst out laughing. 'It wasn't really alive. HAHAHA! They're just made to trick people. They're actually really tasty.' She then proceeded to take some for herself and slurp them into her mouth, still giggling.

Madonny joined them at the table, taking a sip of her drink.

'We've got some time before the stew is ready,' said Lestar. 'Now I need some answers as to what happened, especially as pertains to the missing people.'

Matthew opened his mouth to speak when Daisy began telling the story.

'Well, Daddy, several days ago I was walking home from the library when I bumped into Matthew. He was looking at the street lamp like he'd never seen one before. I walked up to him and he screamed which made me scream when that horrible Officer Doggery came running. Matthew ran down the alley and Doggery followed him. Doggery came out a minute later, grumbling that Matthew had escaped. He was baffled as to how and started interrogating me as to who Matthew was and what he was doing to me. I told him I didn't know and now he scared Matthew off so he should be ashamed of himself. He told me to watch my tongue and walked off in a huff.'

'Daisy!' both Lestar and Madonny shouted in unison. Madonny continued to scold her daughter, 'You need to show them respect regardless of how much of a bully they are. You'll get yourself into big trouble one day if you continue that.'

'Mum. I've seen him do this heaps of times to anyone that he thinks is below him. He kisses the butt of all the rich and powerful.' She turned to Matthew. 'Matthew, you'll have to tell me how you got away.'

'You'll know all by the end of the night,' Matthew replied.

Daisy smiled with satisfaction then continued her story. 'This morning I was on my way to see Kyrral and help people down there.' She turned to Lestar who had a very disapproving look on his face. 'I know, I know, Dad. I wasn't supposed to go down there,' she almost sounded sarcastic. 'Anyway, I saw Matthew crossing the street going toward Sarrus. I didn't know who Sarrus was at the time, though. Then who else but Officer Doggery comes running in to harass Matthew again. So I ran up to him and said that Matthew was under my care. Doggery luckily let us go but threatened to lock Matthew up if he saw him again. I'm telling you, they're corrupt!'

'Daisy! Watch what you say! Apologies for my daughter's behaviour, Sarrus,' Lestar apologised, seemingly fearing insulting the royalty in the room.

'It's quite alright Mr Moon. To be honest my views are more closely aligned to those of your daughter.'

'May I continue?' asked Daisy, not expecting anyone to answer. The Dawn Crew and Kyrral all attempted to hide smirks on their faces.

'So, I took Matthew down to the Scavenger District because we need all the help we can get. We watched someone practicing at the mageball racetrack and then met up with Kyrral at the medical station.

'We were delivering packages to people when we came to a cabin. The man in there wasn't who the package was addressed to. When we wouldn't leave the package with him he got aggressive.

He backed down when Kyrral stepped in. We delivered the last packages and went back to the medical station.

'Matthew had a drink with some guy but had disappeared when we came out to look for him. We knew he wouldn't have left on his own accord and were worried so we told Ganlin who was going to start a search but I'll get to that after. Sarrus, why don't you tell us what happened to you?'

'Gladly, Daisy. I had just dropped off a package of seeds and left the temple when I was attacked from behind by some thugs. They put a hood over my head and bound my hands and feet. When they got sick of me trying to release myself from my restraints someone hit me over the back of the head. I awoke in a cell where they gave me some horrendous food and refused to tell me why they had kidnapped me. A couple of hours later Matthew was brought into the other cell beside mine.'

Matthew then jumped in to add how he ended up next to Sarrus. 'I was pulled in for a drink with some guy and was just going to have a sip to not be rude. It was that purple wombus stuff. When I was on my way back to the medical station some huge guy grabbed me from behind and dragged me away. That little psycho from the cabin was waiting, had a whinge about me disrespecting him and punched me in the stomach. The big oaf then hit me on the back of the head and knocked me out. When I woke up I was getting chucked in the cell. They also gave me crappy food and Sarrus and I got to chatting. She pushes a flower through a whole in the wall-'

'A fundell flower,' interrupted Sarrus, to which Lestar gave an approving nod, obviously having some idea of what was coming next. Madonny was furiously taking notes on what everyone had said.

'Yes. A fundell flower. I blew the flower in the guard's face when he came in and it knocked him out. This guy was huge but went down almost instantly. Anyway, I grabbed the keys and let Sarrus out of her cell. We checked out the room for a weapon but couldn't find anything so Sarrus took some seeds out of her pocket and grew some long vines which wrapped around her wrists to use as whips.'

'You see, Mr and Mrs Moon, I have the power to help plants grow at an accelerated rate,' said Sarrus.

'Very interesting,' commented Lestar. 'I'm a historian and I don't remember ever reading about a Pure with a power like that. What exactly is your lineage? If you don't mind me asking.'

'Not at all. My parents are the High Daitronarchs of House Errothin.'

'You're that Sarrus? Excuse me for asking, my lady, but what is a Progeny of the High Daitronarchs doing walking around town? It could be very dangerous as you've now seen.'

'I can assure you that the men who kidnapped me had no idea who I was. I'm the youngest child. Most would say the least important. My brothers are in line to take over the House before me and I prefer it that way. I have no intention of playing the political games of the rest of the House. I don't show off who I am so when I walk around people assume I'm a Lesser Pure going to help at the temple.'

'How interesting. So whe-'

'Lestar!' interjected Madonny. 'She didn't come here to be interrogated about her bloodline. Shall we continue with what happened?'

'It's quite alright Mrs Moon. But yes, we should continue. Mr Moon, I'd be happy to discuss this further another time.'

Matthew continued from where had been interrupted.

'So we left the room with the cells and went down the tunnel when we came to a room with a whole bunch of crates, barrels and boxes. There were shelves with a bunch of different things on them. There was a man and a woman arguing on one side of the room, behind some shelves, and another big guy sleeping at a table in the middle of the room. We had to get past that guy to get away so we snuck past but I stepped on a creaky floorboard and the big guy woke up. I grabbed a mageball to hit them with but Sarrus started whipping them first.'

Matthew took a quick sidebar to act out some whipping motions with his hands while making noises.

'Then she did some parkour while bringing down the shelves with a vine-whip. The shelves blocked the door which she closed while sliding through it. I put on the mageball glove but took a while to work out how to turn it on. We jumped into a trolley and just before they caught us I managed to turn it on. We blasted down the tunnel in this trolley and crashed in a another room. There were lizard things and more people.'

'Lizard?' Madonny asked.

'I'll explain later. It's not all that important. Anyway, we then ran into the plumpy guy from the cabin again and it turned out we were in the cabin we had been to earlier. The tunnels were on the other side of the cabin wall which they had smashed through to get access. I'm a bit worried they might have done something bad to that Tran guy to get his cabin. Anyway, I cracked that guy in the face with the mageball. We ran out and used the mageball again to fly across the giant cavern and back to the medical tent.'

'It was crazy, Dad,' Daisy remarked, allowing Matthew to finally take a breath and a drink. 'We were with Ganlin getting a search party together and suddenly these two were flying over us. They floated down right next to us. Then a bunch of goons came running up but got scared off when they saw Ganlin and the other guards. They're going to find out what was going on and put a stop to it.'

'Matthew,' said Sarrus, a puzzled look on her face. 'What

happened in that room with the people arguing? There was a strange lifeblood doorway and you said something about a liar?'

Matthew stopped chewing a vegetable he had put in his mouth and lowered the rest back to his plate. Safiri and Sam looked anxious as the people from Dusk stared at him curiously.

'That is a long story. Maybe we should finish eating before I get into that. You'll all have a lot of questions once I've finished and we'll probably have some as well.'

He motioned toward the rest of the Dawn Crew and stopped, waiting for somebody else to move the conversation in a different direction.

'Good idea, Matthew,' said Madonny. 'The stew should be ready now so let's fill our bellies and pick this up again after.'

While Madonny dished up the stew, Lestar poured everyone some warm mead. The slightest sip warmed the entire body and was very welcome indeed. The same could also be said for the stew. Chunks of vegetables and meat made tender in what had become a thickened gravy. The melange of flavours was exactly what Matthew was hoping for and despite the individual ingredients being foreign, the final dish tasted very familiar.

The chit-chat over dinner focussed a little more on Lestar and Madonny while the story of the Dawn Crew was on pause. While Lestar had mentioned he was a historian his specialty was actually artefacts and magical entities which made sense given his curiosities surrounding Sarrus' powers.

'For someone who is so involved with magic your house seems to be quite magic-free,' Sam pointed out.

'Well, Sam, being around magic every day I know how dangerous it can be, especially if not used properly. Kids all think it's fun and games and adults like to show off what they have and what they can do. You wouldn't believe what's out there though.'

The Dawn Crew gave each other a knowing glance, sure that

Lestar would be very interested in the artefacts they had with them.

Lestar continued imparting his knowledge on the dangers of magic. 'There's a black market trade for the most powerful artefacts, runebooks and creatures. History has shown that when good people let their guard down, those with the worst of intentions strike and dark times can last for years.'

'That's enough of the lecturing, dear,' Madonny cut in quickly while Lestar took a sip of mead.

'What do you do for work, Mrs Moon?' Safiri asked.

'I'm a Defender of the Populous. I help people who are wrongly in trouble with The Authority. I also do a lot of work in ethics, trying to root out corruption in all departments of The Authority and keep everyone accountable. The bureaucracy is too much for most people which allows The Authority to get away with more than they should. A group of us decided we wouldn't stand for it any longer so we made a department to specialise in making sure The Authority couldn't keep taking advantage of people. It helps that we're all very stubborn and never back down, no matter how much some of them try to flaunt their power.'

'Is that fear mongering of The Authority, Madonny? Must be where Daisy get's it from.'

A swift slap on the back of Lestar's head abruptly stopped him giggling at his own joke which everyone found quite amusing.

'Very funny, Lestar. Let's clean this all away, refill the drinks and Matthew can tell us the rest of his story.'

Daisy and her parents quickly cleared the table while the jugs were brought to the table.

The Dawn Crew took a couple of minutes in the hallway to get on the same page before the questions began.

'How much are you going to tell them?' Safiri asked.

'I'll answer any question they have. Other than that I'll tell them a bit about us and where we came from. I don't think I need to go into specifics about anything that's not related to Dusk unless they specifically ask. We came here to get answers.'

'Do you trust them enough to talk about Dawn?' asked Sam.

'Daisy's parents seem to be cool and probably would know more than anyone else about most things in Dusk. I doubt they'll give up anything if they don't at least get something in return. The others have all saved me from massive trouble at some point since we've been here. I'm sure it would have been easier for them to just walk away. That earns them a bit of trust, right?'

'Yeah. Just wanted to make sure. The last thing we need are more Finnigans back home.'

'We don't really have any idea how many from Dusk are back home,' Safiri interjected. 'Finnigan's just the only one we happened to come across and there was a lot of luck involved in that. While we're on the subject, Sarrus said there was a doorway when you were escaping. What was that about?'

'I think Finnigan was lying when he said the rift was closed. I think he found a doorway that's somehow permanently open. Judging by what was going on in that room they're smuggling artefacts into Dawn. Come to think of it, if they're the cause of the missing people there must be more people in Dawn, although I can't think of why they would be smuggling people back home.'

The crew went back into the dining room and sat down. Everyone else was already sitting in anticipation of what Matthew had to say, which kicked up his anxiety slightly. Despite the bond that had started to be built between them all, in reality he was still an alien in their world and wasn't sure how they would take it all. Matthew pulled his bag in close next to him, took a sip of mead, a deep breath and began.

'So… You may all be wondering why we look so different to everyone else here.'

'I assumed you were from one of the lessor Houses where

mixing with other races is not unheard of,' Sarrus gave her hypothesis.

'I just though you were a bit deformed,' added Kyrral.

'What the hell, Kyrral?!' Sam blasted.

'Sorry,' Kyrral apologised, lowering his head.

Matthew and Safiri laughed, breaking any tension and allowing everyone else to follow suit.

'You said you were from beyond the wall, right?' Daisy pointed out. Lestar's eyebrows and ears perked up at this bit of information.

'Well, technically I didn't confirm that. I just said we were from very far away and bypassed the wall. '

'Where are you from then?' she asked.

'Sarrus, you know that doorway we saw? Well we're from the other side of that doorway. At least I think we are, unless there are more worlds that we don't know about.'

There was a loud gasp from everyone from Dusk. Before Lestar broke the silence.

'What do you mean, "worlds"?' he asked.

'I mean the doorway that Sarrus mentioned doesn't just take you down the road. It takes you to another world. We came through a different doorway although that one doesn't stay open and you need a sort of key to open it. I don't know exactly how things work, I've only been here a few times and Daisy has seen me both times I've gone outside the alleyway. I know that it's got something to do with the lifeblood.'

'That would explain why you were staring at the street lamp,' said Daisy.

'Yeah. It was all pretty surreal at that point… not that it isn't still surreal. Anyway, this world is called Dusk and ours is Dawn. They seem to be linked by more than just the doorways. Day and night in Dawn seems to align with the change in colour of the ripples in the sky here in Dusk.'

'What happens when you go from day to night?' asked Lestar.

'For us day is when the sun is out and night is when it's not.'

'And the sun is…?'

'How do I explain this?… The sun is a giant ball of burning gas out in space which lights up the planet even more that your lamps do. Everything is super bright. The planet rotates around the sun. When one side is being lit from the sun the other side is dark. As the planet rotates it changes from day to night and back again. We also get heat from the sun. How does it work here with the different colours in the sky and the general temperature?'

'I'm not sure, that's just the way it is,' answered Lestar as everyone else from Dusk had their faces scrunched up trying to think of why things were the way they were. 'It's generally best not to think too hard about the mysteries of the universe. Can give you an awful headache.'

'Does anyone research these things?' Safiri asked.

'Well, there is research into different things. For example I research artefacts, others research lifeblood. There are just some things that nobody seems to look into. Gave up a long time ago, I suppose. At some point if you can't find the answer you just need to accept it.'

'OK, OK. Enough about mysteries of the universe. You can both talk about that later. Back to the story,' Daisy was getting a little impatient.

'There are things that are similar but also things that are much different. I was raised by my Grandad who used to tell me stories about Dusk although I had no idea at the time that they were real. When he died I inherited everything he owned but he also told me that the stories were true. I didn't really know what that meant until I managed to open the doorway the first time.

'There are a bunch of doorways, including the one in the

tunnels. I have no idea how many there are. We mapped a few locations in Dawn but we don't know where they are in Dusk. The doorway we came through is in the alley where I first ran into Daisy and that's how I escaped from Officer Doggery,' he gave Daisy a glance and an accomplished smile as he revelled in his victory.

Matthew then reached into his shirt and pulled out his grandad's necklace.

'The pendant on here is the key to the doorways. It vibrates when a doorway is close and kinda pulls toward it. Once it's close enough it activates and pulses with a white light while the pin here glows with blue lifeblood. Once that happens the pin seems to unlock itself and you can pull it out. The coin spins then locks in place on the opposite side. That opens the doorway, which is a thin line of white lifeblood. When you cross through the doorway it spins around and flashes white and suddenly you're in the other world. Anyone touching the wearer when they go through gets taken through as well. It's like there's some sort of intelligence where it knows to resize itself.'

'This is extraordinary, Matthew. May I take a closer look?' Lestar asked.

After a few seconds mulling it over in his head Matthew took off the necklace and passed it to Lestar who spent a considerable amount of time inspecting every millimetre of the pendent.

'Matthew,' Sarrus commanded his attention. 'You said something about a liar on the other side of the doorway in the tunnels. Who were you talking about?'

'Oh, yeah. Well when I inherited the artefacts from Grandad he didn't tell me anything about them. He just said stuff about making my own stories and that the journey is important and things like that. We didn't really have anything to go off. I had a box which blasted out a cloud of lifeblood when we hit it, although we had no idea at the time what that was, and a bunch of other objects which didn't seem to do anything. We happened to have the TV on-'

'TV?' interrupted Lestar.

'Shut up, Lestar!' Madonny smacked him on the hand, clearly tired of the questions which sidetracked from the story.

'It's a screen that shows moving pictures. Anyway, we recognised a symbol from an advertisement on one of the cards Grandad left me. So we went to this place, it was called The Eye of Dusk, and we got into an altercation with the guy there that was running a bit of a scam. He said he was a psychic but it turns out he had a ring with a mind rune on it which he was using to get bits of information. He used that to scam people out of a lot of money. He had shelves and tables full of strange objects and wasn't overly helpful until we threatened to smash his artefacts.'

'You did what?!' Lestar exclaimed only to, once again, get smacked by Madonny.

'It was the only way we could get him to talk. Anyway, he told us that he was from Dusk and that the world we were in was Dawn. He said he got to Dawn through a rift, which I guess he was talking about a doorway, and that it had closed after a few hours. That's what I think he lied about. I think he's using that open doorway to smuggle artefacts, and maybe people, into Dawn to try and get some power there. He's probably trying to see which artefacts work in Dawn so that he can use them. Once when he got freaked out he fell over and knocked his hat and wig off. Turns out he was a Squaar although nothing like Ganlin. He was short and fat and the tentacles on the back of his head were really short. His face and skin were also pretty close to human.'

'Yeah. Finnigan was really gross,' Sam jumped in.

'I'm sorry, did you say Finnigan?' asked Madonny. 'Did you happen to catch his last name?'

'Yeah. It was Fisk. Finnigan Fisk,' Sam replied.

Madonny, Lestar and Kyrral gasped.

'I thought he was dead,' said Kyrral.

Madonny added some more information. 'Finnigan disappeared months ago. Everyone just assumed he had been killed. He was in the back pocket of a lot of people who had power. He extorted, bribed and blackmailed his way through the Scavengers, into The Authority and I heard he was even being used by some of the Pure. At some point, though, he started getting even more greedy and some of the people who helped him along the way began to turn against him. We all assumed that was the cause of his demise and that his body had been discarded somewhere. It's going to be a busy day tomorrow. I'll need to talk to Ganlin as well as The Authority and pass this information on. The other question is why are they kidnapping people?'

'I have no idea,' replied Matthew,' We didn't see anyone else when we were there although it looked like there was a warehouse on the other side of the doorway so there's no telling how much space he had. Could you possibly not pass on any information about us? We'd rather keep a low profile for now.'

'As you wish, Matthew, although at some point we may need you if they wish to investigate further.'

'We must be very careful who we tell and what we say,' Sarrus cautioned. 'There are a lot of people out there, my family included, who would use this to gain more power. Finnigan isn't the only person with ambition and would jump at the chance to take advantage of a fresh population.'

'Definitely. Finnigan had no idea about my necklace, only that my card had a mind rune on it which tells me that he doesn't really know anything about the doorway that he went through. I actually found my doorway by accident. I had felt the necklace vibrate in a few different places but it was when I was at the lake near my house that I noticed it pulling toward the bushes. I followed it down a stream to a clearing and that's where I found the doorway.

'I have no idea who, in Dawn, knew about Dusk other than Grandad. It's definitely not public knowledge. In our world we don't have magic at all. If someone from Dusk brings through something powerful that actually works, they could do some real damage. Or someone from Dawn could get their hands on it and do the same.'

'What is the most likely response from your world if they found out about Dusk?' Sarrus asked.

Safiri decided to take this question. 'Most people would be scared. A lot of them do really stupid things when they're scared, like shoot first and ask questions later. Our world is full of hatred of things they don't understand or those that don't think along the same lines as them. There's a lot of division which gets fuelled by people wanting power, or thinking they're going to have something taken away if others are treated better. Of course there are a lot of people who try to do the right thing but it's quicker and easier to feed on someone's fear than to come together for the common good.'

'Sounds a lot like here,' Kyrral added, looking very downhearted. 'The powerful keep people like me down. Some different races hate each other. Even paians fight each other.

'What are paians?' asked Safiri.

'Sub-races,' Daisy answered.

'OK. I think we can all agree that the general population on either side knowing about this at the moment is a bad idea,' said Matthew. 'Chances are it could end in a war. Yay for people!'

Matthew stopped talking and took a few sips of mead, allowing everyone to digest the conversation so far.

'You said something about some other artefacts, Matthew?' Lestar passed the necklace to Sarrus as he enquired about more items he could inspect, while at the same time changing the subject to something a little less grim.

'Yes. I've also got a lot of questions about these. We haven't been able to work out what any of them do.'

Matthew pulled his bag onto his lap and removed a plastic container. While those from Dusk gasped in anticipation, Safiri and Sam began to laugh.

'Ahhh. Ignore this,' said Matthew. 'This is just some food that we brought. We had no idea what we would find here and whether or not we could even eat your food.' Matthew could see Daisy was still very much intrigued by what was in the container. 'We'll open it later, OK? Safiri and Sam have some packed away in their bags as well.'

Matthew retrieved the actual items he wished the group to explore from his bag. First he retrieved a cloth which he opened and laid out the ring and medallion on the table. Next he added the deck of cards and lastly the wooden box.

'Where did you get these?' asked Sarrus, picking up the box and medallion. 'That's a House Errothin vault box and seal.'

'I inherited everything here from my grandad. I have no idea where he got them from. We worked out that they had something to do with House Errothin after you guys mentioned the tree symbol at the temple but we don't know what they're actually for.'

'Well we'll need to go to the nearest Treasury Finance Depository to open the box. The seal is required to open it. It's also sometimes used to show that you speak with the authority of House Errothin, although that was more commonly done in the past and is very rare now.'

'Cool. I guess we'll get to that as soon as we can. As I said, Grandad didn't tell me anything useful about them. He seems to have done that on purpose to make sure I learned by experiencing this world. I've been trying to work out how they fit into the stories that he told but I think he fudged the details enough to describe what was happening without being specific on how.

'Right now we're interested in the specifics of what these things are. In the end it's not really that important how they match up to Grandad's stories, even though it's going to keep sitting in the back of my mind, bothering me. I know that the cards here have a rune on each of them with a bunch of other symbols but I have no idea how to activate them.'

Matthew spread the cards out on the table allowing everyone to take some as they pleased and hopefully give him a few answers on what they did and how they work.

Lestar picked up a few of the cards, fixed up his glasses and took a closer inspection.

'Firstly, it's very strange that these runes are on a deck of cards. It's almost like it's a learning game for children.'

'Maybe Grandad got them to teach me about runes and magic… On second thought that doesn't make sense. If he had them to teach me then he wouldn't have kept them secret. The way he was talking before he died, he never had any intention of giving the secrets away at any point. With the mageball and the finger-pointer-glowy-trail-thingy I just needed to touch it and it worked.'

'Yes, well you would definitely need a base understanding of runes to get any meaning out of these cards if used in a learning capacity. That's not to say we can't also use them in this way while we work out how they are activated. There are many ways to use runes and obviously to learn about them you'll need to see them written down. They can intentionally be made to not be activated at all but, as you said, that doesn't seem to fit with your grandfather's intended use. In any case, you can see on these that each one is a combination of three different elements.'

Lestar held up a few of the cards and pointed to the different parts while explaining their meaning. Everyone sat up to attention as even those from Dusk, other than Madonny, had a somewhat limited knowledge on the subject and were quite excited at the prospect of receiving lessons from an expert, despite how little interest they had in it previously.

'They've each got a main symbol in the middle. This is the base element of the rune. This one,' he pointed to a symbol which looked like an upside-down diamond with the bottom line missing, 'is for fire. This one,' now showing a rudimentary house shape with a vertical line down the middle, 'is energy or force. It depends on how it is used.

'Now, these main symbols are surrounded by another symbol which is the element effect of the rune. Back to the fire card again, you can see that it's surrounded by two circles. This means that it will push out in a circle from the rune, like a circle of fire pushing out until its power runs out.

'The energy card has a rectangle around it with a line going through the top. This pushes forward. So the rectangle around the energy will push energy forward from the card. It's effect will likely be similar to a heavy ball being thrown at someone, except it's energy. It will lose power as it encounters an opposing force and gets further away from its origin so it won't continue forever, however it can be useful to push someone over and maybe even knock down a wall. The same symbol around the fire symbol, I presume will throw out a ball of fire or maybe a stream of fire. There are many complex factors that go into the specifics of exactly the form it will take and how powerful it is but as a general concept, that's how it works.

'Now look at the corners of all of these cards.' Lestar again pointed to the cards showing that each had a small symbol in each corner which changed from card to card. 'The cross in each corner of the fire rune card means that it will have immediate effect upon activation. However, I've never seen it displayed this way, usually it will be a single symbol above the other symbols. I'm unsure whether that changes anything though. It's unlikely as it's simply the activation, however I couldn't say for sure.

'In any event the energy card contains crosses with a line connecting the top of the cross and the bottom of the cross. This one means it has a time-based activation.'

'Makes sense,' Safiri said. 'Looks like an hourglass.'

'Indeed it does, Safiri. This one,' Lestar held up another card where the activation symbols in each corner showed a vertical line with two small horizontal lines either side of its base, 'is like a sensor of sorts. It activates when something crosses past it.'

'Ahhhh. Like a trip-wire. Nice!' Matthew was becoming giddy with the possibilities. Although the wide-eyed look on Daisy's face told him that she was far more fearful of what she was being told than having any form of excitement. After thinking about it for a second he had to concede that she had good reason. He wasn't in a video game and the prospect of others having that kind of power wasn't something he was keen to experience.

Safiri was really intrigued and keen to gain as much knowledge about runes as he possibly could. 'So with the card that has a timed activation, how long is that time? You've mentioned what the symbols mean and that has covered all of them. There's nothing else which seems to show how long it lasts. While I'm on it, the proximity, trip-wire activation also gives no indication of how far it goes and nothing indicates how powerful any of these cards are. Is the fire rune card for a few sparks or a massive firewall? It's all very vague.'

'You and I must be kindred spirits, Safiri,' a smile growing on Lestar's face as he continued. 'We see the puzzle that others don't. To answer your questions, I don't know. You see now why I want my house to be as magic-free as possible. Everyone thinks they're in control until they aren't.

'These cards are runes at the most basic level a rune can be, a base, effect and activation. There is a lot of nuance in rune making and also in rune activation. The simpler the rune, the easier and quicker it is to write but also the more that could go wrong if not activated properly. Whereas complex runes take longer to write and require far more knowledge of all aspects of rune making. They are created to achieve a very specific purpose which means they are not volatile. That doesn't mean they are less flexible, though. For this reason there are experts in each field, creating runes and casting runes.'

'Ahhhhh, like James Bond and Q,' said Matthew to confused looks from those from Dusk and impressed agreement from the Dawn Crew.'

'Let's try and keep the Dawn references to a minimum please, Matthew,' Sarrus advised.

'Sorry, mum,' Matthew replied.

Lestar then continued his explanation of runes.

'It's easy for things to go wrong if not handled properly. Symbols can be added to this to specify time, distance, power, size and any number of other things. They can also be layered so different base symbols can be added together to create a different element, for example you could theoretically layer ice and telekinesis, denoted in this card by three decreasing sized, layered arcs going up to a circle on top. In theory, and I must emphasise that I'm not an expert at rune writing, the specific layering of all parts of the rune must be perfect. This could create, for example, an ice dart that could be moved with the mind. Or layer a proximity fire circle with another fire circle to trap people inside the first circle then burn them with the expanding second circle.'

'Dad!'

'Sorry, dear. Unfortunately it's the type of thing people can do with this power in the wrong hands. You could layer time with proximity so that the proximity only activates after a certain period of time. You can see how complex it becomes. The combinations are limitless. There are, of course, shorthand symbols for combinations of symbols, but again, it's an extremely large and complex area of study, of which I am no expert. Some symbols, when put together, have disastrous consequences. Imagine an expanding mind rune. Having everyone's thoughts in your head at the same time. It would drive you mad, and historically it has. Most rune writers and casters, even the most experienced, only specialise in at most a couple of different areas of runes.

'Historians, like myself, tend to know more about runes in a macro, theoretical sense but are usually not very good at writing or casting. We are used by a lot of writers and casters, however, to help them in areas that they don't specialise in or when they need an extra pair of eyes. We all really rely on each other and work as a team. Although there are plenty who work outside the law that do things on their own. It's a very dangerous business indeed and that is why you need a licence to work in the area of magic. Obviously the Pure are exempt from requiring a license for their own innate magic.'

Sarrus interrupted. 'Unfortunately we also tend to have the political means to get away with working outside it for any other magical use.'

'Indeed, that is unfortunately the case,' Madonny agreed.

'So that is just a crash course in runes and how they work. I would be happy to talk about it more another time, Matthew, and go through what each of the runes on the cards can theoretically do.'

'That would be great. Thanks, Mr Moon.'

'Please. Lestar.'

'I still don't get it,' Sam grumbled. 'The mageball, lamps, pointers all just worked when the rune was touched so why don't these?'

'There could be a number of reasons, Sam. Like all magic and artefacts, the lifeblood needs to flow through it. If the cards simply worked on their own I would say that they were written with rune ink which is essentially lifeblood that's had some things added to it to give it the inky consistency. Since it doesn't I assume it needs some other type of activation, maybe from a specific artefact. The engraved runes on the lamps have the lifeblood ink embedded into the engraving. Mageballs are actually two artefacts that work together. The ball obviously does what it does, however the glove is actually an artefact which alone activates the rune on the mageball, preventing accidental activation, while the rune facilitates the connection between the mind and the ball. A complex system indeed.

'There are also artefacts which can draw runes in the air to activate. They create floating, flowing light in the air or on a surface until they are activated and used.

'Artefacts, in general, are single purpose items which are imbued with lifeblood to perform a magical task. The art of creating them has been mostly lost now. We can create simple ones which work with runes like lamps and have managed to create mageballs, however the most powerful artefacts are one of a kind. There's a massive black market for them as well as those that are stored by The Authority and those that are legally owned. All of it, writing or casting runes and owning or using artefacts over a power level of one requires a license.'

Matthew took a deep breath.

'This is a lot to process. Let's say I were to find a way to activate these cards, how would I go about getting a license?'

'Well, you would need to be registered within the Archive of Residents of The Authority, have a very good reason for requiring a license, have three references of a sufficient level of repute, read the two hundred page terms and conditions, complete the twenty pages of forms and pay the hundred gold coin application fee. That's before the interview process which takes a while.'

'So it's not likely to happen?'

'I wouldn't think so, no. What about this ring here, Matthew?'

'I only saw Grandad with it in the last few months. He hadn't wore a ring for a long time before that. There aren't any markings on it.'

'Maybe it's just a ring,' Daisy suggested.

'I don't think so. It's not like Grandad to just start wearing a ring for no reason and it was left to me with the other Dusk items.'

Kyrral picked up the ring and inspected it very closely. He went to put the ring on his finger despite it being far too small for any of his fingers.

'I don't think it's gonna fit, mate,' quipped Matthew.

Regardless of this clear observation Kyrral continued to move the ring toward his finger. As it reached the tip of his index finger it expanded and slid perfectly on. The ring moved down and settled in a comfortable position. The stony, crusty layer covering Kyrral then disappeared to reveal a smooth, blue skin. The removal of the thick layer also slimmed Kyrral down to show more defined, muscly features. His shaggy hair was now smooth and silky, a flowing black mane going down his back. His stubble became a well groomed short beard.

'Damn, man. Is that how you would look with a proper skin routine?' Matthew joked.

'Why?' Kyrral asked. 'What are you talking about? What happened?'

Daisy exchanged an approving look with Sarrus.

'What happened?' Kyrral asked again.

Lestar stepped in to try and make some sense of the situation.

'Kyrral, what do you see when you look at yourself?'

Kyrral quickly scanned his arms.

'The same as what I always see. Nothing is any different.'

Daisy stood up on her chair and poked Kyrral on the cheek with her finger.

'It still feels the same,' she said. She then moved her hand down to where his hair had seemingly grown and waved it through. 'It's not real. It's an illusion.'

Sam retrieved her phone from her pocket, took a photo of Kyrral and checked to see what it captured.

'The camera picks it up. Take a look,' she said as she passed her phone to Matthew.

'You're right. Kyrral check out what we're seeing.'

Kyrral gasped as he stared at this alternate version of himself.

'Is that me?' he asked.

'Yep,' said Matthew. 'It's like you're a completely different person. Pass me the ring. I want to try something.'

As Kyrral removed the ring from his finger he immediately returned to his normal self.

Matthew then put the ring on himself.

'Nothing happened,' said Sarrus.

'Cool. That means I'm perfect the way I am… just kidding. Give me a second.'

After a few seconds of concentration the tips of Matthew's ears grew slightly into a point, his skin turned bronze and his hair developed a tinge of green while straightening out.

'Now you look like me,' she pointed out.

Matthew turned toward Daisy. After a brief period of concentration a coat of blue-grey fur appeared over Matthew's skin. Despite a small amount of movement in his features he didn't really look like a Fenlis, more just a very hairy, pointy-eared man.

'One more test,' said Matthew.

As the fur disappeared and Matthew's features returned to being human his skin began to wrinkle and age. His hair shorted and turned grey.

Safiri looked stunned. 'Oh… my… god… you look just like George.'

Matthew quickly removed the ring and returned to his normal eighteen year old state.

'That's how he did it. That's how he hid the cancer. That's why he'd only been wearing the ring for the past few months. He was hiding it from me. He looked completely different in the hospital. The ring just gives the illusion of how you want to be seen limited to the general layout of your features.'

'Absolutely amazing,' said Lestar. 'What an amazing artefact. You know you can't use that without a license, Matthew.'

'Yeah, I know I can't get caught using it.'

'Excuse me?'

'Don't worry, Lestar. I don't know if there's any side effects so it's safer to not expose myself to it anyway. Grandad knew he was dying so he had nothing to lose.'

'At this point I think it might be better to get some new clothes to fit in,' Madonny advised. 'Lestar, you can take them to The Tailor's Thread tomorrow. Mr Dullage still owes you a sizeable favour. At the very least it will stop the suspicious stares. I'll head down to see Ganlin, update him on everything you've told me, Matthew, and see where they're at down there.'

Sarrus jumped in to give her advice on what they should do next.

'I think we should also go to the Finance Depository and get that vault box opened. I would really like to know what it contains. Maybe it could shed some light on why your Grandad had these House Errothin items in his possession.'

'Sounds like a good plan,' Lestar agreed. 'We'll set you all up here for the night. Boys in the lounge and ladies in Daisy's room… You are male and female, correct? Men and women? Other?

Neither? I never thought to ask and shouldn't have assumed.' The Dawn crew all nodded. 'Tomorrow we'll take the car, get some new clothes and open that vault box… a couple of you might need to hide in the boot to fit everyone in.'

'I'll pretend I didn't hear that,' said Madonny.

For the next couple of hours the Dawn Crew supplied the food as everyone joked around and chatted about various goings-on in their part of town. The lollies were a big hit, especially with Daisy. They all compared each other's tongues after choosing a different flavoured lollipop. Kyrral, Lestar and Madonny were a little more keen on the savoury items. Kyrral loved the nacho flavoured corn chips while the Moons were fascinated by the vast array of different nuts and grains found in the muesli bars.

'One day I'll make you some real nachos,' Matthew said to Kyrral. 'It'll blow your mind.'

They all cleaned themselves up as best they could and got ready for bed. To the relief of the Dawn Crew the plumbing was very similar to what they were used to. That piece of information for them was almost as valuable as any other they had learned since arriving at Daisy's house.

After their time down in the Scavenger District they realised just how lucky they were that they were able to sleep comfortably for their first night in Dawn. While they didn't have an actual bed, making do with couches and cushions, it was much better than sleeping on the dirt, the streets, or in the relative danger of the Scavenger District. With a roof over their heads and their new friends around them they all enjoyed a rejuvenating deep sleep.

Chapter Fourteen
The Tailor's Thread

Matthew awoke the next morning to a delightful scent flowing from the kitchen. Lifting his head he could see, with the help of a small amount of dull light that breached the room from around the curtains, that Kyrral and Safiri were still fast asleep. Standing up, the nearest lamp sparked and slowly increased in intensity, adding a warm orange glow to the room.

At the behest of his stomach, Matthew followed the smell of breakfast to the kitchen where Lestar was stirring a pot on the cooktop while Madonny sat at the table intensely going over a large pile of documents, scribbling notes in the margins with a pen which seemed to use lifeblood to burn writing onto the page.

'Good morning, Matthew,' said Lestar with a smile on his face. 'I hope you slept well?'

'Best sleep I've had in weeks. Probably a combination of exhaustion and the mead,' Matthew replied.

'Glad to hear it, although I'm not sure what weeks are. Would you mind waking everyone? Breakfast is almost ready and we've a lot on the schedule today.'

'No problem.'

Matthew returned a few minutes later with Kyrral, Safiri and

Sam in tow, each taking a seat at the table.

'Daisy and Sarrus will be here soon,' said Sam. 'Daisy wouldn't get up so Sarrus is growing something that will apparently get her jumping.'

Madonny glanced up from her papers, 'Nothing unusual there.'

Lestar dished out breakfast for everyone. As far as Matthew could tell, and as far as he wanted to think about it, breakfast seemed to be the equivalent of a bowl of porridge and honey. It warmed the body perfectly and energised in preparation for the day ahead.

Daisy and Sarrus joined them just as they were finishing up and quickly dispatched all of their own serving of porridge.

After organising themselves Lestar and Madonny loaned some clothing to the Dawn Crew, Kyrral and Sarrus to make them a little less conspicuous on their way to get their own clothes, a selection of jackets, scarves and flat caps. Matthew hoped that once finished they would seamlessly fit in with everybody else and never have to deal with stares on the street again.

'OK. Everybody ready?' Lestar asked to a response of enthusiastic nods. He turned to Madonny and kissed the top of her head. 'We'll be back later this afternoon, dear. See you then.'

'Have fun everybody. I'll let you know if Ganlin has an update.'

Lestar then led everybody downstairs and into the garage.

'Nice wheels!' Matthew beamed as he glimpsed their ride into town.

Consistent with what they had seen in Dusk, the car looked to be straight out of the 1920's. The extended hood took up half the length of the car, leading to a five seat body in navy blue with black fenders and a black roof. As everyone made it into the garage realisation hit them that fitting everybody in wasn't going to be an easy task.

'Gonna have to Tetris this, guys,' Matthew said as Safiri began to whistle the theme tune to confused looks from all from Dusk.

Opening the door revealed black leather seats but also the absence of a steering wheel and dashboard. Leaning in Matthew could also see there were no pedals either.

'Any takers for the boot?' asked Lestar.

Sam was quick to speak up.

'I think it'll be easiest if Daisy and I get in. We'll fit better than anyone else.'

Daisy's eyes opened wide, not expecting to be volunteered.

'Unless anyone else wants in?' Sam added.

'Daisy would be delighted to allow her friends to ride up front,' said Lestar, Daisy now glaring in his direction. 'Kyrral, you take the front seat with me. The rest of you squeeze into the back.'

Matthew sat in the middle of the back bench car seat between Safiri and Sarrus. Looking left and right over his shoulders he then turned to Safiri.

'How the hell do we strap ourselves in?'

The car lacked any seatbelts causing Matthew to start hyperventilating, thinking about his parents and the horrific nightmares he endured on a regular basis. He gripped both Safiri and Sarrus tightly on the forearm.

'Are you alright?' asked Sarrus.

'He'll be OK,' Safiri replied. 'I'm sure they've got some kind of lifeblood contraption to deal with it,' he said to Matthew.

Sarrus took his hand and gave it a motherly stroke, fighting against her impulse to enquire further.

Settling himself into the front seat Lestar pressed a small button on the centre console. The car began to fire up in a similar manner to the mageball charging up. As it did so a blue glow began to emanate from the vents in the hood and the garage doors slowly opened.

Rising from either side of Lestar's seat were armrests with metal domes on the end of each, slightly larger than a hand. A slight blue light appeared on the domes where his hands made contact as would a plasma globe in Dawn.

A polished dark wood panel pushed out from beneath the windshield to sit just in front of the domes. Various gauges and numbers appeared on the panel. Matthew presumed this was the car dashboard.

Lestar slowly slid his hands forward on the domes. Some of the gauges showed some movement and the car gently began to move forward.

As this happened Matthew began to feel his body being pulled back onto the chair.

Safiri turn to him. 'Seems to be a sort of seat force instead of a seatbelt. Either way we're going to be fine, Matthew.'

Matthew eased the grip he had on the arms of his friends and his body began to relax back into the seat.

'Feeling better?' asked Sarrus.

'Yes, thanks. Sorry about the freakout.'

'It's fine. I'm sure you have your reasons.'

As they pulled out onto the cobblestone streets Matthew was amazed at how smooth the ride was. No matter how great the tires and suspension were there's no way it should have been able to take on the uneven surface so smoothly.

'Lestar, how is it not bumpy as hell?'

'What do you mean, Matthew?'

'Well, if you roll a wheel on cobblestones it's gonna bounce pretty badly.'

'Oh, well the tires don't actually touch the ground. They're creating a pocket of air between the tire and the ground which absorbs most of the unevenness of the road. Obviously it has its limits but it works.'

'Ugh. Dawn cars suck.'

Matthew's attention was completely taken by how Lestar controlled the car. At no point did he ever need to take his hands off the domes. Sliding his hands in different directions controlled the speed and direction of the car. It all seemed so simple.

After a brief drive through town Lestar pulled the car into an alley behind a small apartment and retail building.

'OK. Everyone out. Wait for me at the front of the building. I'm just going to go and park.'

Matthew opened the boot to find Daisy asleep upon the lap of a very confused and awkward Sam. Giving her a small nudge to wake her, Sam informed everyone of Daisy's ability to instantly fall asleep at will and sleep through anything.

After a big yawn and quick stretch from Daisy the group slowly made their way around the corner to the front of the building where they waited for Lestar, making sure to keep their features as inconspicuous as possible.

On street level were a number of stores. Where the group happened to be standing, and Matthew assumed where they were intending to go, was a store called "The Tailor's Thread". A large sign was mounted above the door and front windows consisting of a single length of rope shaped to spell out the name. Running through the rope were strands of some kind of lifeblood material, giving the sign a soft golden glow.

Through the windows Matthew could see a number of mannequins, both male and female, showing off some of the proprietor's work. While the designs were varied in style and colour they all resembled the classic styles that was clearly the norm in Dusk. After a few seconds of staring closely at the garments the mannequins began to move like they were on the end of a catwalk, striking another pose. Matthew jumped back into Safiri, startled by the sudden yet graceful movement of what should have been inanimate objects, reminding him of something out of many a horror movie that he had watched.

'Did you see that?' he asked Safiri.

'See what?' Safiri replied.

'The mannequins. They freaking move. Creepy as hell.'

They waited a few moments and the mannequins changed position again.

'Oh god, that's creepy,' Safiri agreed. 'Daisy, is this normal?'

'The mannequins? Only in the higher end shops. You don't have this in Dawn?'

'Hell no,' said Matthew emphatically. 'Why would you want them to move?'

'It shows off how well-crafted the clothes are. They're super flexible even though they don't really look like it. You'll see what I mean when you try on some clothes.'

When Lestar joined them they all headed into The Tailor's Thread. The proprietor, standing behind a counter at the back of the store, was a tall, thin, pale Pure who was immaculately dressed in a grey three piece suit and a monocle. His hair was short and black with a distinguished handlebar moustache atop his mouth. The man's ears were ever so slightly pointed and he looked far more human than anyone they had seen since entering Dusk.

As they walked through the store they were greeted by a couple of politely waving mannequins, which Matthew gave a wide berth.

'Mr Dullage. How are you?'

'Fine indeed, Mr Moon. Who do we have here?'

'These are some of my daughter's friends. They're here to get some new clothes. I told them we would take care of them.'

'Mr Moon, sir, we can't let you pay for this,' Kyrral protested.

'Nonsense, Kyrral. It's our treat. Besides, I'm not sure you all have too many options.'

'We very much appreciate it, Lestar, and we'll find a way to pay you back,' said Matthew.

'Matthew, with my line of work what you all have given me is invaluable.'

Mr Dullage, keen to get everyone going, interrupted the back and forth.

'Pick out whatever you like and bring it back here to try on. Once we've sorted out the styles that best suit you I'll take your measurements. If you have any special requests please let me know.'

The group dispersed to see what took their fancy, splitting off into pairs. Sarrus and Sam went to the women's section to find some outfits for Sam. Daisy accompanied Kyrral and immediately started giving him advice on what she thought he should dress in. Matthew and Safiri took off in the opposite direction to try and avoid what they knew would fast become an awkward situation.

Almost everything on display was a three piece suit with jackets of varying lengths for different occasions. There were ties, bowties, cravats, belts, different styles of hat. The kind of store they would never venture into back home.

Lestar walked up behind them, noticing that they were slightly overwhelmed with the choices.

'Make sure to pick out some clothes for different situations. Everyday wear, parties, balls, the Scavenger District. Mr Dullage can do amazing things and make a single suit extremely versatile. While we're on the subject of Mr Dullage, take a minute to think of anything you may want from your suit, no matter how crazy the request may seem. He has ways of making them work. In fact, he revels in the challenge.'

'So he can make strange modifications to clothing and owes you a favour?' Matthew asked. 'I don't suppose they are both related somehow? A little contraband, perhaps? Mr Moon, are you not quite as committed to the message of lifeblood and artefact dangers as you let on?'

Lestar gave a couple of quick taps of the nose and a wry grin.

'Just think carefully, boys,' he said as he turned and walked away.

'I get the feeling Lestar actually loves all the crazy magical stuff here. I think he really wants us to come up with something he's never seen before. Hides it all well in front of his family, though.'

'Definitely,' Safiri agreed. 'I wonder what types of things we can have added to clothes?'

'Well, we've seen Sarrus' invisible, secret pockets. Let's grab some styles and have a think about some weird stuff we can get built in.'

Everyone met up again back at the counter where Mr Dullage waited, intrigued to see what everyone had picked out.

Kyrral already looked thoroughly exhausted. Keen to get the entire ordeal over with, he stepped up first and quickly handed over all of Daisy's choices. The stack was rather large, possibly more than Matthew could have even carried.

'Enjoy yourself, Daisy?' Matthew asked.

'Indeed, I did. I've been offering to get Kyrral some new clothes for the longest time. This time he couldn't refuse.'

She looked extremely proud of herself. Mr Dullage wasn't quite as impressed with the extraordinarily large and varied range of choices picked out for Kyrral, eyeing the pile with slight annoyance.

'Obviously we're going to have to scale this down before proceeding further,' he said. 'Kyrral, if you would please pick out three of *your* favoured options and try them on that would be ideal.'

The smile quickly faded from Daisy's face causing Lestar to chuckle.

Kyrral sorted through the pile and settled on only two outfits in the end. Both were quite similar, although one was far more formal than the other. It was clear that the only consideration for Kyrral was what he could wear inside and outside the Scavenger District.

He took them both to change and reluctantly give everyone a look at the potential new outfits.

First, presumably for inside the scavenger district, was a white shirt, dark brown trousers and a beige 1700's frock coat. He only chose one set of shoes for both outfits, a pair of thick, black boots.

The second outfit consisted of a white shirt, again, although the trousers were now black and the coat was black with gold buttons, gold floral trim down the length of the coat, around the collar and the cuffs. He also wore a black waistcoat under the jacket.

'Sooooo… what do you all think?' he asked.

'Hot,' replied Sam.

'Yeah. Looking real good,' Matthew added.

Daisy just stared, grinning, seemingly in her happy place.

'Not too much?' Kyrral asked.

Sarrus reassured him. 'Perfect for any situation up here.'

'Excellent choices, sir,' said Mr Dullage. 'Now, lucky for you they are both quite similar. They will merge together perfectly.'

'Merge?' Matthew quietly asked Lestar.

'I said that Mr Dullage could make a single suit versatile. He has a way, for those that know to request it, of merging multiple similar items of clothing into a single set of clothes that will change between the outfits when needed.'

'Nice!'

'Now, Kyrral,' Mr Dullage continued. 'Is there anything else you would like your suit to do?'

'Well, when I go to the Scavenger District I need it to look like I haven't left.'

'Ahhhh. So you'd like them to look a little more… rustic when needed?'

'Yeah, I guess.'

'How about this? When in that situation the suit looks a little more worn and dusty? If you'd like I can also make the waistcoat become part of the jacket, essentially making it invisible to everyone.'

'That would be great. Thank you. Also, if it could possibly grow when needed.'

'Of course. It is my pleasure, sir.'

'Mr Dullage,' Lestar interrupted. 'Would it be OK if we loan a suit for each of them while you do your craft? We have somewhere we need to be.'

'No problem at all, Mr Moon. Select which of the suits you wish to borrow. I have what I need. Now, step over here Kyrral and I'll take your measurements. If the next person would be so kind as to begin changing their clothes that would be much appreciated.'

As Mr Dullage took Kyrral around the counter, Safiri picked up his two suits and proceeded into the changing room. By the time he was changed Kyrral was done and ducked back in to get changed, emerging in the more simple outfit of the two chosen, beige coat and brown trousers.

Safiri was now dressed in a traditional tuxedo with tails and a bowtie.

'Yeah? Nice, right?' Safiri seemed quite pleased with the choice although he quickly saw that nobody else shared his enthusiasm.

'What's wrong?'

'You look like a waiter.' Sam replied.

'What do you mean, a waiter? It's a tux. It's classy.'

'Not feeling it, bro,' said Matthew.

'Agreed,' added Daisy and Sarrus in unison.

'I have to admit, Safiri, it doesn't really suit you,' said Lestar.

Safiri looked at Kyrral who simply shook his head.

'OK. I'll try suit number two.'

Safiri returned a short time later sporting a brand new outfit, this time far more flattering. The new suit was a three-piece, beige and maroon, windowpane-checked tweed suit with a white shirt, and maroon cravat and shoes. The suit also came with an accompanying overcoat and flat cap with the same pattern, although the colours were inversed on the cap.

'Now that is a sweet look!' shouted Matthew.

'Mmm-mmm,' added Sam.

'Hey! I'm not a piece of meat!'

'You look very sophisticated,' said Sarrus as Daisy and Kyrral gave a thumbs up.

'Excellent choice, sir. Would you like to merge it with any other suit?' asked Mr Dullage.

'Ummm… no, thanks. I think I like this… would it be possible to have it change colour and pattern whenever I want?'

'Certainly, sir. I can merge the suit with different colours of the same style. Is there anything else?'

'Well… I'm not sure if this is possible-'

'You'll be surprised, sir.'

'Is there a way… ahhhh… that I could possibly… catalogue information and then bring that information up in my glasses when I need to know something specific?'

'Like some AR glasses? Nice!' Matthew interrupted.

'Now that sounds like an incredible idea and, as I said, I do love a challenge. This, however, is beyond what I am able to achieve with the thread.'

'Ahhh… that sucks-'

'Now, now. I didn't say it couldn't be done. I simply stated that I, alone, could not accomplish it. You see, I do not make glasses. Accessories such as those are created by a friend of mine. She, most definitely could accomplish such a task as to display information to you through a pair of glasses. The question now becomes: *how do you get the information and where is it stored?* That, I may be able to help with. We've worked together to make quite a few interesting combinations. All in an extremely fashionable manner, of course.'

'Excellent! How exactly will you get the information?' asked Safiri.

'Ahhhh… That, my boy, is the tailor's secret. Just know that it will take the information you are after. The suit will, shall we say, increase your sensor range. Now, follow me over here and I'll measure you up.'

'I'm up next,' said Matthew, jumping up from his seat and carrying the single suit he had chosen to get changed.

'Only one?' asked Daisy.

'I think I know my style. I've got this sweet-arse suit back home that's similar to this one.'

'We'll see if you're right.'

Matthew emerged from the changing room in a dark grey three-piece suit with satin lapel trim, white shirt, black shoes and a black tie with grey tartan stripes.

'Matthew, that looks extremely Dawn…ish,' Sam observed.

'Isn't that the suit you wore to the school ball?' asked Safiri.

'Pretty close, yeah?'

'You could've picked anything in here and you picked a suit that was pretty much what you've got back home?'

'I can accessorise. Besides, I'm comfortable in this.'

'Very good, sir. One of my newest pieces. Hasn't attracted much attention at all so far. A bit too *out there* for everyone, I suppose. It is extremely casual. I happened upon this peculiar style very recently and decided to replicate it. I haven't seen it since.'

'We've got different definitions of *casual* Mr Dullage. So I would like it if I could change the style and length of my jacket and maybe play around with the colours occasionally, like Safiri's suit.'

'As you wish, sir. Again, I'll merge the suit with others based on your request. Anything else?'

'Ah… maybe just a few hidden, easy-access pockets will be

good.'

'Excellent, sir.'

'You're up Sam,' said Matthew as he followed Mr Dullage to get his measurements taken.

Matthew returned, still wearing the grey suit and took a seat with his friends. After a short wait Sam still hadn't emerged from the dressing room.

'You OK in there Sam?' asked Safiri.

'Yeah,' came the reply, completely devoid of Sam's usual confidence. 'I'm not sure if this is right for me.'

'Why? What's wrong?'

Sarrus provided a possible explanation for Sam's hesitation.

'I told her she would need to choose a formal dress as well as more casual clothes for… more refined events.'

Sarrus slowly emerged from the dressing room. She was wearing a black, sleeveless, v-neck, empire dress, although taking great pains to obscure the v-neck and lack of sleeves with her hands. Adding to her issues was the unfamiliarity of the black stiletto shoes which had thin leather strings wrapping up her calves. She had pulled her dress up slightly to reveal the shoes and had almost fallen over while doing so.

'I can't do this, guys. It just isn't me.'

'You look beautiful,' Daisy whispered, breaking the silence of the group.

Sarrus joined Sam, pulling her hands down, attempting to boost her confidence.

'It's definitely different,' Matthew added.

'Matthew!' shouted Daisy. 'You're not helping.'

'I mean it in a good way. You look great, Sam.'

Everyone voiced their agreement and approval of the dress.

'I dunno. I don't like dressing like this.'

'Unfortunately people are quite fastidious in that regard. You most likely wouldn't have to wear it very often, though,' Lestar added.

'May I make a suggestion?' Mr Dullage interrupted. 'Give me one moment. I believe I have something here that may make you feel a little more comfortable, my lady.'

A moment later Mr Dullage emerged from a small storeroom at the back.

'What is that? A dead bird?' Matthew joked. Sam smacked him on the back of the head.

Around Sam's neck, Mr Dullage clipped together a high-neck caplet made out of what seemed to be large raven feathers. Small feathers rose up her neck with large ones extending out from the neck, down her chest and around her shoulders and back like wings. The feathers were striking against her silver and black hair, emitting an air of intimidation.

Sam's shoulders relaxed and confidence returned to her face and posture as she inspected herself in the mirror, clearly approving of the new accessory to her outfit.

'We got the Raven Queen up in here,' said Matthew, half mockingly, half quite intimidated. 'What do you command of us my liege?'

Sam giggled. 'Raven Queen, hey? I could get used to that.'

'What's a raven?' asked Lestar.

'It's a black bird in Dawn,' Safiri answered. 'Although the feathers aren't quite as big as what we've got here.'

'We approve of this ensemble?' asked Mr Dullage.

'Yes, Mr Dullage,' Sam wobbled a little, still trying to get used to heels.

'I wouldn't worry about the shoes, my lady. I can make the heels merge into the strings when you would prefer flats.'

'Perfect. Now for the other outfit.'

After a short wait Sam emerged again. This outfit was definitely more Sam and less Sarrus. She wore dark grey breeches with a black leather belt and knee high black leather boots. Her white shirt was covered by a single breasted, Victorian, black longline formal coat. Floral, almost thorny, patterns adorned the slightly exaggerated triple lapel, cuffs and lower back of the coat in dark silver.

'That's badass,' said Matthew and Safiri in unison.

'Love it!,' added Daisy.

'This is much closer to what many of the Pure wear. Suits you extremely well, Sam,' Sarrus grinned, extremely satisfied with the outfits they had decided on.

'There isn't really anything I can do to merge these outfits, unfortunately. They are far too different so you will have to wear them separately. Although, I would be able to merge the coat and the caplet. The density of the feathers should be enough to give a more than satisfactory outcome.'

'Excellent. Thanks Mr Dullage.'

'Is there anything else I can do for you?'

'Ummm… would it be possible if I could have a mask come out from the collar, especially when it's in the caplet form. It would go around my eyes and nose and be kinda bird-like to match the feathers? Also, when in coat form, can I also have a hood extend from the collar that I can put over my head?'

'Intriguing. Versatile for a masquerade party or any other… incognito engagements you may have. If I may say, my lady, this is a very exciting request. I would very much like to discuss how you have used this feature some time in the future. Any more captivating ideas?'

'Well… there is something but it may be waaaay too much. Maybe we can discuss it while you take my measurements?'

'Certainly, my lady. Right this way.'

A short time later Sam returned to the group, seemingly relieved that the ordeal was finally over.

'What was it that you asked for?' Safiri asked.

'I'm just gonna keep it to myself for now. Mr Dullage isn't sure yet whether he'll be able to do it so I don't wanna build it up and everyone gets disappointed.'

'Not even a hint?'

Sam giggled. 'No, Saf.'

'Are we all done here?' Lestar asked the group.

'I think so. We've all got nice shiny suits even if they're just a loan for now,' Matthew adjusted Safiri's cap feeling good that they'll be able to walk around in the open without drawing much attention.

'We'll be back later to pick those up, Mr Dullage,' said Lester, then turned to the group. 'Let's get something to eat and then walk to the Finance Depository to take a look at this vault box.'

After thanking Mr Dullage for his help they all left the shop, Matthew again keeping his distance from the seemingly living mannequins.

'How long will it take to Mr Dullage to finish?' Matthew asked Lestar.

'We'll pick it all up after we've been to the Finance Depository.'

'Really? How will he get it done so quick?'

'We have an arrangement. I don't ask him questions about the process and he doesn't ask me about the supply chain.'

'Fair enough.'

Chapter Fifteen
Money Money Money

After getting a quick bite to eat, of which the Dawn Crew kept to food they had eaten the previous night, the group walked toward a large, miserable-looking, grey concrete building. Matthew had swapped his bag for a more discreet, dark-brown satchel which he had borrowed from Lestar.

Behind the facade of double-height concrete columns were no windows, as Matthew had expected, rather there was simply a long concrete wall. In the middle of the wall was a double glass door the height of the wall. There was certainly no way for anybody to sneak in or out of the Finance Depository.

Sarrus stopped the group outside before making their entrance.

'I think it may be best if only Matthew, Lestar and myself go in. The less people, the less attention we'll attract. It is unusual that anyone would enter a Treasury building, or any Authority building for that matter, in a large group. It'll only make them suspicious of us. I shall take the lead once we go in. The Authority will always react more favourably toward the Pure than anyone else. The vault box and medallion are also of House Errothin so it would make sense that I would have them in my possession.'

After the rest of the group reluctantly agreed to wait outside,

Sarrus, Matthew and Lestar walked through the doors and into a room in stark contrast to the drabness of the facade. White marble floor met black marble walls which stretched four storeys high. A crest was built into the floor as they entered depicting a gold-lined shield. Within the shield was a winged snake. The feathered wings pointed down as if to surround and protect a stack of gold bars in front of it.

'That doesn't look sinister at all,' Matthew said quietly to Lestar.

'The Authority is definitely a fan of the grandiose and intimidating style of branding.'

Down a hallway to the left were a number of uniformed, burly Stroen and Squaar, which Matthew assumed were security guards, sitting at high tables in front of a large door. A man stood waiting as a guard looked through his briefcase before scanning his hand on a device to open the door. This seemed to be where the employees entered the back of the building.

On the right was another hallway. At the end stood a man behind a lectern, behind him an extravagant golden door. He looked like a concierge, dressed in a tuxedo. *That must be the VIP section*, Matthew thought.

Large white columns dotted the massive, lavish foyer in front of them. Circular, floral patterns adorned the ceiling where anything joined to it, whether that be the columns or the extraordinary chandeliers which hung down to provide a plethora of white, lifeblood light into the room. Also contributing to the light were lamps affixed to the walls throughout.

A bearded, grumpy-looking Lorrai sat up on a raised marble box, staring at something, which was obscured by the top of the box, through his tiny glasses on the end of his nose. As they approached him he looked up, apparently none too pleased at the prospect of having to deal with customers. An empty rectangular pad attached to a pole which extended out from the box.

Matthew continued walking, taking in his surroundings. As he went to walk by the box he bumped his nose into something he could not see. An invisible barrier was blocking them from accessing the main area and would explain why there was no sound of chatter coming from the other side. He touched the barrier again with his finger and saw a slight ripple emanate from where he touched it along with some faint, white lifeblood sparks.

The man in the box glared at Matthew, unimpressed at having to deal with this simpleton. Lestar pulled Matthew back and awkwardly smiled up at him.

'State your business,' the Lorrai said, still devoid of any kind of enthusiasm at having to greet them.

'We wish to open a vault box,' Sarrus answered.

'A vault box, you say? And you have the required key and permits to possess such a box and, indeed, to open it?' The Lorrai was now beginning to sound quite smug, still not thinking very much of them at all.

'Shouldn't he be a bit nicer to a Pure?' Matthew asked Lestar quietly.

'He obviously thinks she's from a lesser house given she's wearing Madonny's coat and scarf.'

'Speak up, now. I don't have all day!'

'Sir!' Sarrus snapped. 'You are being quite rude! I have everything a progeny of High Daitronarchs would need, other than the respect myself and my companions should be afforded by the likes of you! So, if you value your current employment I suggest you take a far more cheerful and pleasant tone with me and my companions!'

Sarrus removed the medallion from the satchel and slammed it into the pad which then glowed green. Matthew noticed a quick change in Sarrus' expression from anger to confusion as she looked at the medallion, and back to anger as she returned her gaze up to the man in the box.

The face of the Lorrai drained white with fear and horror as the enormous error in judgement he had made registered in his brain.

'My sincere apologies, my liege. Please forgive me,' the man stammered, praying that he did not lose his job… or worse.

'Is there a problem here?' a Pure man approached from the hallway to the right, flanked by two younger Pure men; two unhealthily skinny, hairless, ghostly white men in cloaks who seemed to be floating as opposed to walking; and four Lorrai struggling to hold an array of wooden boxes and books. The older Pure man had long, flowing red hair and a coat similar to the one that Sam had chosen, although this one was red. An imposing figure, he glared at the petrified Lorrai, awaiting an answer.

Sarrus spoke up to de-escalate the situation.

'Father… brothers… gentlemen… No, there is no problem. A glitch in the system, unfortunately, although all is resolved now.'

Matthew and Lestar stood, heads down, trying not to draw any attention in what was already an extremely tense situation.

'Sarrus? I hardly recognised you. What, in the name of the Gift Giver, are you wearing? We discussed your attire mere days ago. This is unacceptable and unbecoming of your station. Go home at once and change into something more appropriate… absolutely disgusting, the state of you.'

'Father, I have business to-'

'Do not talk back to me, child! Do as I say! You are representing House Errothin regardless of whether you want to or not!'

'Father,' one of Sarrus' brothers interrupted the standoff. 'We must be going or we'll be late for our next appointment with the Senior Masters for Trade.'

Suddenly one of the Lorrai dropped a large book. An echo thundered through the foyer.

Sarrus' father's eyes turned red, a flame erupted from his hand as he bent down and took hold of the shrieking man's neck, causing him to drop the other books he was holding.

'Do you need to be erased you pathetic, incompetent Lorrai?!'

'Apologies, my Daitros,' the man struggled to say through the pain of his neck burning.

'Father! Please stop!' shouted Sarrus.

Her father let go of the man and began to walk toward the door, the others in his entourage following as the, now shivering, Lorrai picked up all his books.

'I'll deal with you later, Sarrus!' he shouted without looking back.

As they walked past, Sarrus' brother, the one who had attempted to move their father along, placed his hand on Sarrus' cheek and smiled.

'Must you always make a scene?' he asked.

'Sorry, Bettinah.'

He laughed as he turned and followed his father. 'It's never boring when you're around.'

Sarrus smiled turning back to the man in the box, raising an eyebrow.

'Go on through, my lady. Apologies again for the misunderstanding.'

'I trust a lesson was learned today?'

'Yes, my lady.'

A ripple ran through a section of the barrier in front of Matthew, creating an open archway. Sarrus walked through, followed by Matthew and Lestar.

'Apologies for that. My father can be very… unreasonable.'

'That was pretty intense. Wouldn't wanna get on his bad side.'

'Unfortunately that is standard behaviour for many of my kind, especially the Daitronarchs and High Daitronarchs. The Faelords and Lesser Pure are slightly more relaxed and understanding, although they are still very much subservient to the upper ranks of the Houses. Let's just be thankful my father didn't enquire as to why we are here.'

'Why is that?'

'He most likely would have taken the vault box and possibly had you two arrested for having possession of it. He would have known it wasn't mine.'

'Dodged a bullet then?'

'I'm not sure what a bullet is but we definitely dodged an awkward situation.'

Matthew was slightly taken aback at Sarrus not knowing what a bullet was.

'What is the name of those floating guys? They're really creepy.'

'Yes. They are Taerith. I don't trust them. They are extremely intelligent although almost always in the employ of those most powerful. They also always have a deceitful smile on their face. I know they can't help it but it's like looking into the face of a smiling dead man. No matter what happens their emotion doesn't show, just a constant smile.'

'One more question and I promise I'll be quiet for at least a short period of time.' Sarrus chuckled at Matthew's near apology. 'I noticed you looked a little confused when you slammed down the medallion. What's the deal with that?'

'Probably nothing… I'm sure I'm just looking for strange occurrences now.'

'Strange like what?'

'Well… the glow from the medallion was green.'

'And? Green for go and red for stop, right?'

'Not sure where you got that from, however that is not correct. House Errothin is red and the glow when the medallion is placed on the pad is usually red… Either way, it's not important right now. Let's get going.'

Moving past the barrier allowed Matthew to get a better look at the business end of the Finance Depository. At the far end and either side was a mezzanine containing rows of bookshelves and desks with people furiously working away.

On the ground floor were a number of offices on either side of the room. All had similar barriers to the one Matthew had just painfully experienced, which went up when people had entered into the office. As soon as a barrier was in place no sound could be heard from the people inside.

Most of those working in the Finance Depository were Lorrai, although there were a couple of Taerith eerily floating among the bookshelves.

Sarrus lead them toward the far end of the enormous room where a Stroen guard and a nicely suited Lorrai stood at each of four doors. As they approached Sarrus returned to a more commanding mode.

'We require a vault room.'

'Certainly, my lady, although wouldn't you prefer to conduct this business in a more… fitting setting?'

'I do not require needless luxuries to go along with my business. I simply need to open this vault box.'

'Of course, my lady. It is… unconventional that you would have it on your person. Is there an issue with our services which you would like to have rectified?'

'No, sir. The business of this box is my own and none of your concern.'

'Of course, my lady. This way, please.'

The door opened as they approached, the guard eyeing them as they walked passed. Once through and into a short hallway they stopped, the door behind them closing. The hallway was the same as the main area, white marble floor with black marble walls and a white ceiling, although this was only a single storey high.

'All personal effects stored before we continue, please.'

Sarrus touched the wall which slid open to reveal what Matthew could only describe as a small locker. Lestar did the same. Following suit, Matthew touched the wall where a locker was soon revealed. He wasn't sure what exactly he needed to do. Sarrus removed the box and medallion from the satchel and left the satchel in the locker. Lestar removed a small box from his pocket and also left it in his locker. They both pressed the wall again just above the opening and the door slid closed and disappeared as if it was never there.

Matthew removed the cards and ring from his pocket and left them, pressing above the opening in the wall, as the others did, to close the locker.

Their guide to the vault room then turned and pressed his hand to the wall on the far end. The light inside the hallway suddenly turned red.

'*All* personal effects, please,' the man said, seemingly very put out at the inconvenience.

'Do you have anything else on you, Matthew?' asked Lestar.

'I don't think so.'

'You have thirty seconds until the guard comes through that door and then things could get unpleasant so if any of you are being... forgetful, then this is probably the time to jog your memory.'

'The necklace?' Matthew asked Lestar, not being comfortable to part with his key back home.

'Yes, Matthew. It's OK. Only you can retrieve it.'

Matthew opened his locker again and quickly added his necklace to the cards and ring.

Once again the man pressed his hand against the wall, this time the wall slid to the side and the light returned to normal.

The hallway opened into a circular stone room. In the center stood a plain stone bench, the middle slightly sunk in to create a small border around a dozen centimetres wide and a few centimetres high. At one end the border was about three times as wide with a circular sunken area which looked, to Matthew, to perfectly fit the medallion.

Sarrus placed the vault box in the centre of the bench and handed the medallion to Matthew.

'I think maybe you should be the one to open it,' she said, smiling.

Matthew took the medallion from Sarrus and slowly walked over to the end of the bench, going through his head everything that had taken him to this point, to finally getting answers to the last of the items he had inherited. After a deep breath he slotted the medallion into the bench.

The edges of the medallion and the embossed tree crest upon it began to glow green and slowly pulse. A green line of light slowly pushed out of the medallion, moving across the surface of the bench, to where the vault box was sitting. Reaching the edge of the border it poured out, revealing itself to be lifeblood, filling the sunken area.

Once the lifeblood had surrounded the box, the patterns all glowed green as the medallion had. A green line, similar to the doorway appeared around the box, an inch down from the top. The box clicked and one side popped up slightly, as if being released from an old fashioned lock. Despite there being no hinges on the box one end held in place.

Matthew quickly moved around to the box, Sarrus and Lestar flanking him, all keen to see what was inside.

Matthew slowly opened the box, the contents being obscured by a note sitting on top. Removing the note revealed a pair of gloves of white mesh with gold veins running through it.

'For the one willing to venture into the dark to expand their world, please accept this gift, to perform your tricks.' Matthew read the note, confusion painted his face as he finished. 'Definitely the kind of cryptic note that Grandad would write.'

'Do you have any idea to what tricks it refers?' asked Lestar.

'No idea.'

'I would advise we take this to my office. We can take a good look there in more controlled conditions.'

'I think that would be wise,' Sarrus agreed, removing the medallion and causing the lifeblood to fade away.

Lestar picked up the box and handed it to Matthew, who now had to hold the lid down.

'All done?' enquired their guide into the vault room.

'Yes, thank you,' Sarrus replied.

The man pushed his hand against the wall as he had done previously, which slid aside to allow access to the hallway once more. Retrieving their possessions, Matthew, Sarrus and Lestar quickly made their way to the exit of the Finance Depository.

Safiri, Sam, Kyrral and Daisy were standing against one of the columns closest to the door, snacking on a few sweets Safiri still had remaining, which he had transferred from his bag to some of the many pockets in his loan suit. This kept Daisy sufficiently busy given her newfound love for Dawn lollies.

Sam spent the wait teaching Kyrral how to play *red hands*. Despite being the clear winner with her superior speed and experience at playing the game, the nature of Kyrral's skin meant that he neither felt any pain nor had a change in the colour of his skin, leaving him slightly confused as to the naming of the game and Sam a little frustrated.

The emergence of Matthew, Sarrus and Lestar brought a welcome break to the dreariness of the wait.

'What was in the box?' asked Sam.

'A pair of gloves,' replied Matthew.

'Doesn't sound too exciting,' Daisy said, a little dejected.

'They also came with a note. It said "For the one willing to venture into the dark to expand their world, please accept this gift, to perform your tricks." I have no idea what it means. We're going to go to Lestar's office to see if we can work out what they do.'

'Another riddle to solve, hey?' Safiri was already mulling it over in his head, seeing if he could quickly discern anything from the note.

The group made their way back to the car, Safiri asking Matthew for all the details of what he saw inside the building. Mentioning Sarrus' family, Daisy gave an account of what had happened outside. A small convoy of cars picking up the group where the older Pure was berating everyone.

On the way they stopped off at The Tailor's Thread once again to pick up their completed attire. The Dawn Crew were astonished at how quickly they had been completed, exiting the store as if still wearing the same clothes they had walked in with.

Safiri put his glasses on and scanned the immediate area. It was as if he had a computer in front of his eyes. Information popped up as he concentrated on what was around him. People's race, approximate height and weight, temperature, lifeblood. Suddenly his face dropped.

'What's wrong, Saf?' asked Matthew.

'It's only showing me what I already know. How is that useful? I wanted it to tell me what I didn't know so that I could learn more quickly.'

'Maybe it's like a blank hard drive. You need to fill it up with information. Sarrus... what type Lof tree is that?'

'That's a plestarium,' the name suddenly appeared through the glasses. 'It's leaves are a browny yellow when they are young, however once they reach maturity they bloom large grey flowers that give a rash to Squaar.'

As Sarrus rattled off properties of the plestarium they continued to list as properties that Safiri could access.

'It's like an endless data repository that I can access instantly. I just need to feed it more information.'

As he continued to try and absorb information his mind went to the places they had been, what extra information he could gain from them and how he could get back, recounting the route they had taken. As he did so a map began to appear in front of him, only displaying where he had a clear recollection of the way they had gotten there. Thinking about each location a small trail appeared in the direction they would need to take, much like the pointers had done when they delivered the packages in the Scavenger District.

'Matthew, I think I underestimated how cool this is.'

'Why? What can you see?'

'Remember when we play those RPGs and there's the map with the fog of war which reveals more of the map as we explore it?'

'Yeah… wait… you've got navigation built in! Hell yeah!'

'So the database builds based on the knowledge that I enter into it, but I can use that data in any way I need to.'

'That's awesome! Give me a look.'

Safiri took the glasses off and handed them to Matthew.

'I'm not seeing anything. Is there an "on" switch?'

'I don't think so. They just worked. Pass them back.'

Safiri once again peered through the glasses and was able to retrieve whatever information he wanted.

'I'm not having a problem. Maybe they only work for me. Hang on… Mr Dullage did accidentally prick me with a pin as he was taking my measurements. I assumed it was just an accident.'

'There was no pinning when I was with him. That must mean that the power in the clothes is secured to your DNA!'

'That's kinda creepy,' Sam pointed out. 'He could be making a clone of you as we speak.'

'I'm sure it's fine. He seemed kinda cool and Lestar vouched for him,' Matthew reassured them.

'What about yours, Matthew?' Sam asked.

'Well, I've got secret pockets everywhere. On the inside, outside, in my sleeves. Even my shoes have secret pockets. I can take stuff anywhere and nobody will know… well, except the Finance Depository. Whatever security system they had running through there, it knew that I still had my necklace on.'

'Maybe hold off on the demonstrations for the moment,' Lestar warned. 'This isn't exactly one hundred percent above board so we don't want to draw attention. Especially not right outside Mr Dullage's establishment. Let's get going to my office where we can have a little more privacy.'

Chapter Sixteen
A Kind Of Magic

After a short drive, in which Safiri insisted on having a window seat in order to expose more of his map of Dusk and take in whatever extra information came his way, the group arrived at The Office of Magic. The building was located a little way outside of the built-up area they had experienced so far.

Despite there being a number of large buildings around, they were each situated on their own large plot of land surrounded by grass and trees, with a pebble driveway and carpark out the front.

It was like visiting a large hotel in the countryside. Five storeys high and grandiose, The Office of Magic was a U-shape with a large courtyard in front of the entrance, which itself was curved and adorned with a dome on top.

As the group walked through the courtyard there were a few people sitting amongst the serenity of the flora. Some were studying books, some were writing furiously as though inspired by their surroundings, others were writing runes in the air with lifeblood. Symbols glowing in the air for a time before fading away.

A driveway surrounded the courtyard, presumably for drop-offs and pick-ups. *Probably for the more important people with their chauffeurs,* thought Matthew.

A set of stairs, curved in keeping with the building in front of them, led up to the double height, metal front doors. Matthew noted that Dusk people loved a large door. Strangely the doors were completely surrounded by a single, curved pane of glass, stretching the entire width of the curve and three storeys high.

As they reached the top Matthew tapped the glass with his knuckle.

'Surely this isn't secure,' he said.

'You'd be surprised,' Lestar replied.

Lestar pressed his hand onto a pad next to the door, which responded by pushing back and sliding behind the glass a little faster than what Matthew expected based on its size and thickness.

'Keep your hands to yourselves and don't say anything until we reach my office. There's a chance you may not be allowed in, however given most people have the day off it may be OK with me showing my daughter and her friends around.'

They all nodded their acknowledgment of the instructions and followed Lestar to the reception desk.

While Lestar explained the situation Matthew took the opportunity to have a look around. Where the Finance Depository had surfaces of shiny marble, The Office of Magic was far more classic. Matthew put it down to the abundance of natural light through the large number of windows and the glass dome that sat atop the open reception area. He paused, momentarily forgetting that there was not enough light outside to create the amount of light which was shining through each of the windows, akin to full sunlight.

Matthew tapped Safiri and Sam to get their attention, pointing out the appearance of sunlight shining through the windows. Despite the desire to investigate they decided to follow instructions and stay put, so as to avoid attracting any attention.

A mix of stone, wood and glass was the feature of the

architecture, along with the many books and artefacts sitting on the array of shelves and tables that lined the walls.

Behind reception was a massive gold statue of a robed Pure with her arm raised. Sat upon her palm was a gigantic orb as tall as she was. The orb was etched all over with runes and circular patterns. Red lifeblood pulsed through the patterns while yellow sparks periodically burst from the runes. In all the statue rose almost three storeys high. A pond sat at her feet, water flowing down her arm and body from the top of the orb.

Mezzanines connected levels on either side of the open reception, following the curve around the back of the statue.

'OK, kids. Let's go. Each of you needs to place your hand on this pad to sign in and we'll get going.'

Each of the group placed their hand on the pad which sat on the reception desk as they followed Lestar toward the statue. They walked around the back to what looked like a row of four elevators.

The doors to the closest one opened as they approached and they all walked in. While the doors that opened were the kind the Dawn Crew were used to, thick, metal sliding doors, the inside was a cage of vertical bars with a thick mesh floor and ceiling.

Strangely, outside the floor and ceiling the vertical bars which made up the walls of the elevator curved to form a dome at the top and bottom, creating a pill shape.

The odd light along the wall of the shaft, both up and down gave somewhat of an indication of where they could possibly be heading.

Looking down was quite disconcerting for Matthew as the shaft extended down farther than he could judge and he didn't much enjoy looking down at the large drop.

Lestar touched a combination of runes on a wider bar by the side of the door.

'Whatever happens just remain calm. Nothing is going to

happen to you,' Lestar remarked, a smile appearing across his face somewhere between mischievous and an attempt to comfort, seemingly unsure which way to go.

Safiri turned to stare at him. 'Why? What's going to hap-'

The elevator suddenly dropped. While they never felt like they were going to fly around the cage, the air blasting past them had them all scared. All except Lestar who stood calmly as if this was all completely normal.

Matthew could see the bottom quickly approaching when the shaft curved, the pill-shaped cage now flying horizontally through the tunnel. Everyone holding tightly to the bars of the cage.

The curve of the cage, it became apparent to Matthew, was there to facilitate moving in any direction.

'Oh, apologies!' shouted Lestar, who touched another rune. Metal sheets slid out all along the cage, completely enclosing it. With the air no longer blasting in their faces it felt as if they were not moving at all.

'Dad! What are you doing!' Daisy screamed.

'Just a little office gag. Too far?' he chuckled.

Matthew, Sam, Kyrral and Sarrus laughed. While they were all genuinely scared they respected the prank that was pulled on them.

Daisy turned away from her father, clearly not feeling the same way.

Safiri was still catching his breath, trying to make sense of what happened.

'You OK, Saf?' asked Sam.

'You have no idea how fast we were going. We're kilometres from where we got in.'

'Really? How do you know that?'

'I captured all the data.'

'Nice! Do you know exactly where we are?'

'Not really. It's not anywhere we've been before, at least not on the surface.'

The cage made a *ding* noise and the doors opened.

'Strange how the most random things are the same across worlds,' Matthew commented, which had the added effect of somewhat relaxing Safiri.

They all stepped out into a large stone room, lamps switching on as they entered.

'Welcome to my office,' Lestar said proudly as they all filed into the room.

Stacks of books sat alongside various objects of all shapes and sizes on benches and shelves in the room. It was quite a mess.

A massive screen turned on on the far side of the room, spanning almost the entire width and height of the wall, and it was quite a large wall, almost ten metres in length and four metres high. The screen depicted some parkland, similar to that which the Dawn Crew had traveled through to get to the Scavenger District. A slight breeze caused the trees to sway.

'What's that for, Dad?' Daisy asked.

'The screen? Just to keep us sane. We spend a lot of time studying books and artefacts and we're a long way underground so a serene view of the park is calming, even if it's not really there. Each of the artefacts here have been brought in for us to try and uncover its history and properties. If we can get enough information we're hoping we can uncover more about our own history and get some answers to some of the bigger mysteries we have. Some of these artefacts could be very dangerous, some useful and some just silly. We research them, catalogue them and get as much information as we can. They then get packed away for storage in another part of the facility, although sometimes they go out to be used or go on display.'

'Would you say you have a lot of information here?' asked Safiri.

'Yes. Why?'

A massive smile stretched across Safiri's face.

'You thinking about filling some of that data storage, Saf?' asked Matthew.

'I most certainly am,' he replied.

Giving it a test run, Safiri found a book open with some information relating to a nearby artefact. Safiri simply looked at the page and it was absorbed by his clothing, the information suddenly appearing around the artefact as he looked at it through his glasses.

'This is so cool,' he said, picking up a few books and taking them to a desk.

Lestar cleared another desk.

'Let's take a look at those gloves, Matthew.'

Matthew took the box out of his satchel and set it down on the desk. Everyone gathered around, eager to discover what the gloves could do. Even Safiri tore himself away from absorbing data to see what Matthew had discovered.

Carefully, Matthew removed the mesh gloves from the box.

'Come across anything like this in the books, Saf?'

'Nope. Nothing like that.'

Matthew slipped the gloves onto his hands, the length taking them slightly past his wrists. Like the mageball glove they resized to perfectly fit, however the mesh disappeared as soon as the resizing was complete. At a quick glance it would seem like he wasn't wearing any gloves at all, although on closer inspection the gold veins were still somewhat visible.

'Do you feel anything?' asked Lestar.

'Not really. It doesn't even feel like I'm wearing gloves.'

'Maybe pick up some things and see if anything happens. Everyone else keep some distance just in case.'

Everyone moved back and took cover behind pillars or shelves, peeping to still watch if anything happened.

Matthew slowly began to touch objects and books, pick them up, squeeze them, just to make sure nothing had changed. He waved his hands around and tried to do some parkour over some benches to see if his agility was improved. Tripping over and falling flat on his face proved that wasn't the case.

'I've got nothing, guys. Maybe they're just some rich man's mageball gloves. The note did say something about tricks. Maybe I'm destined to become some kind of mageball champion. Anyone got anything we can light up? See if it burns?' Matthew asked

'Let me see… Ahhhh, yes. Here we go.'

Lestar picked up an object that looked like a large pot. Setting it down in a small, empty stone room he touched a rune on the side and jumped back. A jet flame of blue lifeblood shot out from the pot.

Matthew removed one of the gloves and hung it from a pole Lestar was holding in front of him.

'If this thing burns up we just wasted a whole lot of time,' he remarked, worried about the possibility of losing something he took so long to find, regardless of how little he knew about it.

Lestar walked over to the room and, using the pole, moved the glove over the flame and held it for a few moments. Taking it away, the glove looked slightly charred although it quickly faded away. Matthew touched the glove quickly and found it to be at room temperature.

'That's something,' he said with a slight smile. 'Doesn't really tell us too much other than the possibility that it is a fancy-arse mageball glove.'

'I can't believe that would be it,' Sarrus remarked. 'To go to all the trouble of locking it away in an Errothin vault box and store it in Dawn seems far too much effort for simply gloves for a game, no matter how stylish they may be.'

Kyrral took hold of the glove and tried to rip it in half, his crusty muscles bulging as he tried with all his might to tear it apart.

'Whoa, calm down, mate.'

'I was just trying to see if they would break. Sorry,' Kyrral apologised, dropping his head.

'All good, big man. Just give us a heads up next time before savaging inanimate objects.'

Matthew tapped him on the shoulder and took the glove from Kyrral. Putting it back on his bare hand, Matthew turned to Safiri.

'How about you check some more books and see if you can find anything.'

'Sounds good to me,' Safiri replied as he sat back down to continue where he had left off.

Lestar roamed the bookshelves taking anything that may contain something useful, adding them to the pile of books next to Safiri.

While Kyrral walked around looking at artefacts and reading the tags on them, Sam and Daisy sat listening to Sarrus recount the story of what had taken place in the Finance Depository with her father and brothers. *Looks like a good, old-fashioned gossip session,* thought Matthew as he sat on a chair, balancing on the back legs, feet upon a desk.

'This is so boring,' he complained. 'Why couldn't they just come with an instruction manual or a marketing brochure. Everything is always some damn riddle.'

Succumbing to his usual routine when bored, Matthew took the deck of cards out from his pocket, deciding this was a good a time as ever to practice his aim. Removing the first card from the deck he held the card between his fingers ready to flick it across the room.

As he lifted his hand the gold veins intensified to the point of emitting a golden glow. The card then burst into flames. Matthew froze, shocked at what was happening.

'Matthew!' screamed Sam.

'What do I do! What do I do! What do I do!' Matthew shouted, too scared to move.

'Throw it into the small room over there!' Lestar commanded, pointing to the room where they had attempted to burn the glove.

With a flick of his wrist the flaming card flew in the direction of the room. As it left Matthews hand, flames engulfed the card as it morphed into a fireball. With perfect accuracy the fireball flew through the doorway and crashed against the wall on the opposite side, exploding and filling the small room with flames.

Lestar grabbed a nearby hose, not dissimilar to that used by firemen in Dawn, and turned it on, dousing the flames and relieving the situation.

'Are you OK, Matthew?' Sarrus asked as they all ran to check on his wellbeing.

'Yeah. I'm fine. I couldn't even feel it other than the force of the flame blowing my hair.'

'That, children, is why we have the blast room. Anything that has the smallest hint of getting out of control we throw in there. I guess we've also solved the mystery of the gloves... and how to activate the runes on the cards.'

'You have no idea how many questions this answers,' said Matthew, a huge grin having overridden the shock on his face moments prior. 'Grandad must have been training me since I was a kid. The cards, the box, the stories. He must have known that some day I'll come here and discover all this for myself. And the note! Tricks! Card tricks! It was so obvious!'

'You're like The Traveler come to life,' Lestar said, chuckling to himself.

'The Traveler?' Matthew asked.

'Oh, just whispers and rumours that I heard from some people when I was young. The Traveler, the trickster with his cards of magic. I had completely forgotten about it. It was only around for a little while and not widely circulated. Faded away quite quickly. The Traveler from afar, reluctant hero serving justice. A little bit of a scoundrel with an eye for the ladies.'

Matthew, Safiri and Sam all looked at each other and chuckled.

'Maybe The Traveler was Grandad,' Matthew said laughing.

'Oh I'm sure it's just a tale that spun out of control as the whispers passed along. Nobody gave any indication any of it was actually true.'

'It doesn't answer everything,' Sarrus interrupted.

'What do you mean?' asked Matthew.

'Well, it doesn't explain why the gloves were in an Errothin vault box. They are supposed to be for House Errothin use only.'

'Maybe somebody in House Errothin gave them to George,' Sam suggested.

'Maybe, however that would be extremely irregular. These vault boxes aren't available for everyone to use and those that do have access to them wouldn't simply give them away to a stranger from another world.'

'Well, what would this little adventure be without another question to answer,' said Matthew.

'I think you're going to need some lessons on runes, Matthew,' said Daisy. 'Don't want you to blow yourself up.'

'Very good idea, Daisy,' said Lestar. 'Although we have to keep this all very hush hush and do it all as safely as possible. You shouldn't even have artefacts like this, Matthew.'

'Time to hit the books,' Safiri suggested.

'We'll hang around here for a little while before heading home. I've got a few things I could be getting a head start on. Matthew, you should go through the basics so at least you'll know what each card does.'

As they all went to find something to pass the time Safiri turned back to Matthew.

'You know how my clothes can absorb information and I can access relevant things when needed?'

'Aha.'

'There's a lot of info about runes and writing them,' Safiri pointed out, tapping his nose.

'Nice,' Matthew replied.

Matthew studied the basics of runes, mostly covering what Lestar had already told them the previous night at the dinner table, although he now had a grasp on the meaning of a few more of the symbols that made up the runes on the cards.

The *ding* of the elevator rang and everybody stopped what they were doing.

'Everybody hide!' Lestar ordered.

'Why?' asked Daisy.

'In case whoever it is asks questions about our new friends.'

They quickly took cover behind whatever was closest and large enough to obscure them.

'Mr Moon? Are you here?'

'Ah, Mr Santhorn, sir. What brings you down here?'

'I heard you had come in on your day off. Everything alright at home?'

'Yes, yes. Just had an epiphany on one of the artefacts I was looking into and thought I would quickly run down and see if I was right.'

'And…?'

'It would seem not. I made a little bit of a mess in the blast room.'

'I heard you brought your daughter and some of her friends?'

'I did. I was in town with them and brought them along to take a look at where I work.'

'Where are they now?'

'They got bored quite quickly. You know how kids are these days. They left and went for a walk outside while I quickly tested my hypothesis. I'll meet them at the car once I'm done here.'

'Very well… Look, Lestar. The reason I'm down here is that there are some officers upstairs that would like a word with you.'

'Really? What about?'

'I'm not sure. It's quite serious, Lestar. There were quite a few of them.'

'OK. Well, I guess I'll come up with you then?'

As the elevator doors closed everyone emerged from their hiding places. Daisy in a state of shock.

'We need to find out what's happening. What if something happened to Mum?'

'I'm sure she's fine,' Sarrus reassured her. 'Everybody collect your belongings quickly and we'll head back up. We'll have to be careful though. Your father told that man that we had left.'

As quickly as they could manage they gathered up everything they had brought with them and headed for the elevator, the doors opening as soon as they were close enough. As they stepped inside they stood and waited, Matthew and Safiri stared at the runes working out in their head the combination that Lestar had pressed previously.

'I have no idea, Saf,' Matthew conceded. 'Lestar was pressing runes to get in. It's probably not the same to get back.'

'Some of the runes are in my database,' Safiri said. 'But I don't really have enough information to know for certain what to press.'

'Just take a guess, man. It's the best chance we've got.'

'OK. Give me a second.'

Safiri pressed a combination of runes. Luckily he had seen which one had been pressed to enclose the cage.

'Why is this even an option?' he asked rhetorically.

The elevator began to move, although they had no indication of the direction they were going. The silence was soon broken by the *ding* to indicate they had reached their destination, although whether it was the right destination they did not know.

The door opened to a dark corridor, a small amount of light emanating from next to a thick metal door with a barred window a few metres ahead of them.

It was completely silent and nobody moved. Suddenly echoes of screams and menacing laughter made its way toward them. Through the bars a light could be seen growing larger and brighter, heading toward them.

'Safiri, press something now,' Sam begged.

'Press what. I don't know what I'm doing.'

'Anything. Press anything,' she said, clearly panicked.

'I don't like this, Safiri. Take us anywhere else,' Daisy joined the calls to leave as quickly as possible.

Safiri pressed another combination of runes. The doors closed and they began to move once again. Nobody said a word, however it was clear on everyone's face that they were quite shaken by the experience.

The doors opened again to a large open plan office. Apparently the only part of the building which had a large number of people working.

A Pure man stepped in and keyed in some runes to his desired destination. He looked around at the others sharing the elevator.

'Afternoon, sir,' said Matthew, trying to put on his most charming smile.

'Indeed,' the man replied in a somewhat arrogant tone, seemingly taking no pleasure at having to share the elevator with Matthew and his friends.

The elevator stopped and the man stepped out, hastily walking to wherever he needed to be. This time their stop was something slightly familiar. In front of them was a balustrade. On the other side was the back of the orb with pulsing runes and patterns.

'We're on one of the mezzanines,' Matthew told the group.

They all rushed out and ran as quietly as they could in the opposite direction that the other elevator passenger had exited, to the side of the statue to see down into the reception area. Lestar was standing next to the man from the office, in front of a group of ten officers. In the middle, closest to Lestar and looking like the ring-leader of the group was Officer Doggery.

'What do you mean she's leading a takeover?' Lestar asked, exasperated.

'Her and those other good for nothing Scavenger guards have barricaded themselves in. Clearly it's a hostage situation. Now, enough of the questions. Either you come with us willingly or we're taking you.'

'Taking me where? To do what?'

'To the Scavenger District. You're going to talk her down and let us in. If not, we'll have to take it by force.'

'She's a Defender of the Populous. There's no way she would do anything unless she had good reason and it was lawful.'

'Enough!' shouted Officer Doggery. 'Arrest him. We need to get down there now.'

Doggery turned and walked out toward the cars waiting at the bottom of the stairs. Each car had a crest on it. Presumably something relating to The Decree although it was too far away to make out any of the details. Two other officers shackled Lestar with some sort of energy cuffs before leading him out toward the waiting cars.

Matthew and his friends ran along the mezzanine, around the curve of the building where they could see through the glass.

After Lestar had been shoved into a car and driven away, another officer stepped out of the remaining car and walked over to Doggery, who was still standing where the other car had left.

After a brief discussion they turned and walked back to the car, still in discussion, allowing Matthew to get a good look at him. His jaw dropped.

'Are you guys seeing this?' he asked Safiri and Sam.

'Yep. That's definitely him,' Sam answered.

'Agreed,' said Safiri.

'Who is it?' mumbled Daisy, grabbing hold of Matthew's arms, on the edge of tears.

'It's Finnigan Fisk.'

'Finnigan Fisk?' asked Sarrus. 'Are you one hundred percent sure?'

'One hundred percent,' Matthew confirmed.

The Decree cars pulled away from the stairs, through the carpark and out onto the road where they began driving back toward town.

'We need to follow them!' screamed Daisy.

Kyrral pushed past them all, up to the glass. He clenched his fist which seemed to become solid stone, no longer just a hard skin.

Pulling his arm back he rocketed his fist forward into the glass, keen to exit The Office of Magic as quickly as possible and not considering that they were a few levels above ground.

The glass, responding to the force of Kyrral's punch, rippled like water. A glow intensified where Kyrral's hand connected and exploded, throwing Kyrral back through the air where he crashed and rolled a few times before coming to a stop.

'Crap,' Matthew responded, now knowing what Lestar meant regarding the security of the glass.

'Hey! You kids get down here now!' the man who summoned Lestar was still standing at reception. He spoke for a second to the receptionist who began speaking into a round object in his hand.

'I think security will be on us soon. We need to find a way out of here,' said Sam.

'This way!' commanded Sarrus who began running down the hallway, away from the main entrance. The others quickly followed.

'Do you know where you're going?' Matthew asked.

'No idea.'

They took a sharp left at a large archway assuming it would take them to the far end of the U-shaped building and close to the car.

Either side of the hallway were study rooms filled with bookshelves and desks. There were a few people attempting to get work done, glaring at the doorway to see what the commotion was as the group ran past.

Reaching a room at the end of the hall they ran in and shut the door. Windows on the opposite side of the room proved their navigation was correct.

'Kyrral! Block that door!' Matthew shouted as he ran to the window in the corner of the room, nearest to the car park. A quick tap on the window confirmed his suspicion that the same protection was also in effect throughout the building. Tapping the stone walls, however did not have the same effect.

'I think this force field is only the windows. Care to try again, Kyrral?'

With a grin he jogged over to the wall, having placed a couple of desks up against the door. Kyrral clenched his fists and began punching the wall as hard as he could. Chips of stone fell to the floor as dust began to fill the air around him. In quick time the remainder of one of the stones which had taken the brunt of the punches fell out of the wall and to the ground below. Having severely weakened the wall a large hole was quickly created, large enough for each of them to get through.

'Now we just need a way down,' Safiri pointed out.

'Everyone take a look around. See if you can find any rope,' Matthew commanded.

They opened cupboards and desks as quickly as they could, finding nothing but books and rune writing equipment.

'How about this?' asked Daisy.

She was standing at a wardrobe where a fire hose, similar to that used by Lestar, was wound up on the back.

'Perfect,' said Matthew. 'Bring it over here.'

Daisy took the end of the hose and pulled it over to where Matthew was standing. Matthew took it from her and threw the end through the hole, over the side of the building. He began pulling the hose to lengthen their makeshift rope to freedom. Quickly the slack ended and the hose was at its longest.

'Dammit! That's nowhere near far enough!' he shouted.

Banging came from the blocked door.

'Open this door! This is your one and only chance!' came a shout from the other side.

Matthew paused for a second then reached into his pocket and pulled out a card.

'Perfect,' he said, grinning.

Do I wanna know what you're planning?' asked Safiri.

'Nope,' Matthew replied, pulling the hose back up. 'Kyrral, fire the water out the hole on a downward angle. Make sure you keep as low to the ground as you can and start spraying from just inside the room.'

Kyrral did as requested. The powerful jet sprayed out the hole angling down toward the ground, curving slightly down with gravity.

'Let's hope this card does what I think it does.'

As the banging on the door intensified Matthew took a breath and activated the rune. A jet of ice flakes coned out from Matthew's hand. Upon touching the water it froze solid, creating a thick sheet of ice.

'Grab a desk and turn it upside down. We're gonna ride this

thing out of here.'

With no time to argue and no better ideas the group complied. They upturned two desks, fitting three per desk and set them upon the sheet of ice sitting on the edge of the wall, one behind the other. Kyrral was still spraying water out over the ice ahead of them.

'Everyone get on quickly.'

Matthew, Kyrral and Daisy took the leading desk. Matthew in front, Kyrral sitting behind, holding the hose beside Matthew and spraying it out in front of them. Daisy held onto Kyrral as tight as she could. Safiri, Sam and Sarrus sat on the second desk.

'Follow us as soon as we go. Kyrral, let go of the hose once it's stretched out as far as it will go. Oh, and push us off.'

Kyrral nodded acknowledgment and pushed them forward, gliding smoothly along the ice.

Matthew activated the rune again, freezing the water in front of him, creating a slide of ice as they continued forward, gaining speed. The force of water reduced quickly as Kyrral discarded the hose, increasing the steepness of the slide, stopping completely a few metres off the ground. The speed of the desk allowed them to travel through the air and safely onto the grass in the field beside the car park, albeit with an uncomfortable bump. They quickly slid to a stop with the grip of the grass.

Matthew, Kyrral and Daisy quickly jumped off as the second desk crashed in the now empty lead desk.

'I can't believe that worked,' said Matthew, puffing for air as he lay on his back.

Kyrral lifted him up by the shirt and they ran as fast as they could to the car, not wishing to push their luck any further. Daisy opened the doors and jumped into the driver's seat, Kyrral beside her in the front. The car seemed to react to her touch as it did Lestar. Safiri, Sam and Sarrus took the back seat before Matthew dove onto their laps.

'Let's get out of here!' he shouted.

Chapter Seventeen
Sneaky, Sneaky

As the crew neared the park under which the Scavengers lived, the presence of the police arm of The Decree became more notable. Small groups stood on street corners keeping watch. Deciding to remain as indiscreet as possible they drove around to the other side of the river and parked a little way down the street.

As they walked alongside the river, past the townhouses, the thought hit Matthew that nobody else was around.

'Where is everybody?' he asked the group.

'I don't know,' Daisy replied. 'But it's pretty strange that nobody else is on the street. I get that sometimes it's quiet but never like this.'

Continuing on down the street Matthew could begin to hear an announcement over some kind of public address system.

'The park and surrounding area is now under the control of The Decree. Vacate the area immediately or you will be arrested… The park and surrounding area is now under the control of The Decree. Vacate the area immediately or you will be arrested…' The announcement continued on loop.

Taking refuge in the front hedges of the nearest townhouse discussion was had as to what the next course of action should be.

'Has anyone actually seen any police yet?' asked Sam.

'No, however we still have some distance before reaching the Scavenger District. Someone will need to scout ahead,' Sarrus replied.

'Daisy and I will go,' offered Matthew. 'Daisy doesn't look a threat and I can pass as a lower class Pure, right? It'll look like we're just taking a stroll if anyone asks and come straight back without getting into any trouble. Anything you can pick up with your glasses, Saf?'

'No. We're still too far away for my suit to pick up anything.'

'OK. You ready, Daisy?'

'Yes. Let's go.'

Kyrral turned to Daisy and took her by the arm.

'Don't react to anything you see or hear. Just have a look and come straight back,' he said to her.

'Don't worry Kyrral, I'll take care of her,' Matthew reassured.

The remainder of the group stayed in the cover of the hedges while Matthew and Daisy walked up the street. It wasn't too long before they could see the area surrounding the entrance to the Scavenger District.

Squads of police were gathered at the top of the ramp that led down to the door. A couple of Stroen officers stood behind a short force shield creating a barrier across the bridge near the entrance.

'Oi! What are you two doing there! Announcement says to keep away.'

'Oh, apologies officers,' Matthew began. 'We live down the street and wanted to see what all the commotion was about. Say, what is going on here?'

'Apparently the Scavengers are causing trouble. Being led by some Fenlis woman,'

Daisy gripped Matthew's arm who promptly rested his other hand on hers for comfort.

'Strange,' said Matthew. 'We haven't heard any trouble.'

'Yeah, well they've got a hoard of dangerous, illegal artefacts so we had to act quickly after the tip off. Can't be too careful with these types. Need to nip it in the bud before it gets out of hand. Anyway, you two better get back home. We've got it all under control here.'

'Certainly, officer. Thank you for your service.'

Matthew turned and began walking back to the group, pulling Daisy who hadn't moved. He took this opportunity to look across the river to see if there was anything else of note. He could see on the other side of the bridge Lestar, still handcuffed, standing beside a couple of police officers. One was Doggery, the other, who looked more high ranking based on his uniform, Matthew didn't recognise from The Office of Magic. Matthew decided to shield Daisy from seeing her father for the moment and avoid any possible issue that may arise from it.

Crawling back into the hedges Matthew updated the others on the information he had gathered.

'There are heaps of police who look like they're ready to bust in and start taking out Scavengers. Lestar is there with Doggery and another officer.'

'What! Why didn't you tell me?!' Daisy shouted.

'Calm down,' said Matthew. 'This reaction is why. You completely froze when they mentioned your mum.'

'Who did?' asked Sarrus.

'There were two officers on the bridge and some kind of force barricade. We told them we lived here and that we were just trying to find out what was going on. Apparently someone has tipped off the cops that the Scavengers have a hoard of artefacts, that they're causing trouble and are being led by a Fenlis woman.'

Daisy interrupted. 'It's all lies. There's no way that mum or the Scavengers would do anything like that.'

'We know, Daisy,' said Sam, giving Daisy a hug.

'Madonny has only been there for, at most, a few hours. There's no way The Decree or The Authority could've approved an operation of this size this quickly, especially not based on evidence this weak,' Sarrus said trying to work out how it had gotten to this point.

'I don't think they got approval,' Matthew said. 'The officer said they had to act quickly after the tip off. The other guy with Doggery looks like he might have a bit more authority based on his uniform. I didn't see Finnigan there, though.'

'We need to get a closer look at what's happening over there,' said Sarrus.

'I can't see how. There's police everywhere. They'll see us coming.'

'Not if we approach where they aren't looking,' Safiri interrupted. 'There's a brick overhang under these paths, over the river. If someone can stick to the beams that go between the solid wall and the overhang then they should be able to get to the bridge and underneath to the other side without being seen.'

'Did you have a bit of a look around while we were away?'

'Maybe just a quick peek. That, coupled with everything Sarrus and Kyrral could tell me about the structure allowed my suit to give me a pretty accurate blueprint of what is there.'

'Do you have any more of those vines?' Daisy asked Sarrus.

'Yes. Why?'

'How long do they go?'

'As long as you need them.'

'OK. I need them extra long. We'll tie one end to the beams and I'll get the other ends over to the bridge. Then do the same across the bridge. That way a couple of you can get across.'

'How are you going to get through to tie up the vines?' asked Sam.

Daisy lifted a hand up in front of her face. Long, sharp claws shot out from the ends of her paw-fingers. 'I'm also quite agile when I want to be,' she added.

'Are you sure you're OK to do this Daisy?'

'Yes. I can't sit around and wait. We need to do something now.'

Matthew took a quick look over the barrier to try and get an idea of what they were dealing with.

'OK, guys. Daisy goes first with the vines. When you get to the bridge tie them off and give one a big tug. Kyrral will be holding them at this end. When you give the signal we'll tie them here and work our way across. We can do the same to cross the bridge once we get there. I'll head down first to make sure it's all good. Saf?'

Matthew looked at his friend who stared back, slowly registering what was happening.

'Oh, hell no. No way.' The penny finally dropped for Safiri.

'Saf, I need any help your suit can give or at the very least to keep a record of what we hear.'

'I can't do it, man. I can't walk along there.'

'What about crossing through all the branches and stuff to get to the doorway?' Sam pointed out.

'That was different. The worst that could've happened is that I fell into the stream.'

'And? What's the difference?'

'For starters this is way higher… And I don't know where that goes, how to get out and what's in there.'

Matthew was beginning to get frustrated at the amount of time it was taking.

'Mate, there would have been snakes or leeches in that stream. You've got a platform to walk on from start to finish with the vines and beams to hold onto. You'll be fine. We gotta get going now before it's too late. I'll shout you burgers and pizza when we get home if you just come now.'

'You got this, Saf.' Sam took a more positive approach to get Safiri's confidence up to which everyone else promptly joined in.

'Fine. Can I get an extra vine to hold onto?'

'Good idea, Saf.' Said Matthew. 'We'll tie one each around our waist. Kyrral, you good with that?'

'No problem.'

'Cool. Sarrus, get cracking on those vines so Daisy can get over to the bridge. Daisy, once you get there tie them up as tight as you can. Let's go team!'

Sarrus reached into her pockets and retrieved handfuls of seeds. Sitting on the ground and crossing her legs she closed her eyes and concentrated, appearing very much like she was in a state of meditation. As her hands began to glow emerald, vines emerged from the sides of her fists, thickening and intertwining around each other to create a thick, strong rope.

Once the vines had become long enough Kyrral tied the end around Daisy. Waiting a little while longer in order to create a sufficient amount of slack, Daisy climbed over the barrier to be lowered down by Kyrral.

Reaching the bottom of the overhang Daisy took hold of the beam and disappeared out of sight.

'OK. I'm in!' Came the call from Daisy. 'Just let it thread through, Kyrral, and I'll let you know once I'm at the bridge. I'll give it a few seconds before I go to let the slack get out some more.'

'Be safe, Daisy!' Sam called out as the faint tapping of Daisy's nails could be heard on the metal beams.

Daisy proved her agility as Kyrral soon felt the tug of the vines in his hand. He gave a light tug back to confirm the message had been received.

'OK, Sarrus. Cut that one off. Kyrral, tie it to the barrier. We need to start on our ones. How are you feeling Sarrus?'

'Don't worry about me,' she replied. 'I can keep this up far longer that what you'll need. It just takes a bit of concentration to get them done quickly.'

'Cool. Sam, you just chill here until we get back.'

'Ahhhh, nope.'

Sam jumped over the barrier and grabbed hold of the vine that had been tied up. Climbing down, she was quickly out of sight by the time Matthew and Safiri peered over.

'Ah crap!' said Matthew. 'We gotta get going, Saf.' Before Safiri could protest he added. 'At least you've got a bunch of info being fed through your glasses. You've got nothing to worry about. Get going and I'll be right behind you.'

Kyrral tied one of the vines around Safiri's waist and lowered him down as Safiri guided himself with the tied vine. As soon as Safiri called up that he was in Matthew did the same.

Once he had reached the bottom of the overhang, where a metal beam ran along the bottom of the bricks, Matthew pulled himself underneath, taking hold of another beam which stretched across from the solid wall on the other side. Pulling himself up, he shouted out to Kyrral to confirm that he had safe footing.

From inside it looked like a tunnel of crossing beams. Some crossed along the base between the main beams from the wall and some crossed from the base to the top. The crossing of the beams made it impossible to see too far ahead, taking away any view of the end and his friends in front of him.

As Matthew walked along the vines and climbed over crossing beams he couldn't help but think back to the trail along the stream to get to the doorway, chuckling to himself that he was once again in a similar situation.

The structured and repetitive nature of the beams actually made it quite easy to get through, although the vine didn't exactly take the same path as Matthew given Daisy's size and advantages at traversing the tunnel.

Reaching the bridge, Matthew found his friends casually resting against the final beams that were still obscured by the overhanging wall.

'Feels like we've done this before, hey?' Matthew said with a smile on his face.

'Kinda felt like crossing all those branches,' Sam confirmed.

'What do we have out there, Daisy?' Matthew asked.

'Well, the bridge is made up of a load of beams which arch. It's pretty similar to what we just went through except we don't have the cover of the wall. We also need to be really careful when we get to the middle. The arching of the beams leaves it a little exposed.'

'OK. Well have a little more rest while we get these other vines through.'

Matthew and Safiri removed the vines from their waist and gave a hard tug to make sure Kyrral knew that they were in place, allowing Sarrus to finally stop creating vines and take a rest of her own. After a minute of waiting to be sure the vines were free they began pulling them through the tunnel.

Once they had the full vines wound up in their possession they tied an end of each around Daisy and once again let her scurry through the beams, as close as possible to the stone decking underneath the bridge, to create a marginally safer route to the other side.

Again, Daisy tugged the vines to indicated she had reached her destination and tied her ends to the beams.

'OK, guys. Let's take it slow, safe and quiet.'

'Got it,' confirmed Safiri as he began climbing to get to the highest possible point before moving out of the cover of the overhang and into the beams within the bridge.

'Surprised to see Saf keen to go first,' said Sam.

'I get the feeling that his glasses are telling him exactly where he needs to go. Gives him an extra bit of confidence that he'll be safe.'

Sam followed Safiri, taking the exact same path, followed by Matthew. Once inside the beams of the bridge they followed the vines which were threaded through by Daisy. The extra width of the bridge compared to the tunnel made their pathway the same and quite easy to negotiate. The only factor slowing them down was ensuring that they remained quiet so as not to draw any attention from the officers standing on and around the bridge.

Reaching the other side of the bridge they hugged the wall, getting as close as they could to where Doggery was standing with the high ranking officer.

Matthew closed his eyes in an attempt to extend his hearing. He should be able to pick out Doggery and Lestar and work from there.

'High Inspector Morssel,' Said Officer Doggery. 'I've just been informed that we have the entire area closed off. Nobody is coming anywhere near here. Every officer can be trusted. They're either on board or know enough to ensure the perimeter is enforced by order of The Decree and follow through on those orders without question.'

'Excellent work Doggery,' said High Inspector Morssel, 'Our mission will soon be accomplished after so long.'

Matthew sensed something was off. His brow furrowed, Matthew looked at Safiri and Sam, mouthing the question *Finnigan?*

They both nodded their confirmation.

Matthew ran through his mind what he had seen earlier. The man who sounded like Finnigan most definitely didn't look like him from a distance. He decided he needed to take a closer look. Not wanting to take the time to second guess his decision he quickly moved toward the side of the bridge.

'Matthew!' Sam hissed as she, Safiri and Daisy all reached out to grab him.

Matthew was too quick for them, reaching the beams that

obscured them from the officers of The Decree and climbed out into the open, poking his head out slightly first to see if anyone would spot him.

He quickly, but quietly, climbed the decking of the bridge where it met the wall. Nearing the top, Matthew put his right hand on the wall, as well as his right foot, while keeping his left side gripping onto the top of the bridge. Slowly he moved his head up until his eyes could see over the top of the wall at the base of the black iron fence.

Matthew held himself steady as he listened to the conversation between Doggery and Morssel.

'Soon we'll be rid of these Scavengers for good and the cavern will be ours. Once I'm established here again we'll look at expanding past the wall.'

Despite the appearance, Matthew was now one hundred percent convinced that High Inspector Morssel was Finnigan.

'Do you have any idea what's beyond the wall yet?' Doggery asked.

'Not yet, Doggery, but it's just a matter of time. As for right now, make sure everyone knows that Madonny Moon is the leader of the Scavenger uprising and that everyone is in place once we get in to ensure there's no peaceful resolution. Anyone who is alive after we're done will be working for me.' Finnigan put up air quotes as he said *working* just in case there was any doubt that he was intending to make them slaves.

'Start sending down the troops to bash down those doors so we can get this ov-'

Matthew's foot slipped on the wall causing him to let go and swing back into the bridge, hitting it with his chest and just managing to keep hold with his left hand. Some debris from the wall fell into the river and Matthew could hear footsteps on the path heading his way.

Quickly, Matthew dropped down under the decking and moved inside the bridge before any of the officers made it to the fence, blowing their cover. He sat, huddled against the wall and beam, as small as he could holding his chest, trying to take in air without making a sound.

Safiri, Sam and Daisy froze in position, staring at Matthew who stared back, eyes wide with fear of being found.

'Must be a crinler,' came the voice of Doggery after a few agonising moments. 'I hate those things. Can't see why we can't just wipe out the lot of them.'

The sound of footsteps started again and faded away as Doggery walked back to Finnigan.

Matthew took a few deep breaths and headed back over to his friends.

Safiri punched him in the arm. 'Don't you ever do that again!' he hissed, trying to keep quiet.

'Sorry. I had to know if it was him.'

'And?' Sam asked.

'It's definitely him. He must have a ring or something, like mine. Daisy, he's going to fake an uprising and pin it all on your mum. He wants the Scavenger District all to himself.'

'He must be looking to use the entire cavern as his headquarters,' Safiri deduced.

'He definitely sounds like he wants to get back into Dusk. Maybe the psychic trade isn't working for him anymore or maybe he's sick of artefacts not working.'

'In any case, we've got what we came for,' Sam interrupted. 'Let's get back to Sarrus and Kyrral and work out what the hell we're going to do about it.'

It didn't take them long to get back, although it was far harder getting back up than it had been getting down. Daisy had no trouble using her claws to climb up the vines. Sam also managed with relative ease. Safiri got through, although with plenty of struggle and groaning. The pounding of Matthew's chest caused him to stop shortly after reaching the bottom, before beginning his climb up.

'What's the problem?' Daisy asked, as they all watched Matthew.

'I can't do it. I'm stuck. My chest is killing me!'

'What are we going to do?' asked Safiri.

Daisy climbed over the fence one again and ran down the vine with her long nails. She leaped over Matthew, grabbing onto the vine on the other side of him.

'Kyrral, when I cut, you pull, OK?'

Kyrral gave a nod and took hold of the vine in his hands just below where it was tied to the fence.

'Just hold on Matthew. I'm going to cut the vine and hang onto your neck while Kyrral pulls us up. Don't let go or we'll be crinler dinner.'

Daisy climbed onto Matthew's back with one arm around his neck and chest, causing Matthew to wince in pain. With the other hand she extended her claws and sliced down onto the vine, cutting it clean, then putting her other arm around Matthew.

Matthew wheezed as Kyrral pulled them up and over the fence. Once over he fell onto his hands and knees, gasping for air.

After a few moments Sarrus gave Matthew some seeds.

'Eat them for the pain. You'll be OK.'

Matthew sat against the fence and swallowed the seeds. A warmth grew in his chest and then subsided, along with the pain.

'Thanks, Sarrus. You too, Daisy and Kyrral. Without you guys I would've been screwed.'

'You're welcome, Matthew. Please, tell me what happened.'

Sarrus and Kyrral were updated as to how the group faired and all that they were able to discover about Finnigan and his plans.

'What are we going to do, Sarrus?' Daisy pleaded for some

direction.

'I'm not sure, Daisy. Clearly we can't get in through the tunnel and we don't have the location of the entrance that Finnigan's men were using to kidnap people.'

'Why wouldn't Finnigan just use that entrance?' Matthew asked.

'I suspect it's too small to get all those officers through quickly. No doubt it would also create more questions as to how they knew about the secret entrance. I would try and plead a case to The Authority to put an end to it all, however we have no evidence.'

After a few harebrained ideas that quickly fell flat Sarrus finally spoke again.

'I've got an idea, however I've never tried anything like it before and have no idea if it will work. It could kill us all.'

'At this point it's all we've got, ' said Matthew. 'If we do nothing Daisy's parents are done.'

'Please, Sarrus. We have to try.' Daisy begged.

'Alright. Let's get back to the car and take it to the other side of the park. We need to get to the Gift Giver as quickly as we can.'

Chapter Eighteen
Make Your Own Path

The group took the long route around the park to the opposite side, safely parking the car a fair distance from where they assumed The Decree would be keeping a perimeter.

The green ribbons in the sky had transitioned to purple as day turned to night. The extra darkness an added advantage in their attempt to reach the Scavenger District.

After a short walk through some streets and into the parkland, the group crouched behind a dense collection of bushes and poked their heads out in an attempt to get an idea of what they were dealing with. Safiri's suit helped map out a possible route to the Gift Giver and clearly show him where the main group of Finnigan's men was situated, despite the darkness.

As luck would have it they were all positioned on the opposite side of the Gift Giver, close to the entrance of the Scavenger District, seemingly ready to storm in once they had bashed open the main doors.

Pairs of officers patrolled the outskirts of the park, although they were scattered far enough apart to manoeuvre quite easily between them. More often than not they were deep in conversation, most likely not privy to the seriousness of the operation.

Sarrus and Daisy pointed out the trees and bushes they needed to avoid to prevent an unwelcome pickup.

It didn't take long for enough data to be stored and analysed by Safiri's suit to plot a safe path through to where Sarrus needed them to be, setting off as soon as it was complete. Reaching the Gift Giver they once again crouched behind some bushes to conceal themselves.

'OK. What now?' Matthew asked Sarrus.

'Now you all wait while I see if I can actually do this.'

Sarrus turned and placed her forehead as well as both hands on the Gift Giver, her hands glowing emerald on the bark. After a few minutes watching and waiting for something to happen, some of the lifeblood pulsing up toward the canopy began to move toward Sarrus.

Matthew instinctively reached out to pull Sarrus away when Kyrral intercepted his arm and pulled him back.

'Wait,' he whispered, calmly.

The lifeblood seemed to flow into Sarrus' hands and head and pulse out again, emerald, returning to blue as it made its way up the massive tree. This continued for some time until Sarrus slowly pushed herself away and turned to the group smiling.

'What happened?' Daisy asked.

'She… spoke to me. Her lifeblood pulsed through me. It was amazing.'

'What did she say?'

'She said she could see through me. She could feel what was happening around her, feel the intentions of the officers at the entrance to the tunnel. I told her what was happening and asked if we could have passage to the Scavenger District.'

'Have passage? How?' Matthew asked.

'You'll see. She's agreed and is willing to help guide me.'

'And you can definitely trust her, right?'

'With our lives,' Sarrus smirked. 'Now everyone keep close. It's going to take a lot of concentration to do this and the tunnel will close behind us.'

A loud bang exploded in the distance, from the other side of the Gift Giver. Everybody froze in place, all concentration going toward listening for what was happening. The bang repeated moments later, then again.

'I think they've started trying to take down the door,' Matthew deduced. 'We gotta do this. Now.'

Lining up close to one another, still crouching low, Sarrus once again placed her hands on the Gift Giver and closed her eyes, her hands glowing emerald. The bark between Sarrus' hands began to split and the trunk unknotted itself to open into a small tunnel.

Sarrus walked forward on her knees as the tunnel began to form and made her way inside, the rest of the group following close behind.

A short way into the tunnel the height increased to the point where they could stand and walk normally. Being upright helped Sarrus concentrate and move through more easily, speeding up their progress.

Following the guiding hand of the Gift Giver, Sarrus steered the group in what felt to be a downward trajectory, occasionally turning for reasons nobody knew.

Finally Sarrus' tunnel broke open to clear air and they each filed out onto a ledge.

'This definitely isn't the Scavenger District,' Safiri pointed out, not that anyone really needed to be told.

'Where the hell are we?' Matthew asked.

'I'm not sure,' Sarrus replied. 'I followed where the Gift Giver was guiding me.

The ledge seemed to be part of a staircase although they could not see to where. Looking up the faint glow of blue lifeblood could be seen as a hazy cloud somewhere far higher than could be judged, at the end of blackness.

A leaf shaped cup jutted out from the wall just above them, golden lifeblood flowing from it and lighting a small area around them. To the left the stairs went up and to the right they went down.

'Which way?' Daisy asked, gipping tightly onto Kyrral's arm.

'Based on how far we've gone and the angle at which we descended there's no way we're anywhere near low enough to get into the Scavenger District,' Safiri deduced. 'I say we go down.'

'Makes sense,' Matthew agreed. 'I'm with Saf on this one.'

'Me too,' Sam confirmed.

After quickly coming to a consensus they began, in single file, to descending the stairs.

As they continued down the stairs a streak of blue lifeblood would occasionally pulse down the wall and ignite one of the cups, further lighting their path.

After a few more minutes walking down the stairs the group came to another ledge. Looking up Matthew could now get a better idea of what they were traversing.

'Take a look guys,' he said. 'The stairs are spiralling down the walls of this place.'

'It looks like a giant cylinder,' Safiri added. 'We must be in the centre of the Gift Giver. I would have never though that it would be hollow.'

'Why are stairs already here?' asked Sam. 'Did she just build this for us? She did say she'd help.'

'I don't think so,' said Daisy, who was standing on the other side of a doorway in the wall. 'There are more tunnels here.'

Daisy disappeared down a tunnel with more lights seemingly being turned on by the Gift Giver as she moved through.

'Come look at this!' came a shout from Daisy.

The others scrambled down the tunnel following Daisy's voice. They found her standing in a small room. A number of crude beds were carved into the walls. A pile of soft leaves covering each, although most of the leaves had died and disintegrated on touch.

A large opening in the side wall exposed the room to the main hollow centre of the gift giver, a few wooden cups and bowls sat on the ledge.

'Who the hell lives here?' Matthew asked.

'The Gift Giver didn't tell me anything about this,' said Sarrus. 'Look at this on the wall.'

Sarrus pointed out a number of carvings in the wall, some partially worn away. They depicted men with wings, long hair and spikes jutting from their forearms and lower legs.

'Looks like the kind of stuff you'd find on the walls of the pyramids in Egypt,' Sam noted. 'The pyramids are giant structures created by people thousands of years ago. Maybe these people cleared out a long time ago as well.'

'Definitely doesn't look like anyone is around here anymore,' Matthew agreed.

'We should get going, guys. We need to get to the Scavengers and warn Mum.' Daisy reminding everyone of the task at hand.

'Agreed. Let's keep moving,' Sarrus added, Kyrral also nodding agreement.

Continuing down the stairs was more of the same, occasionally reaching a ledge where tunnels branched off to rooms which housed the mysterious occupants of the Gift Giver.

Finally they reached the bottom of the stairs. A cloudy pool of blue lifeblood emanated from the knotted wood floor, sparking upward. Pulses of lifeblood in the walls converged on a point in front of Sarrus.

'This must be where we have to tunnel out. Everyone get behind me.'

Sarrus once again touched the walls and activated her power, opening a tunnel toward their final destination.

Sarrus' tunnel opened to the plaza surrounding the base of the Gift Giver in the Scavenger District. Where it was a jovial scene when last the group were there, it now looked as if they had walked in the morning after a riot.

Mason and Tark were at the edge of the plaza facing the entrance, shouting orders and directing where upturned tables and benches were to be placed. The marketplace in front of them had been torn down and replaced with rows of stacked furniture and whatever else could be found to create makeshift cover, trenches also having been dug in-between.

'Seems they know what's coming,' said Matthew.

'We need to find Mum and Ganlin,' Daisy reminded them. 'Mason! Tark!' she shouted as she ran over find some answers, the others close behind.

'How did you guys get in here?' asked Mason.

'It's a long story. You know what's waiting outside?'

'Yes. We were out patrolling the area when they all turned up. They herded everyone out of the park and set up a perimeter. I've never seen so many of them in one place. We were lucky to get back in before the doors were locked up and barricaded. Everything was already being taken down by the time we got here. We're making sure there's as much protection as possible. If you want to help, get all the families to the amphitheater. Everyone's holing up in the tunnels behind it.'

'We need to find Mum and Ganlin. Do you know where they are?'

'HQ is in the tavern next to the medical station. You'll probably find them there. Battlements have been set up around that area with a path cleared to retreat to the amphitheater if it starts to fall.

I don't know what we did but they're not messing around out there.'

Daisy immediately turned and began running to the other side of the plaza to find Madonny.

'Thanks guys!' Matthew shouted as the rest scrambled to follow.

The battlements hadn't yet been completed making it an easy task to get in. The ingenuity of the Scavengers was again on show, making impressive structures out the scarce resource they had, in incredibly quick time. The battlements were constructed of a combination of stone, metal and wood repurposed from the markets, mageball track stand, parts of the residential platforms and wherever else the Scavengers could salvage them.

A large table was set up in the middle of what used to be the tavern, a number of smaller tables were set up around it with small groups in discussion. Occasionally some people would run around passing along notes and orders. Ganlin was deep in discussion with a number of other senior guards. Madonny was standing next to Ganlin, passing on what intelligence she could about The Authority and The Decree that was relevant to the situation.

'Mum!' Daisy shouted running straight into her arms.

'Daisy! Children! How did you get here… Where's Lestar.'

'They took him, Mum,' tears welling up in her eyes. 'We were at Dad's office and they just arrested him… for no reason!'

Sarrus interrupted, trying to add a steady voice to the exchange of information.

'They said you've staged a takeover of the District, that there are hostages. They expect Lestar to talk you down. He didn't go willingly.'

'Oh, my dear Lestar. What have we gotten into?'

'I don't think they'll hurt him. He serves a purpose for them at this stage.'

'I can shed some light on why this is happening,' said Matthew.

'We managed to do a bit of scouting before getting in. It's all being led by High Inspector Morssel.'

'I've never heard of him… and I know all the big players in this game.'

'That's because he doesn't exist. It's Finnigan Fisk. I saw him when they took Lestar at The Office of Magic. When we got to the river, and managed to get close enough to get a bit of intel, we worked out he's using something to disguise himself. I know that voice anywhere, though.'

By now Ganlin had finished strategising and was listening intently to the new information Matthew was providing.

'How did you get close enough to get any of this?' he asked. 'And while we're on the topic of impossible feats, how did you get in here? We've got this place locked down.'

'Let's just say it turns out we're a pretty resourceful crew. We can give you all the details after we've gotten out of this mess.'

'The point is,' Sarrus cut in again, 'Finnigan has plans to take over the entire cavern for whatever scheme he's got in motion and is planning on doing something outside the wall. Most of the officers out there are in on it and the others are too low on the hierarchy to question the orders.'

'The wall? What's he gonna do out there?' asked Ganlin.

'I don't think he even knows yet,' Matthew answered. 'I think he just really hates it here and Dawn isn't working out too well for him. In any case, he won't get that far if we stop him here.'

'How are you planning on stopping him?' Safiri asked Ganlin.

Ganlin showed them over to the large table. There were various pieces of paper lined up together to create a large map of the cavern. Ganlin pointed to scraps and objects that were plotted on the map to depict different groups of guards and people who are fit and able to defend their home.

'You getting all this, Saf?' Matthew asked.

'Yep.'

'Cool. How about you guys work out the best way to hold Finnigan back? We need to think of a way to put an end to it, otherwise they'll just keep coming until they overrun us.'

'They're The Authority,' said Sam. 'How can we put an end to it? They control it all.'

'Not necessarily, Sam,' Madonny stroked Daisy's head as she pondered the situation. 'Finnigan has a lot of enemies which is why he fled initially. The fact that he's commandeered the constabulary is sure to anger even more. If we can get word out to the right people, powerful people, then they can stop him.'

'If we can get my mother involved she can quickly get word to those in power in The Authority,' Sarrus was beginning to form a plan. 'If you can hold out here until they send support then we may be able to get through this.'

'But why would they help us?' asked Sam. 'They all detest the Scavengers.'

'Because the Scavengers mine the lifeblood. If Finnigan gets control of the lifeblood he'll have the power to change who's in control of everything. That will be him. The Pure and The Authority won't want to give that up. The way it is now at least the Scavengers have autonomy over their own space. Finnigan will make slaves of everyone here. I'll take Madonny with me back to the surface and try to convince everyone we need to that Finnigan is trying to take over.'

'Sounds like a plan,' agreed Matthew.

'I'll go with you,' Daisy demanded.

'No, Daisy. You stay here and make sure your dad is OK if they bring him in.'

'Before you go, why are they putting all the blame onto you, Maddony? How do they even know you're here?'

'I ran into Officer Doggery on my way here. He warned me not to be messing around with the Svangers today unless I wanted to be counted as one of them when they finally get what's coming to them. I tried to warn him about unprovoked attacks against the Scavengers, or anyone for that matter. It did confuse me how brazen he was about this, especially with me. He's not the most intelligent but he's usually smarter than that. I assume he told Finnigan and they both cooked up this story to make me the scapegoat for all of it. It's no secret that I'm not well liked in those circles. I think Lestar is just a smokescreen to make it look like they're trying a peaceful approach first.'

'This is our fault,' said Matthew, bowing his head in shame. 'If we hadn't gone to Finnigan, if we hadn't come here, then this wouldn't have happened.'

'It's not your fault, Matthew.' Kyrral reassured, to everyone's shock. 'You said yourself that he told you he had no way of getting back. He was clearly lying to you. This was probably his plan from the start. There's no reason for him to even know you're here.'

'You're probably right, Kyrral. Thanks. Strangely insightful.'

'It's not that strange, Matthew,' Daisy corrected him.

'We better get going, Madonny,' said Sarrus. 'There's no knowing how long this could take, and that's after we get out of here and get to my mother.'

'Agreed. Daisy, you stay strong. Hopefully we can stop this before it begins,' added Maddony.

Sarrus and Madonny disappeared, running out of the battlements and toward the Gift Giver, following the same route the group took through the enormous tree.

Matthew, Sam, Daisy and Kyrral joined Safiri and Ganlin at the map to work out exactly what they were going to do.

'Sarrus and Madonny have gone to try and get the Pure and The Authority to intervene,' Sam updated Safiri and Ganlin on their part of the plan. 'What have you guys got?'

Safiri pointed to the various objects on the map as he explained the situation. 'We've got groups here, here, here and here as the initial line in front of the main stairs. The makeshift trenches should do a pretty good job of giving cover to everyone. The tunnels will funnel Finnigan's men in pretty tight so they'll be slow to come through. We've got more lines behind who can push forward when needed. These guys,' Safiri pointed to a group of pins. 'Will be running between the groups passing messages. We've also made some different coloured flags that they can hold to give quick status updates.

'Ganlin's men have been split up. Half are going with the groups. Two in each to command the Scavengers. A quarter are here to man the battlements and control the war room. The other quarter are with the rest of the Scavengers at the amphitheater tunnels.'

'Where do the amphitheater tunnels go?' Matthew asked.

'Some go to the lifeblood mines,' said Ganlin. 'Others we have no idea. Most are blocked either by cave-ins, old traps or force shields that have been there longer than any of us. We can try them if we're desperate but nobody has them mapped so there's no telling where we'll end up, if they lead anywhere at all. Speaking of, you should all head there now. I can't imagine it'll take them too much longer to break through.'

'Hell no!' Matthew barked, surprising even himself. 'We're not going to sit and wait this out. We've all got things we can offer. Kyrral is a tank, Safiri is apparently a strategic genius, Daisy is spritely and has some super-sharp nails, I've got my rune cards and Sam isn't scared of anyone.'

'Fine, but you're not going to the front lines. You can stay here with me. Keep an eye out on the battlements until it all kicks off. But if they get too close I need you to run as quickly as you can to the amphitheater. I can't protect you all if they make it this far. By then we're in real trouble.'

'I guess we can agree to that,' said Matthew with a wry smile on his face. Despite having no idea where this newfound confidence came from all he could think to himself was: *If things get bad there's nothing you can do to hold me back.*

Chapter Nineteen
The Siege

Matthew, Sam and Safiri stood upon the battlements, watching out over the Scavenger District at everyone scurrying about, trying to complete preparations before the unwelcome guests bashed through the doors.

Safiri occasionally passed messages down to Ganlin when he noticed anything that didn't quite match up to their plans. The combination of suit and glasses giving him a perfect picture of where everything and everybody was supposed to be.

Daisy was helping the nurses prepare the medical tent for the inevitable influx of injured Scavengers while Kyrral joined the ranks of the guard and kept close to Ganlin as a backup messenger should they need more resources in that department.

Sam turned to Matthew as they both leaned against the parapet which was to provide cover for those stationed as the last line before a retreat was necessary. 'How did we get here, Matthew?' she asked with furrowed brow. 'Two days ago we were back home working at a café and now we're about to go into battle.'

'I know. It all escalated pretty quickly. I probably should have seen it coming. Grandad's stories weren't always all fun and games. I always found those the most entertaining. Looking at it from this perspective it doesn't seem so cool. I'm pretty much crapping my pants right now. What's even more surprising, though, is Saf. He's always so hesitant but look at him now.'

They both turned to look at Safiri who was shouting reports down to Ganlin.

'I guess he's gone into autopilot now that he's got a problem to solve and all the information to process,' Sam offered up the only conclusion she could come up with. 'I've definitely seen a bit of a change the more he's used his suit. Maybe the advantage it gives him has given him more confidence.'

Safiri joined them once again, looking out over the soon to be battlefield.

'How are you doing, Saf?' Matthew asked. 'You look like you know what you're doing out here.'

'I've never been so scared in my life. I dread the second that my suit stops giving me info. Right now it's keeping me busy and distracted from what's going to come. Look at what we're dealing with here.' Safiri pointed down to a pile of rocks and stones in a basket next to them. 'With everything we've seen in Dusk there's no way we can hold them off by throwing stones at them. They're guaranteed to have some laser guns or something. What the hell were we thinking coming here? This is no place for us.'

Matthew and Sam glanced at each other before both wrapping their arms around Safiri.

'What's happening here?' he asked.

'Nothing,' Sam replied. 'You're still our Saf.'

Safiri shrugged them off. 'You've both gone nuts.'

'Can't dispute that,' Matthew agreed, allowing a moment of levity.

BANG! Finnigan's officers had made it to the inner doors, a thunderous echo exploded through the cavern with every attempt to take the giant doors down.

'Everybody in position now!' shouted Ganlin, the message echoed by those in the makeshift trenches.

Daisy ran out from the medical tent and embraced Kyrral. 'Be safe… You guys too!' she shouted to Dawn Crew up on the battlements.

'And you! Stay out of trouble!' Matthew shouted.

Kyrral gave a nod in their direction, already looking the part of a soldier.

'This is it, guys.' Matthew said to his friends. 'Let's make sure we get home.'

After giving each other a hug they spread out slightly along the battlements, each in front of a basket of rocks, Safiri closest to where he could communicate with Ganlin.

After a few more thunderous explosions the doors blasted into the cavern allowing the officers to pour in and spread out along the massive ledge above what used to be the market.

An eerie silence filled the Scavenger District as both sides held and awaited instruction. The tense atmosphere getting to Matthew as a bead of sweat formed on his brow and ran down his cheek. Reaching into his shirt he took hold of the necklace George had left. He closed his eyes and begged his grandad for help to keep he and his friends safe from the impending attack.

'Grandad… If you can hear me, I'm in a bit of a crappy situation. I suspect you've been here before. Please help get us out of this. I'm way out of my depth. I've got no idea what to do. Please help us.'

A slight scuffle could be seen from Finnigan's men as they parted to make way for Finnigan and his entourage. Finnigan, still under the guise of High Inspector Morssel, reached the front of his army with Officer Doggery and, a still restrained, Lestar Moon.

Above him appeared an enlarged lifeblood projection of the top half of his body.

'Scavengers!' his voice boomed out through the projection, filling the cavern. 'By order of The Decree, acting on behalf of The Authority, I order you to stand down, surrender and hand over Madonny Moon on charges of conspiracy to incite riots and violence against The Authority.'

Ganlin ran up to the battlements. 'And who are you?!' he shouted.

'Jeez, that man's voice can carry,' Matthew said to Sam, who didn't move.

Sam was frozen with fear. Her eyes were wide, staring straight at Finnigan's men.

'I am High Inspector Morssel… and who am I speaking to?'

'I'm Ganlin, Captain of the Scavenger guard! I've never heard of a High Inspector Morssel and I know everyone who's in charge at The Decree!'

'Apparently not, sir. Now stand down and hand over Mrs Moon. I will not ask again.'

'Apologies… sir! I don't recognise your authority here! You are in violation of our treaty with The Authority and I advise you vacate this district immediately!'

'How dare you speak to me this way! I am The Authority here!'

The projection dissipated and moments later a regiment of officers began descending the stairs toward the no man's land that was cleared in front of the front line trenches of the Scavengers.

Once the officers finished descending the stairs and lined up, three rows deep, they stood and waited. After a brief pause the first line threw grenades at the trenches in front of them. As they arced through the air they hit some kind of invisible barrier, bursting open with flashes of electricity and falling harmlessly to the floor metres short of the trenches.

A smile appeared on Ganlin's face.

'What just happened, Ganlin?' Matthew asked.

'We did a bit of work on creating some barriers based on the grav-boots. We were counting on them wasting spark grenades first. They'll soon work out that the barrier doesn't go very high and also won't stop them walking straight underneath and into the trenches. We had to decide what angle would give us the most impact with its limited range. Hopefully they'll be out of grenades by the time they smarten up to what's going on.'

Another round of grenades flew from the officers and fell to the dirt with no harm to the Scavengers.

The first line drew batons from their belts and with a touch of a device on their forearms extended an oval-shaped force shield in front of them. In addition, they also activated a blue ring of energy which pulsed around the top of their black batons.

Holding their shields in front of them they began to march forward. Half way into no man's land they stopped and bent down to one knee. The second line, who were marching behind them, threw another round of grenades. This time, as they were much closer, they were able to throw the grenades higher and further, clearing the barrier and sailing into the maze of trenches that the scavengers had created. Shocks of electricity shot from the grenades where they impacted.

Any of the Scavengers within range of the blast seized as electricity raced through their bodies, after which they collapsed to the dirt. Whether they were dead or just knocked out, Matthew could not tell.

The first line marched forward again. Reaching the discharged grenades which had been sacrificed previously, the officers stopped. Reaching their batons forward they slowly crept forward, expecting to hit the invisible barrier.

A few meters beyond the line of grenades was the point where they knew there was nothing stopping them from proceeding further. They were so close to the trenches they could almost see in.

'Looks like the ruse is done.' Ganlin conceded.

He pulled a large bone horn from his belt and put it to his mouth. The horn split off into two symmetrical, looping horns. Ganlin blew as hard as he could. A deep, resonating echo filled the cavern.

Shouts reverberated from the trenches as Scavengers rose to meet their attackers with tools, planks of wood and whatever they could find that they could swing at the enemy. Some lifted their head just long enough to throw objects, mostly rocks, at the officers who were advancing upon them.

Ganlin took his leave from the battlements and returned to the war room, awaiting status updates in order to continue strategising and hold the cavern for as long as they needed for help to arrive.

The officers blocked whatever was thrown at them with their shields, seemingly impervious to the force of whatever object flew in their direction. Whenever a chance presented itself they thrust their batons at the Scavengers, shocking wherever they connected on their opponent. This was usually followed up with a hefty swing of the baton to bludgeon and disable their hapless victim.

As the first line of officers descended into the trenches the second advanced with their shields and batons ready, leaving the third line to continue launching grenades at the Scavengers who were yet to be engaged.

The next regiment of Finnigan's men made their way down the stairs to take the place of the first wave. As they pressed forward each line took the place of that which proceeded it.

The maze of trenches was quickly being overrun as some Scavengers retreated in order to try and regain their footing and hold off the oncoming force.

Matthew looked to his left and right. Safiri was shouting at Ganlin, trying his best to update him on the progress of the defence of the Scavengers' home.

Sam was still petrified, eyes wide.

'Sam! Sam!' he shouted to snap her out of it, although it was to no avail.

'We're outnumbered and out-armed!' Mason shouted from a couple of trenches in front of the battlements. He had better luck than most at slowing down the enemy and removing some from the fight, although Matthew knew it was more skill than luck.

Most of the untrained Scavengers were now lying motionless on the battlefield, either as a result of grenades or the unstoppable advance of the infantry through their defences.

Those that remained were beginning to get pinned back to the walls of the battlements.

Rocks were being discharged from above as best they could while avoiding the Scavengers that were still fighting in the trenches.

'Tark!' shouted Safiri who was looking down at the man now surrounded and taunted by five officers. Each of them began beating down on the hapless man who attempted in vain to cover himself from the blows.

Mason, after a quick punch to the face of his nearest assailant, ran as swiftly as he could to aid his friend, while those on the battlements attempted to clear his path with a shower of rocks.

Matthew spotted two officers emerge from the trench nearest to Mason, on course to intercept him before he could reach his friend.

'Mason! Look out!'

It was too late. The first officer barged Mason with his shield, sending him flying into a large metal plate which made part of the wall, the second quickly running past to commence the beating.

A wind rushed from beside Matthew as a giant figure leapt over the parapet to the ground below in support of Mason.

'Kyrral! No!' he shouted once Kyrral had passed into his eye line.

Kyrral's huge frame landed on the ground producing a massive dust cloud. Without taking a second to collect himself he was off running the short distance to aid Mason.

The two officers lifted their shields and braced for impact, their batons ready behind them to swing immediately. They underestimated both Kyrral's size and conviction, sending both flying backward, flat onto their backs.

Kyrral helped Mason back to his feet and they sprinted as fast a they could to where Tark was curled up on the dirt, still taking a beating.

Kyrral bashed through the back of the nearest two while Mason engaged another. They both made quick work of their opponents to give Tark a reprieve. Despite managing to get to his feet Tark was no longer in any condition to help.

Those Scavengers that remained upright coalesced around Kyrral and Mason. They were severely outmatched despite Finnigan not sending any more of his troops forward. They remained watching in no man's land while the first regiment had pushed through and decimated the Scavengers.

'We're screwed,' Matthew said, dejected. 'This is still the first wave and we're almost out of people on the ground.'

'We just need to buy some more time.'

Matthew, startled, turned to see Daisy standing next to him.

'What are you doing out here, Daisy?'

'The medical tent is fine without me. I'm going to help Kyrral.'

With that she leapt over the parapet and down to the ground to join the remaining Scavenger soldiers.

'We need to do something!' Matthew shouted over the Sam.

'What the hell can we do?' she asked.

'I don't know but I can't just stand here and watch.'

'Matthew, don't do anything stupid.'

The officers were slowly moving around the Scavenger group,

taunting them with every slow step and smug smile.

Matthew looked down at the group as Sam and Safiri stared at him.

'Matthew, please don't,' Safiri begged.

Matthew looked at both of them and jumped down to the ground.

'Ah crap,' said Sam. 'Saf, don't you even think about going down. You're Ganlin's eyes.'

'I wasn't plan-' Safiri was cut short as Sam joined Matthew, against her better judgement. As she fell she pulled her hood from her collar and over her head. Once in place Sam pulled down from just inside the front of the hood to reveal a black mask which moulded into place once down. The mask, now a hard shell perfectly contoured to Sam's facial features, covered the entirety of her face bar her mouth and chin.

'Sam, what are you doing here?' asked Matthew as she landed next to him, flinching as he noticed her intimidating hood and mask.

'Same thing you are. Being insanely stupid. What the hell are we gonna do to help?'

'I don't know but I had an idea come to me while we were standing up there. I kept getting this feeling that something was touching my wrists. Turns out that even though I put the cards in my pocket they kept trying to get into my hands whenever I thought of maybe using them, through my sleeves. It's like the suit knew I wanted them and somehow fed them through my jacket to the sleeves and into my hands.'

'So you plan on throwing some fireballs?'

'No. There's too many of them.'

'So what are you going to do?'

'I don't know yet but when I do I'm sure I'll have what I need.'

As he said this Kyrral clenched his hands. Matthew noticed a change in his skin. The crustiness disappeared until Kyrral looked like solid blue stone.

Matthew also noticed a change in the demeanour of the others around him. Their fatigue seemed to be fading and they stood with more determination, readying themselves for the final stand.

Kyrral bent his legs slightly.

'He's gonna charge them,' Matthew said, astonished. 'They're all gonna charge. We're gonna charge.'

Matthew took a deep breath and readied himself. 'Sarrus… Please hurry the hell up.'

As Kyrral took off, prompting the others to follow, Matthew had an epiphany. He finally had an idea and hoped he had a card to make it work. Instantly a card slipped from his sleeve into his hand. The rune depicted a caret in a circle with an arc above it. In each corner of the card was a cross. He touched his thumb to the rune and the golden veins of his glove glowed.

A dome of energy erected around them just before Kyrral reached the line of officers. Where Kyrral was expecting to make impact with the shield of his enemy, the officer was thrown back as she made contact with the dome, allowing Kyrral to continue to run. Laying on the floor as the dome reached her again, the officer got caught against it, pushing her through the dirt, giving her no opportunity to recover.

The dome, with the Scavengers inside, ploughed through Finnigan's officers as they broke the lines. Although with every impact on the dome Matthew could feel his energy drain and needed to concentrate more to keep it up, knowing that if it were to collapse that they would be done for.

'What's wrong, Matthew?!' Sam shouted as she sprinted along with the group.

'The energy to keep it up… It's too much!'

'OK. I got this!'

Matthew looked at her in confusion.

'Time for your magic, Mr Dullage,' she whispered.

Sam closed her eyes and concentrated as best she could as she ran. Black lifeblood began to rise from her back and shoulders, slowly at first but quickly increasing speed and intensity.

The lifeblood began to take shape above them, taking the form of a gigantic raven, twice the width of the dome. As the last of the lifeblood from Sam joined the raven it flapped its massive wings and swooped down toward the officers in front of the group.

The officers turned and ran in any direction that was away from the gigantic bird, screaming as they did so.

In the commotion Matthew let his concentration slip and the dome faded.

The regiment still waiting in no man's land let fly spark grenades in the direction of the on-running group of Scavengers.

The grenades passed harmlessly through Sam's raven and Matthew was able to strengthen the dome just in time before they hit, electricity exploding above them on the top of the dome.

The intensity of the grenades sapped the last of Matthew's energy and the dome finally succumbed and dissipated to nothing.

The officers readied another round of grenades to finally finish off the Scavenger charge and allow them to move onto taking down the battlements.

The Scavengers had reached the edge of no man's land, although they had no plan on what they were going to do once they had reached the officers.

Just as the next round of grenades were about to be released a large blue flame appeared between the two groups. Then another, this one purple. Many more appeared of varying colours, lingered for just a second and disappeared leaving tall, long-haired men and women dressed in a similar fashion to Sam, although more regal. Emerging from some of the flames were other well dressed ministers of The Authority, as well as some high level Decree officers.

The Scavengers stopped where they were, gasping for air.

From the last flame appeared Sarrus and Madonny.

'They did it,' said Matthew, at this point down on one knee, depleted.

Madonny ran to Daisy and embraced her.

'ENOUGH!' shouted one of the Pure. 'YOU WILL ALL STAND DOWN IMMEDIATELY!'

Matthew recognised the man now in charge as Sarrus' father. His command was redundant as the abrupt entrance of the reinforcements had already shocked all on both sides to freeze in place.

'I have better things to do with my time than to come to this wretched place. Ordinarily I would expect nothing more than the squalor of my city to be fighting down here, however, I have it on very good authority that something happening here is very much amiss.

'I see on one side we have utter filth,' this made many of the officers chuckle, 'and on the other some Scavenger trash,' their laughs abruptly silenced. 'Now why would I call Officers of The Decree utter filth? Well that would be because all intelligence suggests that this raid of the Scavenger District is very much illegal pursuant to the correct documentation… or the absence of any at all!

'It strikes me as very strange that the number of officers here at this moment could have coalesced in this magnitude without orders from the top. It also strikes me as very strange that this happened so very quickly without the knowledge of those around me here. One strange message from The Office of Magic does not a conspiracy make, however, a coordinated gathering and unlawful invasion does make me ever so curious. As does the intelligence received from my progeny and a bothersome, yet strangely respected, Fenlis.'

Sarrus' father turned and stared directly at Finnigan. 'Good sir… Yes, you. The High Inspector. You look strangely unfamiliar. I have been told that you are responsible for this, however I cannot recall ever seeing you before… at least not in this form…'

Finnigan pulled out a revolver and pointed it at Lestar. Everyone looked confused except for Matthew and Sam who gasped in horror.

'Well done, Torriah. Or should I say well done to your human spies. For anyone who doesn't know, they would be the ones who looked scared of the weapon I'm holding. Nice to see you made it. You know what this does and you should also know that I have many more of these. They happen to be in the possession of my friends over there.'

Finnigan motioned to the living platforms where a number of officers were crouched, holding rifles. Through the charge Matthew hadn't even noticed them.

Torriah, who Matthew now knew was Sarrus' father, was in no way intimidated. 'Stop this nonsense, Finnigan Fisk. You are under arrest for this attempted takeover of the Scavenger District, as well as all crimes previous to your disappearance.'

'HAHAHA! I am done with you, Torriah. I'm done with this entire place. TAKE THEM OUT!' Finnigan shouted as he and Doggery began running toward to living platforms.

Lestar, still restrained, bumped Doggery off the ledge and onto the regiment of officers standing below.

Hearing the scream from Doggery, Finnigan turned and shot his gun.

Lestar looked down as red began to stain his shirt from his stomach.

Chapter Twenty
A Final Push

'DAD!' Daisy shouted and began to run on all fours, Madonny close behind. They quickly scaled the jagged wall up to the ledge while a nearby officer removed the restraints from Lestar.

Finnigan's gang on the platforms had begun shooting their rifles down into those standing in no man's land.

The officers without guns on the ledge ran for the tunnel and back to the surface, apparently not willing to be tied to Finnigan's takeover, while those stuck in no man's land activated their own shields to protect themselves from the bullets.

The Scavengers leapt into the trenches behind them while the Pure and The Authority ministers shielded themselves. The Pure used their magical abilities to fire back at the officers. Some, like Torriah, had fire, some ice and some lightning. Generally the colour of their hair and clothing matched the magic that they used, at least to some degree and mostly just the trimmings. Those with fire wore red, ice was white and lightning was blue. Matthew thought it to be a little pretentious, it was completely oblivious to him that Sarrus was the same.

'We need to help Lestar,' Matthew said to Kyrral and Sam.

'How?' Sam asked.

'I don't know but I'm not sure anyone here knows what to do with a bullet wound.'

'My mum does but how are we gonna get her here?'

'I think we'll have to get Lestar to her. We'll need everybody to storm the platforms so we can get to the doorway. Once through we can call your mum. We'll be able to see where the doorway leads to on the maps.'

'Matthew, he's a cat.'

'One problem at a time, Sam. We'll leg it to the end of the trench and let Sarrus know to get Lestar to the doorway. We'll get the Scavengers to help clear the platforms while I protect us in an energy bubble thingy for as long as I can. The officers shooting down are mostly distracted by the Pure. Kyrral, you just bash through them all.'

Both nodded acknowledgment of the plan, having no better suggestions themselves.

Matthew, still holding the rune card for the protective dome, activated it once again although this time only to cover Sam, Kyrral and himself. He could feel the reduced strain that the smaller dome was taking on his energy.

'Let's go!' he shouted. 'Storm the platforms!'

Those around him headed the call and followed them out of the trench, keeping as close as possible behind the dome for at least a bit of cover. As more in the trenches saw what was happening those too joined the attack, having pulled off parts of the trench or grabbing hold of other debris around them to use as a shield.

Some of the shooters on the right hand side of the platforms saw the offensive move and changed target from the Pure to the Scavengers.

A small group of Scavengers with the shortest route were first to reach the ramp to the first level. The closer they got the smaller the group became. While doing as best they could to shield themselves, a lot of them fell to bullets to their legs. Those that could still run pressed on as hard as they could. Matthew could see that the one leading them was Rackma, a few of those he had shared a drink with were also part of the group. Once they reached the ramp they took a few seconds to rest and regroup under the platform.

'Wait there!' Matthew attempted to shout to them. The dome was the most effective cover any of them had and he planned to use it to bash through as many of Finnigan's people as possible before letting the Scavengers take over.

Unfortunately Rackma and his group could not hear them through the gunfire and explosions of the elements against the platforms. After regathering their breath they raised their makeshift shields and stormed the ramp.

By the time Matthew, Sam and Kyrral had reached the ramp, Rackma's group had reached the first platform and begun taking care of some of the shooters, who soon found out that the guns that Finnigan had supplied them weren't as easy to use when their target was close. Once face to face they became little more than a heavy staff.

Rackma had a slight advantage being Stroen with his skin adding an extra layer of protection.

As they bashed their way across the first level they had little trouble eliminating Finnigan's people once they were close enough. The trouble they had was reducing the distance without drawing the attention of those who were still completely focussed on the Pure in no man's land.

Once the rumblings began and the realisation washed over those on the platform that they were under attack they turned their guns quickly toward the Scavengers, shooting in their direction regardless of the risk of hitting their own. A large portion of their own numbers on the platform were taken out simply as a result of fear of the Scavengers reaching them, however the more that fell the more exposed the Scavengers became.

Rackma's group began to reduce in numbers although the haphazard aiming of the officers meant that they were rarely lethal shots. Those that were injured managed to take cover in the areas that had already been cleared.

The first platform was won before Matthew had reached the top of the ramp. The bottom of the next ramp and the ladders up to level two had been secured with Rackma's group taking a short rest before continuing.

The above platform and barricades created by Finnigan's cronies allowed them to ignore the attacks from the Pure in no man's land, especially given their fire was concentrated toward the higher levels.

'Rackma! Hold up!' Matthew shouted at him before he could continue to push up through the platforms. He also let go of the dome while they were in the protected area to conserve some of his own energy.

'Matthew, my boy!' Rackma called back. 'Glad to see you're still in the fight.'

Matthew could see the toll the fight had taken on the old Stroen despite his cheerful demeanour. Blood stained his ragged clothing from the glancing blows he had taken. Strapped to his right arm was a thick piece of metal, large enough to cover his face and part of his upper torso. A number of small dents marked its outer side where bullets had struck.

'Are you OK, Rackma?' Matthew asked.

'Yeah. Just a few scratches is all.'

Rackma winced and touched his side as he started laughing.

'You need medical help, Rackma. We've got it from here.'

'Nonsense, Matthew. I've still got enough in me to make sure the Scavengers win the day.'

'Fine, but we go first. You stay behind us where you're

protected.'

'Yes, sir,' Rackma mocked as he saluted Matthew.

'You all ready to go again?' Matthew asked Sam and Kyrral.

'Let's do it,' Sam replied.

Matthew took a deep breath and activated the dome.

The Scavengers, headed by Matthew, barged their way up the platforms, level by level. The lack of communication between the shooters meant none were expecting them, nor had a coordinated plan to deal with the shield pushing through. As the realisation hit them they all shot at the shield in vain before they were either pushed off the platforms, falling down to the ground, or pushed down the rows of tents and cabins where they were immediately set upon by the Scavengers closely following Matthew.

The Pure had noticed the Scavengers taking each platform and concentrated their fire on the platforms above as the Scavengers continued moving up.

The plan could not have worked any more perfectly for Matthew, until they reached level seven. Much of Finnigan's remaining army had coalesced near the cabin which housed the tunnels, once Finnigan had run through. The area had been abandoned by the Scavengers as people were moved to the amphitheater or joined the Scavenger soldiers, which gave Finnigan a simple escape route.

The momentary rest before attempting to take the final platform which led to Dawn, and help for Lestar, allowed Matthew to recover a small amount of energy. The fatigue had set in after scaling so many platforms and keeping the dome activated for so long while being shot at.

'Are you OK, Matthew.' Sam asked, as Matthew was doubled over, hands on knees, trying to take in some air.

'Yeah. Just give me a second.' Matthew walked over to the ramp for one last climb. 'One more to go. We got this.'

Sam and Kyrral stood next to Matthew as he activated the dome for the last time. Running up the ramp they barged through officers once again, reaching the row that led to the tunnels.

The dome suddenly faulted. It had taken all of Matthew's strength to keep it activated, however he could not hold it any longer. Despite having taken out most of those on the platform there were still some that were surrounding the entrance to the cabin and those in the following rows.

The realisation hit the remaining officers that the Scavengers were now completely exposed and they began to ready their rifles to retake the platform.

Kyrral bashed through those that emerged from the next row and Scavenger guards raced past Matthew to help.

With a rifle now being lifted to point in Matthew's direction from an officer beside the door that they needed to get to, he froze in place, having no idea what he could do. Matthew heard a loud bang then found himself laying on his side on the floor. The face of Rackma stared back at him as Scavengers swarmed those guarding the cabin door.

'You saved me.' Matthew managed to say, his lips trembling.

'I did… and you're saving us. It's a rare thing for outsiders to do things like that… but you're special aren't you. Our meeting was no accident, Matthew. You're quite alike, you know… My promise is now fulfilled. We're even George.' Rackma closed his eyes and his breathing stopped, although even death could not take his smile.

Matthew's shock intensified with the small, yet mind-blowing piece of information Rackma just gave him. The shock then turned to anger that Rackma had been taken from him before he could be told any more. Holding onto that anger Matthew stood up, Sam taking hold of his arm to help.

'Are you OK?' she asked.

'No holes in me. Rackma saved me. He knew Grandad. He said his promised was fulfilled and that they're now even.'

'Oh my god.'

'And now he's dead. He could've told me so much.'

'What are we going to do now?'

'The plan stays the same. We're gonna stop Finnigan and save Lestar.'

Matthew and Sam jogged over to the cabin door where Mason was standing guard. 'When Sarrus and Daisy get here take them through. Sarrus will know where to go. We could do with a couple of guards to help us when we run into trouble.'

'No problem, Matthew.'

Kyrral ran over to join them at the door. 'This platform is secure,' he informed them.

'Great. Let's get Finnigan,' said a determined Matthew.

Matthew opened the door and walked into the cabin, leading the group toward the open doorway that he was sure Finnigan had run to. There was nobody in sight as they made their way through the tunnel and into the small storage room, the doorway still active.

'You two stay here,' Matthew said to the Scavenger guards. 'Make sure nobody else comes through unless it's Sarrus, Daisy and her parents.'

The guards stood in the middle of the room, one facing the doorway and the other facing the tunnel they had come from.

Matthew, Sam and Kyrral slowly walked through the doorway, the blue tinge disappearing as they crossed to the other side.

They were in a large warehouse. The doorway was against a brick wall in the corner of what was the last aisle of giant shelves. A forklift sat nearby, as did a workbench.

'Sam, plug your phone in there and call your mum,' Matthew whispered. 'Open your maps to see where we are.'

They quietly crept over to the bench which allowed Sam to get a small amount of charge into her phone before they could turn it on. As soon as the phone was working again she opened the map to check their location.

'Matthew. We're right behind Finnigan's shop. Look at what's on these shelves. It looks like this is a massive warehouse for artefacts he's stolen. The artefacts in his shop are just a small portion of what he's got.'

'Call your mum and get her over here. We need to deal with Finnigan in the time it takes her to get here.'

Sam called her mother and whispered into the phone. 'Mum, I need you help… I can't talk any louder… Gunshot wound to the stomach… We can't go to the hospital… We can deal with that later I just need you here now. I'll text you the address.'

Slowly they crept down the aisle toward a large break in the middle. Matthew presumed that was the main thoroughfare in the warehouse. Kyrral jumped back as something scurried across the aisle in front of them, bumping into Matthew who fell into the shelf and knocking down a cast iron pot.

'Is that you, boy!?' came the voice of Finnigan, echoing through the warehouse. 'I must say I didn't think you'd be this resourceful… or this much of a pain.'

'You should give yourself up,' Matthew replied. 'You're surrounded. There's no escape. I'm sure it'll be easier on you than if you resist.'

'Quite the cheek to walk into my warehouse and tell me to give up. You forget that I know what everything in here does.'

A loud pulsing sound began and rapidly sped up. For a second all the sound seemed to get sucked out of the air before a *whoomph* sound filled the warehouse followed by the crashing of objects and shelves heading toward them.

The shelves in front of them cascaded down with everything on them crashing to the floor. Matthew and Kyrral dived out the way as a ring of rippled air hit Sam, throwing her back into the wall where she fell down, unconscious.

'You lied about artefacts not working in Dawn, then?!' Matthew shouted.

'I never said that there were no artefacts that worked, only the ones that happened to be on display. In any case, you were a fool to believe that none of them worked when I told you the mind ring worked.'

'Kyrral, I've got an idea.' Matthew whispered.

'What is it?'

'A leap of faith, I guess. Watch my back.'

A rune card slipped into Matthew's hand from his sleeve as soon as he thought of what he needed. Taking a look at it, just to be sure, he confirmed that it was the card with the mind rune that he showed Finnigan when they had met the first time. Touching the rune he closed his eyes and concentrated.

In his mind Matthew could see within a few seconds the past, present and future, all from Finnigan's perspective. He could see Finnigan making his way up The Authority, bribing, extorting, blackmailing. He could see Finnigan getting caught and escaping to the Scavenger District, finding the doorway, discovering Dawn and setting up his business by defrauding his clients and extorting and blackmailing money from people. He could see how Finnigan recruited Scavengers and Officers of The Decree with help from a few still loyal to him. He could see how all the planning for the attack on the Scavenger District came together. More importantly, Matthew could see where Finnigan was at that very moment, what was around him and what he was planning on doing.

Matthew motioned for Kyrral to move around the other side of the warehouse to flank Finnigan and the three loyal Scavengers who Matthew now knew were surrounding him.

He played along with Finnigan's plan for the time being, moving into the thoroughfare and exposing himself.

'Stupid boy,' said Finnigan, who had reverted to his natural, plump appearance. 'How could you possibly think you could best me? I've been at this for a long time. You have no idea what you're dealing with. If The Decree weren't so incompetent I wouldn't have to deal with you now… but deal I must.'

The door to the storefront was still open behind him from where he and his accomplices had come from after hearing Matthew's unfortunate crash into the shelves earlier.

'Hey, Finnigan. What was it that I showed you when we first met?'

'A card with a rune on it, why?'

'And what was the rune that was on the card?'

Finnigan took a moment to contemplate why Matthew was asking him about a rune. His eyes widened as he realised what had happened.

'Your arrogance has betrayed you, Finnigan. Wanting nothing more than to brag to everybody about what you've done.'

As Matthew finished pointing out how foolish Finnigan was, Kyrral, his skin turned to stone, ran along the back wall, barging into the closest man and sending him flying into Finnigan. The weapon he was holding, which looked like a glass trombone, fell from his hands and shattered on the concrete floor.

A card slipped into each of Matthew's hands which he flicked forward simultaneously toward the two remaining cronies standing either side of Finnigan.

As the cards spun their way toward their targets sparks began to generate, growing in intensity as they continued to fly. They then morphed into balls of intense, white light with blue sparks emitting from ever growing streams of spitting electricity.

As if sentient, the streams embraced their victims, holding them in place as the white ball of plasma crashed into their chests, contorting their muscles. A second later they both lay unconscious on the ground.

As the cards flew forward Daisy had whizzed past Matthew, sprinting as fast as she could toward Finnigan.

Regaining his footing, Finnigan once again retrieved his revolver from the back of his trousers, bringing it forward to fire at his foes.

Daisy leapt forward, claws extending as the gun came into line. She latched onto his chest, forcing Finnigan to shoot wide. She scratched at his face as he fell backward, landing face up with Daisy continuing her attack from on top of him. Finnigan's threw his arms in front of his face in an attempt to block the attacks, although it didn't stop Daisy from ripping through his sleeves and drawing blood from his forearms, to match his bloodied face.

Kyrral rushed over and pulled a ferocious Daisy from the fallen man, holding her tight as she continued to try and strike out.

Finnigan lay on his back screaming and crying in pain. Matthew struggled to feel any sympathy for the man who had put them through hell for the past half a day and shot Lestar as he ran like a coward.

Chapter Twenty-One
Consequences

Matthew ran back to the doorway as Sam was regaining consciousness. Madonny, Ganlin and Safiri were holding Lestar while Sarrus was applying some concoction she had made to the wound.

'How's he going?' Matthew asked.

'I've been trying to keep him from bleeding out,' Sarrus replied. 'However the wound won't heal.'

'The bullet is still in there. We've got someone coming to help but Sam, Safiri and I need to be the only ones there. Ganlin and Saf, help me take him through to the front. Madonny and Sarrus, you take care of Daisy. Kyrral is holding onto her at the moment. She scratched the hell out of Finnigan who's a bloody mess on the floor. Ganlin, you can take him out with you when you come back. Let's go.'

Matthew helped a groggy Sam back to her feet as they went through the doorway, guiding her toward the storefront while Ganlin and Safiri laid Lestar on a trolley that was under the bench.

'Ganlin, all the missing people are through a door on the far side of the warehouse. Finnigan has the keys in his pocket.'

'How do you know that?' Ganlin asked.

'I had a cheat code,' Matthew replied, grinning.

Ganlin and Safiri moved Lestar from the trolley onto the wooden table in the storefront. Sam unlocked the front door and waited for her mother. Matthew wiped off whatever Sarrus had put on Lestar's wound in case any questions were asked.

'Thanks, Ganlin. Make sure Finnigan gets what he deserves. We'll be back as soon as we can.'

'No problem. I'll leave Finnigan with the guards and come back for everyone who's been locked up. Thank you… all of you. I don't know what we would've done if you weren't helping us.'

'You're welcome, Ganlin.'

Ganlin took off back into the warehouse with a couple of minutes to spare before Sam's mother arrived. Matthew removed the ring from his pocket and placed it on Lestar's finger.

'Lestar, can you hear me?' Matthew asked.

'Yes… yes, I can hear you.' Lestar was struggling to talk.

'Lestar, I need you to concentrate on looking like us. No matter what happens you need to keep concentrating.'

'Daisy… Madonny. Are they-?'

'They're fine, Lestar. They can't be here right now but they're close by and you'll see them soon.'

'Finnigan?'

'We got him. Don't worry about that. We need to fix you up. Make sure you keep concentrating on looking like us.'

Lestar closed his eyes to concentrate. His fur disappeared and was replaced by dark skin while his features morphed form cat to human.

'Looks like your dad, Saf,' Matthew joked.

'Really? You're gonna do this right now?'

'Sorry. Just trying to deal. You know how I get.'

'I know. Let's just try and get through this without any questions.'

'We've got a man with a gunshot wound to the stomach. Not sure how we're gonna avoid questions,' said Sam. 'OK. She's here… In here, Mum.'

'What the hell is going on? What are you all wearing?' she asked as she walked through the door.

'We need you to save him, Mrs Walker. He's been shot in the stomach. The bullet's still in there.'

'Once I'm done you need to tell me everything… EVERYTHING!'

'Yes, Mum. We will.'

Sam's mother set her bag down on the table and got to work helping Lestar. After extracting the bullet she applied some alcohol to the wound. Lestar screamed and momentarily returned to his true self. Luckily Mrs Walker didn't notice as she concentrated on the wound and all the dressing surrounding it.

Mrs Walker finished patching Lestar up. 'The bullet missed his organs. I've done what I can and he should be OK but you need to take him to a hospital. Something didn't seem right when I was in there. In any case I need to report this to the police. I don't know what you've gotten yourselves into but I have an obligation.

'I can't let you do that, Mrs Walker. I'm sorry I have to do this.'

Matthew retrieved the mind rune card from his suit and held it behind his back. *I hope this works* he thought to himself. Touching the rune he closed his eyes and concentrated. The markings on the card glowed a dark pink in his hand.

'You're going to pack up, go home and clean your equipment. Once you've done that you'll go to bed and forget everything that happened from the time Sam called you. Anything you do happen to remember you'll put down to a strange dream you had.'

Mrs Walker immediately packed everything into her bag and exited the store, Sam locking the door behind her. Nothing else was said by Mrs Walker as she followed her commands.

Matthew sank down onto a chair, completely exhausted.

'What the hell did you just do?' Sam asked.

Matthew showed them the card. 'The mind rune. Turns out this is a pretty powerful card. I used it to read Finnigan's mind as well when we were in the warehouse. I saw everything he had done and what he was planning. He's so egotistical he wanted everyone to know and tell him how smart he was. The info he gave us about the mind rune turned out to bite him in the arse. Go get the others and tell them that Lestar is going to be OK. Sarrus' paste stuff should finish the job now.'

Safiri ran out to the back and returned with Daisy, Madonny and Sarrus.

Matthew retrieved his ring from Lestar while they waited.

'He's going to be fine,' said Matthew. 'Sarrus, you can do your thing on him now.'

'How are you going, Matthew? You don't look too good.'

'I'm stuffed. I've had to concentrate so much with these runes that I've got nothing left.'

Sarrus gave Matthew some of the seeds he had eaten earlier in the day. The aches and pains in his muscles subsided and a little bit of energy returned to his body.

'How did you help Lestar?' Madonny asked.

'My Mum helped him. She's a doctor. More specifically a surgeon,' said Sam.

'Where is she? We'd like to thank her.'

'She's gone. She won't remember what she did. It's safer for everyone that way. Matthew used the mind rune card to make sure she forgets everything.'

'The runes work here? I thought Finnigan said nothing worked?'

'A lot of artefacts don't work,' said Matthew. 'Some things do work though. My ring worked on Lestar. Finnigan's ring worked. He had a big sonic weapon thing that he shot at us. I think

Grandad locked the gloves up in the vault box to make sure the card's couldn't be used unless they really had to be. Did Ganlin sort everything out there?' Matthew asked.

'Finnigan has been taken away,' said Daisy. 'He's alive but he's in a lot of pain.' She smirked at what she had done to him after he shot her father.

'Everyone who had been locked up has been freed,' Madonny added. 'Ganlin is taking them to the medical tent and I'll interview them all tomorrow. We need to make sure we get all the information and find everyone who's responsible.'

'What are we going to do about this place?' asked Safiri. 'We can't have people wandering through the doorway.'

'Sam, get Ganlin to bring Finnigan back here,' said Matthew.

'OK. What do you have in mind?' she asked.

'When I was looking into Finnigan's mind I saw a few things that might help us keep control of access to the doorway. Safiri, can you grab the laptop over there?' Matthew motioned to the counter at the back of the store. 'The password is scavs suck, one word with capital S's for each part and three exclamation marks at the end'

Safiri sat on the other side with the laptop and Sarrus took Lestar back into the warehouse to tend to his wounds.

Sam returned a few minutes later with Ganlin, who was dragging a sobbing, restrained Finnigan. Ganlin dropped him down onto a chair at the wooden table, now stained with blood.

'Haven't you done enough?' Finnigan sobbed, staring at Matthew.

'You literally tried to take over and enslave an entire community, and that was just the first part of your plan,' Matthew answered. 'You're not really in any place to have a whinge about what we did to stop you. People are dead because of you.'

'What do you care? They're not your people.'

'Maybe not, but they *are* people and nobody deserves to go through that.'

'I did what I needed to survive.'

'Maybe at first, when you were a Scavenger. But then you got greedy and every decision you made was for yourself. You never even considered helping anyone else.'

'You have no idea what it's like!'

'No. But these people do and they choose to help those around them. You're a disgrace.'

'Whatever. Ganlin get me out of here. I'm tired of listening to this human.'

'Safiri, print out a *Transfer of Ownership* form for this property.' Matthew requested.

'We're going to need more than just a form, Matthew. There's a bunch of other documentation that's needed,' Safiri advised.

'Didn't think that through, did you boy,' Finnigan mocked.

'You're not one to trust banks, are you Finnigan,' Matthew retorted. 'Something tells me you've got everything we need here. In a safe, maybe? You don't seem to be grasping this, Finnigan Fisk. In your arrogance you left your mind completely open. You gave me everything.'

Finnigan's face dropped. 'If you've got everything then why am I here? Just so you can throw it in my face?'

'No. I still need you for one more thing.'

Safiri retrieved the form from the printer and handed it to Matthew. The faces of those from Dusk were a mixture of confusion at what was happening and satisfaction that whatever was happening was punishment for Finnigan.

Matthew put the form down on the table in front of Finnigan along with a pen.

'Ganlin, let him have a hand,' Matthew waited for Finnigan to have a hand free. 'Sign it.'

'No,' Finnigan refused.

'Sign. It.'

'No. Looks like I've got all the leverage now.'

Daisy moved in close to Finnigan's ear. 'Looks like you've still got some skin left on your face,' she whispered as she extended a single nail and slowly, gently ran it down his cheek, leaving everyone wide-eyed in shock at how dark Daisy had become since Finnigan had shot Lestar.

Finnigan's breathing quickened and he started to sob once again. He picked up the pen and signed the form.

Daisy stood up straight, retracted her nail and smiled. 'Thanks Finnigan. You've made the right decision.'

'Ganlin, if you could bring Finnigan over here please.' Matthew walked over to the other end of the store, in the back corner, and moved a chest of draws aside exposing a safe in the wall. 'And if you could pass me the keys that you used to free the Scavengers.'

Ganlin passed Matthew the keys he had taken from Finnigan earlier. Matthew unlocked and opened a flap on the front of the safe to expose a screen. Touching the screen lit up a keypad allowing Matthew to enter a code. The keypad then turned into blank screen prompting a finger print. Matthew took hold of Finnigan's free hand and pushed his thumb onto the screen. The entire screen turned green and the safe door unlocked and opened.

'You can take him away now, Ganlin. We're done with him.'

Ganlin tied Finnigan's hand once again, picked the man up from his knees and dragged him out, all the while Finnigan continued to sob.

Matthew emptied the contents of the safe. First was a folder full of original documents, a large portion of them not legally created or obtained. Second was a large box.

'You'll find everything you need in here, Saf.' Matthew handed over the folder. 'You finally get to live your dream of dealing with forms and documents. Matthew and Sam laughed.

'You better stop mocking me if you want me to do this,' Safiri threatened, jokingly. 'Who are we transferring it to?' he asked.

'Us three, I guess.' Matthew replied.

'What are we going to do with it?' asked Sam.

'Not sure yet. I guess we've got time to work that out.'

'How are we gonna afford to do anything? We've got no money.'

Matthew placed the box on the table and opened it. He retrieved from the box stacks of cash and put them on the table.

'Like I said, Finnigan didn't trust banks.'

'I dunno, Matthew,' said Safiri, looking concerned. 'This kinda feels like stealing.'

'Think of it more like a reclamation from a criminal. Finnigan stole this for his own selfish purposes. We can put this place to good use. For Dawn and Dusk. For the sake of the doorway between our worlds I don't think we have a choice.'

'I agree,' Madonny interrupted. 'Finnigan has caused so much pain. There's no telling what he could've done, having the benefit of the doorway into both worlds. He would've continued to become more powerful on both sides.'

Sarrus and Lestar walked back into the storefront, Ganlin having taken Finnigan back into Dusk. Daisy and Madonny both hugging him the second they saw him.

'How are you feeling?' Matthew asked.

'Pretty good,' Lestar replied. 'Sarrus can do amazing things with those plants. I'm a little sore still but whatever Sarrus put on it is healing it up very quickly and these seeds are helping with the pain. Thanks to all of you. Without you I wouldn't be here. What's going on now?'

'We're discussing the ethics of taking everything from Finnigan,' said Safiri.

'Do it. There's nothing unethical here. He's a criminal. You saved the Scavenger District and countless more people from what Finnigan could've done in the future. In any case, the doorway needs to be protected and we need to get all these artefacts safely back to Dusk and catalogued. As far as I see it there's an obligation to take over this place.'

'Sarrus, Daisy, Kyrral?' Matthew asked for their input.

'Agree,' they said in unison.

'OK. You good with that Saf?'

'Yes. I'm in.'

'Me too,' added Sam.

'Cool. Saf, finish all the paperwork and get it all approved. We can discuss what we're going to do here later on. It would be awesome if everyone here was involved. You all cool with that? Great. Let's pick this up again tomorrow. We'll meet at the doorway in, say, 10 hours?'

Sarrus walked up to Matthew as everyone got themselves ready to leave. 'Matthew, there's still so much we don't know. The biggest being how did your grandad get the House Errothin vault box and seal? We don't just give those things away to anybody.'

'Sarrus. That's a great question. It's also a question for another time. I'm tired as hell. Lestar got shot. Rackma and so many others are dead. I can't deal with anything else right now. We all need a rest and I damn sure want to spend tonight in my own bed, whether I can sleep or not. It's been the weirdest, craziest couple of days of my life and if I've learned anything over the past few weeks it's that Grandad's secrets will reveal themselves in time, in exactly the way he intended.'

'I suppose you're right, Matthew.'

'Please try and get some help to the Scavengers from the outside. Their home's been completely destroyed… And maybe get Ganlin to put some of his most trusted guys at the doorway to make sure no Finnigan types sneak though again.'

'I will. You all stay safe and rest as much as you can. I'll see you tomorrow.'

'Bye Sarrus.' Each of the Dawn Crew called out as she turned and walked back to the warehouse.

'OK. Who's got the keys?' Matthew asked.

'I've got them,' replied Sam. 'Let's get out of here.'

All three of the Dawn Crew walked out the front door, Sam locking up. Completely depleted of energy they held each other up as they stood by the street.

'Sooooo… how are we getting home?' asked Safiri.

Matthew's head dropped. 'Ahhhh crap.'